"Don't you know that I would never hurt you intentionally?"

Jessica shook her head. "I'm not afraid of you. It's what you do that frightens me."

"Selling farm equipment?" Damon asked, raising one brow.

"You don't sell equipment; you make contracts." And what else are you involved in? She wished she could come right out and ask him if her suspicions were correct, but she knew Damon would deny any other activities.

"What are you trying to tell me?"

Jessica took a deep breath. "I don't want to get involved with you. I don't want to constantly live with fear for your safety. I want more than nightmares as my only companion in the dead of night." She stopped, then added, "I don't want to fall in love with you."

Dear Reader,

Over the years, we at Silhouette Books have taken advantage of this space to do many things. We have introduced whole new lines of books; we have told you what kinds of stories to expect; we have alerted you to future appearances by some of your favorite authors. Last month we told you about an exciting group of new authors coming from Silhouette Intimate Moments, and now the time has come for them to make their appearance.

Nancy Morse may be familiar to those of you who also read historical romances, but this is her first—but not her last—contemporary romance. Our other three authors this month—Sibylle Garrett, Paula Detmer Riggs and Marilyn Pappano—are all publishing their very first books with us. Let them take you on a trip around the world, from the deserts of the American West to Hollywood, from an Indian reservation to Afghanistan, proving that no matter where you travel, love is always the same.

On their behalf, as well as the editors', I hope not only that you enjoy this month's Silhouette Intimate Moments novels, but also that you will take the time to write to us with your comments. Your opinions and suggestions are always important to us, and I thank you in advance for sharing them.

Sincerely,
Leslie J. Wainger
Senior Editor
Silhouette Books
300 E. 42nd St.
New York, NY 10017

Sibylle Garrett

September Rainbow

Silhouette Intimate Moments

Published by Silhouette Books New York

America's Publisher of Contemporary Romance

SILHOUETTE BOOKS
300 East 42nd St., New York, N.Y. 10017

ISBN: 0-373-07184-1

First Silhouette Books printing March 1987

America's Publisher of Contemporary Romance

Printed in the U.S.A.

SIBYLLE GARRETT

was born a Berliner, but considers herself a citizen of the world. After years of moving across the globe, first with her parents, then with her husband of twenty years and their two children, she finally settled down on Long Island. She began writing as a way to pass the time during a lull in her career as a physical therapist. What began as a hobby quickly became a passion to be a published writer.

To my husband. Thank you.

Chapter 1

Lights flooding the front lawn reflected off highly polished limousines and chrome mirrors, casting a chaotic interplay of painful brightness and murky dark. Balancing on high heels, a slim, trench-coated woman slowly picked her way up the circular driveway, moving through the shadows to the big house. Her left shoulder sagged under the weight of a large traveling bag. She stopped at the worn stone steps leading to the house's imposing front and tilted her head back to look at the carved oak door. For a long moment she hesitated, as if debating whether to use the heavy brass knocker. Then, turning aside, she stole past flowering rhododendrons, quickly vanishing among the bushes.

A small metallic click alerted the man in the shadows that she had found the garden gate at the side of the house. He heard the faint rustle of leaves, then only silence. Resting easily against one of the limousines, he stared at the spot where she had disappeared.

Who is she? he wondered. Surely not a guest at the party. His invitation had specified black tie. All the women present were wearing an abundance of jewels, expensive perfume and long gowns. They would not have been caught dead arriving in a trench coat. The heavy purse, too, was out of place.

"What is she doing in the garden? Trying to shoot pictures for one of the tabloids?" Grimly he smiled. Like most of the guests at the party he valued his privacy. "Good luck."

For privacy, all windows were tightly shut and blinded by heavy drapes. Security was supposedly tight at Gloria Barton's diplomatic receptions. Inside, the house swarmed with bodyguards, some dressed as waiters, some as maids and others as guests in tuxedos, their jackets bulging with shoulder holsters and beepers.

Frowning, he looked around for the guards hired to patrol the grounds this night. Where are they? And where are the drivers of the limousines? He swore softly. Together. Playing poker somewhere, most likely.

He looked back at the rhododendrons. What is keeping that woman? His neck prickled with apprehension. No guards. No woman. Only darkness. And quiet.

Silently he slid past the cars and eased through the rhododendrons framing the garden gate. Even with the protection of the guards, tightly closed windows and heavy drapes were flimsy barriers for a terrorist. Glass could be cut without sound and curtains shifted easily through very small openings to toss bombs among the guests.

The latch didn't make a sound as he carefully opened and closed the garden gate. The garden beyond was shrouded in darkness. For a moment he stopped, listening intently as he let his eyes adjust. Everything was quiet. Too quiet for his taste.

The dark cloth of his tuxedo blended with the gloom. His shirtfront, however, shone like a beacon in the night. He turned up his collar and closed the front of his jacket, folding the dark lapels across the pleated white linen. Then he moved forward, a tall shadow intent on stalking its prey. Despite his considerable height he was light on his feet, his body moved with an athlete's smoothness. His ears were attuned to the sounds of night—the occasional light rustles in the undergrowth, the faint stirrings of leaves as the May breeze caressed them.

Where was she?

He listened for the small sound of a breaking twig, the occasional roll of a pebble, even the slight sucking noise high-heeled sandals made against a woman's foot as she walked.

He heard nothing.

His eyes skimmed past bushes and flowers, searching the back of the house. He looked for a moving figure, searched for a crouching object.

He saw nothing.

He left the path and stepped onto grass, expanding his search. She couldn't have left the garden. Not unless she had climbed the high fence surrounding the property.

The air was filled with the fresh scent of pines, the light fragrance of flowering lilacs and a hint of jasmine. Suddenly he stopped. Jasmine? He knew the garden well, yet he could not remember a jasmine bush, not here, mingling with the branches of the tall lilacs. Besides, the scent wasn't strong enough. He followed his nose and found her. She was sitting on the old stone bench, hidden by blooming lilacs.

The spot was one of his favorite retreats; the thick leaves provided a perfect hiding space from Gloria's garden parties. Resentment flared. Never again would he return to this place without remembering what it was being used for tonight.

As he watched, the woman opened the zipper of her purse and groped among its contents. Then she unloaded a few items, placing them with care on the bench. Unfortunately it was too dark to make out more than vague shapes.

What's the oval ball she's stuffing into the pocket of her trench coat? It was small, but big enough to turn the party into a bloodbath.

The woman replaced the rest of the objects and closed the zipper. Leaving the large purse on the bench, she rose and meandered through the garden. He followed her, a silent, watchful shadow. She stopped at the rosebushes and cupped a large bloom to sniff its fragrance. The gesture reminded him of his own habits. He, too, often enjoyed their intoxicating smell in much the same way. His anger grew. She had tarnished still another of his simple pleasures. Yet as he watched her, resentment gave way to puzzlement. How could she contemplate destruction one moment and stand there drinking in beauty the next?

Could she be innocent? Could there be another explanation for why she had slunk into the garden? He couldn't think of one.

Suddenly she turned, moving across the grass, back toward the house. He followed her, crossing the patio without a sound, watching her as she pulled on the sliding door leading into the den. He heard a slight sound of frustration when the door stayed shut. For a moment she stood, as if in thought, then she walked past him toward the far end of the house.

Damn! His blood chilled, remembering the big bay window in the living room with its profusion of plants. He remembered, too, that for years Gloria Barton had successfully resisted all of security's pressures to hide her jungle behind curtains.

Jessica, too, had remembered the window. The moment she had spotted the lines of cars, many with diplomatic license plates, she wished she hadn't dismissed the taxi. Gate crashing one of Aunt Gloria's receptions had not been part of her plan for the evening. She had looked forward to spending her last night in the States quietly visiting with her parents, not spending it listening to the latest Washington gossip and answering questions about her life in Pakistan.

"I should have called mother before I left New York," she muttered, walking toward the far side of the house.

The last five days had been hectic. Her interviews by the members of the U.N. delegation had seemed endless. She had really wanted the job and had felt as tense as a bowstring. After six years spent overseas in countries where women still wore veils, she needed a change from the restrictions imposed on female diplomats.

Between interviews she had run from Saks to Bergdorf Goodman, and then to Bloomingdale's, with a list of items her friends in Islamabad just couldn't do without.

Over lunch today, she had learned that the job was hers and had been ecstatic. In her hotel room she had packed a small bag, then rushed to the airport to take the shuttle to Washington. Who would have thought that an hour's trip would stretch into five? She hadn't. Not after living in countries where only the privileged owned cars, and where time moved at a snail's pace.

When she finally reached her parents' apartment she had found they were out. The sensible thing would have been to relax and wait their return. But when she'd read in her mother's appointment book just where they had gone, she'd quickly changed her clothes and dashed across town.

"I should've stayed at the apartment," she muttered. "Now I'll either have to join the circus inside, or walk two miles to the nearest phone."

She looked at the sky. The moon was in its first quarter. Even in daylight she wouldn't have enjoyed the long trek in high heels. This late at night it would be stupid and dangerous. "I guess it's the circus."

She rounded the corner of the house and stopped. Light streamed through the big bay window into the garden. As she walked closer, she heard subdued party music drift through the hanging plants and out into the night.

She grinned. So little had changed since she had left this house six years ago. She could still walk through the garden at night without stumbling into bushes and Aunt Gloria still remained victorious in her constant battle to keep the bay window undraped.

"I wonder if someone removed my blocks?" Spreading the yews apart, Jessica searched for the concrete blocks she had piled up in her childhood. "There they are." Smiling, she gingerly stepped through the plants, careful not to snag her nylons. Grabbing the windowsill for support, she stood on the blocks and peered past the blooming hoya and flowering hibiscus into the crowd of designer gowns and glittering medals. Her parents were not in the living room.

But she did recognize a German diplomat, a former ambassador to India, several senators, and a well-known socialite.

She stifled a groan. This was not just an ordinary circus, but a Barnum and Bailey sized one. There would be no opportunity for privacy with her parents or with her aunt and uncle. Her attire wasn't for the occasion either. Beneath her trench coat she wore a strapless black dress of silky synthetic. It was the type of dress that didn't crush and could be worn most places, but not to one of Aunt Gloria's official receptions. She also wore no jewelry. In the heat of Pakistan, even gold left dark smudges on her skin. Jessica had deposited her few good rings and bracelets in a safe so long ago she couldn't even remember exactly what she owned.

Suddenly her nose itched. Now she really wished she had stayed in New York. At this moment she could be lying in her hotel room bed, watching a golden oldie on TV and stuffing herself with pizza instead of hiding in the spring-scented, pollen-filled garden. If she didn't knock on the front door soon, she would have to face everyone with a runny nose and watery eyes. She sneezed, muffling the sound with her hand.

He had followed her, carefully watching his step. He was a tall man and knew that his weight would crush every branch he trod on. So far, he had been lucky. Not once had she halted to listen for unusual sounds. Instead she had moved with a confidence and sureness that spoke of familiarity with her surroundings.

When had she searched the garden? And when had she placed those blocks under the window? He drew closer, his eyes trained on the small figure outlined by the light.

How innocent she seemed with her face pressed like a curious child's against the window. How radiant she looked in the stream of light, her fiery hair a halo of burnished gold. He shivered. The night air was cooling rapidly. The lure of warmth was as potent as the scent of jasmine accosting his nostrils. Silently he slid closer.

Her perfume reminded him of the treacherous Near East, where children threw bombs into unsuspecting crowds and the hot sun never penetrated the cold cloud of fear. He crouched low, a long black shadow, ready to pounce should she make a wrong move.

Suddenly she raised her hand. Was she testing the strength of the window? She reached into her pocket.

He lunged.

A strong blow numbed her arm as Jessica reached for her handkerchief. Her feet slipped on the mossy blocks. As she opened her mouth to scream, a hard hand covered it, stifling any sound. She felt herself falling backward. Wildly she clawed with her free hand at the windowsill to regain her hold. But the vicelike grip across her waist drew her back relentlessly, dragging her through the yews. She felt her nylons tear. She flailed her free arm and kicked out with her legs, trying to shake off the force that bore her backward. Then her back fell against a hard wall of bone and muscle.

Stars danced before her eyes. The light streaming from the window began to fade. Her chest struggled against the constricting force. Stunned, she stood motionless.

"Don't move." The harsh words came from somewhere above her, a whispered threat barely audible above the roaring in her ears. She didn't—she couldn't—respond. The steel arms relaxed slightly.

She took rapid shallow breaths. Slowly the light in the window brightened again. She waited until the vines came clearly into focus.

Then she kicked, her spike heels hammering against her assailant's legs. With satisfaction she heard him swear at the sudden pain she inflicted. She twisted in his arms, her free hand clawing at the small finger of the hand covering her mouth, twisting it outward and up.

For a second she thought she had won. The hand eased away from her mouth and she opened her lips to let out a scream.

The next moment she was choking again as his arm tightened across her throat. Once again the light began to fade. Then she was half carried toward the house.

Her arms were wrenched behind her back. Strong legs flattened her body against the wall. She leaned forward, utterly helpless, but unhurt.

"Don't try that again," the harsh whisper warned her.

She couldn't talk; she was still trying to catch her breath. But she nodded briefly to let him know that she understood the implied threat if she didn't obey.

"Good. Raise your arms above your head. One at a time."

Slowly Jessica obeyed until her palms were pressed flat against the brick wall. While she leaned spread-eagled against the house, she breathed deeply.

Panic receded with each breath of night air. What a crazy situation! For years she had walked through the bazaars of the East without being accosted. Yet here, outside her childhood home, she had been attacked like a common criminal. She opened her mouth to explain who she was and that she had every right to roam the garden. "I am—"

"Don't talk."

The cold threat of his voice silenced her immediately. She would deal with him later. No security guard had the right to treat her so roughly without first finding out what she was doing in the garden.

Suddenly strong fingers slid over her, beginning their search at her hair, sliding expertly over her shoulders and down her back. They dipped into her pockets, prodded along her hips. His touch was impersonal. Yet the feel of his hands was a violation of her privacy. Angrily, she stiffened in response.

She could still hear the faint sound of music. The garden was so silent. So isolated. What if the fingers searching her didn't belong to a security guard? On her walk up the drive she had seen no one. Not even the drivers of the limousines parked in front.

She jerked as his hand began to slide down her legs. She clenched her teeth, stifling the shudder of revulsion sweeping over her.

"Stop it!" she hissed as he lifted one foot to examine her shoe.

She heard the swift movement as he straightened. His hand curled lightly around her neck in warning.

''Silence,'' the cold hard voice hissed into her ear.

Jessica could feel the strength of that hand. Fear spread within her, tightening her stomach into knots and clogging her throat.

He must have taken her silence for acquiescence because he withdrew his hand. She almost jumped when she felt him search her other shoe.

For a moment she considered kicking him. If she was lucky she might strike with her heel straight into his face. Would the surprise attack give her enough time to reach the front door?

She doubted it.

Agents and terrorists—for that's what she thought he was—were a different breed; they did not react to pain like ordinary people. Years of training had honed their reflexes to respond swiftly and accurately despite injury or pain. Jessica had no intention of finding herself thrown to the ground.

But when his hands slid upward again, she burst out, ''Take your filthy hands off me.''

He paused, hesitated, his eyes burning into her back. He was a nameless, faceless man with a strength far superior to her own.

Her fear spread, invading every part of her body, shaking her and leaving her weakly clinging to the wall for support. She wanted to plead with him not to violate her further. Yet, even engulfed in terror, she knew that pleading would get her nowhere. Cowardliness seemed to fan cruelty, unleashing frustrated anger in the face of submission. Jessica had no intention of becoming a victim.

She bit her lip to hold back the words. She stiffened her body to stop the trembling.

Suddenly the hands were gone. She felt him step back.

''Take your hands down.''

She obeyed.

''Turn around.''

Slowly she rolled her body against the wall, until she faced him.

He was tall, taller than most men. He towered above her, still faceless and nameless, but no longer threatening. If he had wanted to hurt her, he would have done so already. She sagged with relief. Her knees began to shake, and her teeth started chattering. Tears flooded her eyes. She made no attempt to stop their flow. The darkness that hid his face also covered her weakness.

"Who are you?" His voice was softer now. His search had produced nothing, neither bomb nor weapon of any kind. Just a wadded ball of a handkerchief. He felt puzzled and a little foolish.

She hesitated a few moments, trying to control her trembling lips. "Jessica Stanton," she finally said, her voice still slightly shaky.

"What are you doing here?" His voice had softened further at the sound of her tear-roughened response. He remembered the softness of her skin, the small size of her feet. Even in her high heels she barely reached his shoulders. How many bruises had he inflicted? The thought filled him with remorse.

"Looking for my parents." Her voice sounded firmer now. "I know I must have looked odd with my nose glued to the window, but you didn't have any right to handle me so roughly. Damn it, you tore my nylons."

He smiled faintly. She was recovering fast from her ordeal. Any moment now she would yell abuses at him. His ex-wife certainly would have showered him with curses. But nothing happened.

"Your parents?" he prompted, breaking the silence. He knew most of the guests, some personally, others by sight. He was fairly certain that no one named Stanton had been invited. Suspicion surfaced once again. "Why didn't you simply knock on the door?"

Jessica hesitated. She could have given him the excuses she had used herself: her dislike of mingling with that crowd, her inappropriate dress. Or she could have told him the truth: that she was reluctant to enter the house because she was afraid to face the past. Either answer would make her look ridiculous. She resorted to anger instead. "I don't have to stand here and answer your damned questions. If you don't believe me, call my aunt. She will vouch for me."

"First your parents, now your aunt." His voice was heavily laced with sarcasm. "Just who is your aunt?"

"Gloria Barton."

"Good try," he jeered softly. "Gloria Barton doesn't have a niece." He had known the Bartons all his life. Gloria Barton had been an only child, her husband, Howard, had one younger, unmarried brother.

"She's really my godmother." Jessica was too tired to respond to his sarcasm. All she wanted was to go inside the house with its bright lights and music.

There was a goddaughter named Jessica. Gloria had mentioned her less than an hour ago. In fact, within the small circle of close friends, the name Jessica cropped up with predictable regularity. His lawyer, Fred Dowel, was married to Alicia, Jessica's sister. Even Howard Barton's stern face softened whenever he mentioned the young woman's name.

At first he had resented the unknown Jessica's constant intrusion. With his divorce only recently finalized, every one of his friends seemed intent on matchmaking. The woman Jessica seemed to be their prime candidate. Only her name was Jessica O'Connor.

Also, Jessica O'Connor worked in Pakistan. When Gloria had mentioned her goddaughter earlier, wouldn't she have also mentioned her arrival in the States? He felt sure of it.

This woman had to be an imposter.

"Are you finished now with your questions?" Jessica's cool voice broke the silence. She had sensed the subtle shifting of emotions within him. "It's getting rather chilly out here. If you don't mind, I'd like to go inside to find my aunt."

"And what about your parents?" he asked pointedly.

She pushed herself away from the wall. "And my parents," she added, hoping she sounded more confident than she felt. Despite the note in her mother's appointment calendar, her parents might have made last minute changes.

He didn't answer. If she really was Pat O'Connor's daughter, she would meet her father soon enough. If she wasn't... He frowned. Somehow he hated the thought of handing her over to security. If only he could put her into a cab and send her on her way. But too much was at stake. "What did you do with the bomb?"

Her head snapped back at the harsh question. "Bomb? What bomb?" She caught her breath. "Is that what you think I am? A terrorist?" So that was why he had handled her so roughly and frisked her so thoroughly. "I'm no terrorist," she denied firmly. "Do I look like a terrorist?"

"Lady, terrorists come in all shapes and sizes." His voice was cold.

"And there's no way I can convince you that terrorism makes me sick. Look, I've got IDs. I can show you my passport and my driver's license. They're in my purse."

His silence told her what he thought of IDs. Jessica herself knew just how easily passports could be falsified.

"What did you stuff into your pocket earlier?"

She stared at his face, wishing she could make out his features. What was he talking about? She couldn't remember putting anything into her coat pocket. She'd been too occupied with her thoughts of the past.

The stone bench amid the lilacs had been where Michael had asked her to marry him. The rosebushes had witnessed their wedding. The rose she had cupped was his favorite kind. Only eighteen months later she had thrown one fresh bud into his grave.

That had been six years ago. Six years of fighting pain and loneliness. Six years of building a new life from the ashes of shattered dreams.

Visiting the garden had been one way of testing her recovery. She was glad that only sadness lingered where pain once ruled, pain that had driven her overseas. The thought that this stranger had witnessed her pilgrimage angered her.

"I don't know what you're talking about," she snapped.

"When you sat on that bench, you emptied your purse. What were you searching for?"

She suppressed a smile. "My handkerchief," she said, her voice mocking him. "Don't tell me you followed me like a common criminal because of that?"

A handkerchief? Remembering the wadded ball he'd found in the pocket of her coat, he felt a touch of remorse. Perhaps he should have confronted her the moment she had taken it from her purse.

Abruptly he dismissed the thought. Only the very young or naive would have responded to that gesture without suspicion. He hadn't been that for a long time. "Let's go inside. I'll give you to security and let them figure you out" was his icy response.

Her brief amusement vanished. She couldn't take any more! She began shaking again, this time with weariness. For a moment she even considered sitting down right here at his feet and letting him carry her into the house. Only the thought that someone might witness such an undignified arrival kept her head high.

She turned jerkily, her lips pressed together.

"Move, lady!" His voice was filled with impatience. He wanted to get this affair over with as swiftly as possible. "First let's pick up your purse."

The harsh words stiffened her back and she began walking, carefully placing her high heels on the uneven ground. She didn't want to stumble. If he touched her again she'd lose her cool and hit out at him. Or even worse, she might break down and cry. Just a few more minutes, a few more minutes, she told herself in rhythm with her steps. Don't break down now, don't break down now. Don't give him the satisfaction of seeing you cry. All the way to the garden gate she fought her tears. The silent shadow following her was unnerving. Slowly her eyes filled with tears.

She stepped past the bushes into the brightly lit front, waiting for him to close the gate. Then she turned to reason with him once again. "I am not a terrorist," she repeated. "And I don't want to be handed over to security to be taken away for questioning. Ask one of the guards in the foyer to call my uncle. He'll vouch for me.''

He stopped, the tall bushes framing him. Until now darkness had blurred her features. For the first time he clearly saw the pure oval of her face.

She wasn't beautiful. Not in the classical sense of the word. Her eyes, which at the moment were huge with distress, were spaced too far apart; her nose was tilted and her mouth was too wide. Her lips trembled slightly at the corners and her chin wobbled as she fought for control. A single tear ran slowly down her cheek.

Sharply he sucked in air. Where was the hardness that marred even the most beautiful face of a terrorist? He saw none. All he saw was weariness and a vulnerability she was trying desperately to hide. He wanted to draw her against him, to cradle her in his arms and soothe away the hurt he'd inflicted. Yet he sensed that if he were to reach out for her, to touch her in any way at all, she would withdraw from him even further.

Briefly he nodded. "I'll call Howard the moment we get inside."

"Thank you," she said, wishing she could see him more clearly, but the shadows blurred his features. Abruptly she turned. Walking swiftly, she almost raced up the steps to end the nightmare.

When the door opened, he was right behind her. Before Jessica could identify herself, she heard him say, "I found her outside wandering in the garden. She claims she's Jessica Stanton, Ambassador O'Connor's daughter and Mr. Barton's niece."

"I *am* Jessica Stanton. And Mr. Barton is *not* my real uncle. He's my godfather," she corrected smoothly, staring into the impassive faces of the two security guards in front of her. With her head held high, she walked past them to one of the chairs by the telephone. Sitting down, she briefly closed her eyes.

"I'll get Mr. Barton," she heard one of the men say. She listened as the French doors separating the foyer from the living room opened and then closed. When she opened her eyes to look around for the stranger, he was gone. Only one guard remained. He stood next to her chair, dangling her heavy purse from his hand.

Feeling oddly disappointed, she closed her eyes once again. Yet, strangely, she could still sense the man's presence. Who was he? If he was a guest, she'd see him again soon enough. It should be easy to pick him out of the crowd. Few people were as tall and broad as the stranger, with his black hair and rock-hard body.

She raised her head. This episode had unnerved her more than she'd thought. Why else would she even contemplate looking for that man? He had scared her, frisked her and reduced her to tears.

She lifted a hand and wiped her face. Fine grit covered her skin. Startled, she sat up. What a wreck she must look. She stretched out her legs and gazed at the torn nylons.

Her hazel eyes began to blaze with green fire. Oh, she was going to find that stranger. She owed him something for turning her surprise into a nightmare. She was going to pay him back. The thought was uplifting, a formidable restorative that did wonders for her weariness. She turned toward the hovering guard, asking him for her bag.

After handing her over to the two men, he had crossed the foyer to the shadow cast by the curving staircase. With his shoulder propped against the wall, he watched as she raised her face, talking to the guard hovering near her.

Her face was cool and composed, as if the incident in the garden had never happened. The man was smiling at her like a big guard dog turned gentle pet. Resentment flared. He inched closer, trying to catch her words.

Suddenly he stiffened. The guard was handing her the bag, without checking the contents first. He couldn't believe the man's stupidity. Striding forward, he warned, "Don't open it."

Jessica's head snapped around. She glared into the harsh, bronzed face of the stranger, her fingers clenched around the tassel of the zipper. "I need a tissue to clean my face."

"Use the handkerchief in your coat," he suggested pointedly, meeting the furious green fire in her eyes with an implacable look.

Jessica's lips tightened angrily. Silently she handed him her bag. Turning away, she reached into her pocket and withdrew her handkerchief. A muffled "Damn you" reached his ears as she wiped the grit from her face.

At that moment the French doors were flung open and Howard Barton entered the foyer, a tall, slim man with graying hair and a strong, lined face.

"Jessica. What are you doing here?" He held out his arms in welcome.

With a swift, triumphant look at her tormentor, Jessica rose to her feet. Then she turned to her godfather, a smile of such warmth brightening her face that the man held his breath. "It's a long story," she said, her voice husky with emotion. "I got the job. When I heard the news, I needed to tell someone."

"Congratulations. It's about time you returned stateside. Your aunt and I have missed you."

Jessica tilted her head back to look into the familiar face. He hadn't changed much, she thought; a few more gray hairs and a few more lines, but his gray eyes were as piercing as ever. "I'm looking forward to working here myself," she admitted. "I've missed you, too."

With a mixture of relief and remorse, the man watched the scene. He felt awkward and ashamed at the way he'd handled her. If there had been some way of leaving the foyer without disturbing their reunion, he'd have left immediately.

Instead he retreated a few steps. His eyes were drawn to Jessica's radiant face. Then they moved to her thick hair confined in a French braid. Her skin tones were slightly lighter than her hair, a golden bronze, unusual for a redhead.

Studying her closely, he could now see some resemblance to her father. She had the same stubborn set to her chin and way of tilting her head as she talked to her uncle.

Yes, she was definitely her father's daughter. She had neither her mother's fine blond hair nor her sister's cool classical beauty. Instead she had inherited Pat O'Connor's dark brows and Titian hair. His hand itched with the desire to loosen the silky mane and feel it cascade over his hands, to bury his face in its jasmine scent.

Jessica reminded him of the warmth spread by glowing embers on a cool winter night. He wanted to move closer, to be warmed by those embers. He had lived in the dark coldness for a long time. Too long, he thought grimly, remembering the scene in the garden. Other men would have treated her gently, asking questions first instead of attacking her. But he had seen too much cruelty. He had lived so long in a world of destruction, terror and hate that he had forgotten about glowing embers, about decency and innocence.

The French doors opened once again. Gloria Barton rushed into the foyer in a cloud of green silk. "Jessica. Of all the days to choose from, did you have to arrive tonight?"

Jessica hugged her godmother, grinning broadly. "I can always go back to the apartment," she suggested.

"Don't you dare." Gloria Barton blinked, trying to trap the moisture in her green eyes. "I'm so happy to see you, I could cry."

"Could?" Howard teased. "Jessica, take her upstairs before she turns into a waterfall. I'll look for your parents while you two talk. Do they know you're here?"

Wiping her godmother's tears away with her handkerchief, Jessica shook her head. "I didn't have the time to call before I left New York."

"Don't tell them just yet," Gloria pleaded with her husband. "I want a few minutes with her alone. I promise I won't keep her too long." She turned toward the stairs, then stopped abruptly. She looked at the man standing a few feet away.

"Damon." A look of dismay clouded her face. "Don't tell me you're going already."

Damon shook his head. All thoughts of leaving early had fled from his mind. "I only went out for a breath of fresh air," he answered, a crooked smile lifting the corner of his mouth. His dark eyes shifted from Gloria to Jessica. "I bumped into Mrs. Stanton and escorted her inside."

Jessica's brows rose sharply at his description of the events that had left her body trembling with fear. The scene was still too vivid for her to feel amused, especially in her present grubby state. Holding out her hand, she said, "I'll take my bag now."

Her eyes bright with curiosity, Gloria watched the bag change hands. "I don't believe you two have met before. Jessica, this is Damon Noble." She smiled at him affectionately. "Damon, you must have heard me mention Jessica. I'm glad you two finally met."

Dismayed, Jessica realized that her godmother was actually fond of the man. She nodded politely, wishing he would leave.

With a hint of laughter in his voice, Damon responded, "Your name comes up constantly. Sometimes, though, I doubted you actually existed. I wonder why we've never met."

"Jessica has been abroad for six years." Howard Barton joined the conversation. He turned to his wife. "If you two want to talk, you'd better go upstairs before someone comes looking for you."

With a nod and a light, "I'll see you later," Gloria led the way up the stairs. Relieved, Jessica followed her.

Crossing the foyer, Damon asked Howard thoughtfully, "What happened to Jessica's husband?"

Howard Barton shot him a piercing look. He didn't usually divulge personal information but Damon was a good and trusted friend. "Six years ago he was killed in Libya in a freak accident. They'd only been married a short time. Jessica took it hard. She's been overseas ever since. I'm glad she finally decided to come home."

Once inside the living room, Howard Barton excused himself. Damon wandered through the spacious rooms in search of Patrick O'Connor. He intended to find out more about Jessica Stanton. And what better source than a proud father?

Chapter 2

In the blue and white master bedroom upstairs, Gloria Barton closed the door. "Take your coat off, Jessica."

While Jessica unbuttoned her coat, Gloria went to the mirror to repair the damage her tears had caused.

Jessica dropped her heavy purse on a chair, draped her coat over it, then went to the adjoining bathroom to wash her hands. She gasped. The mirror reflected a face lightly streaked with dirt. Swiftly she removed all traces of her ordeal before joining her godmother once again.

"Tell me, did you get the job?" Gloria turned, holding a comb suspended in the air.

Smiling, Jessica bowed. "You see before you the most junior member of the U.S. delegation to the United Nations."

The comb dropped. Gloria jumped to her feet, rushing to embrace Jessica once again. "I'm so glad," she said, her voice shaking. "God, how I've missed you."

Jessica hugged her tightly, tears shimmering in her eyes. How selfish she had been, so wrapped up in her personal misery she hadn't thought of the pain she was causing others.

While her parents had moved from embassy to embassy, Aunt Gloria and Uncle Howard had given her a home. They had cared for her through chicken pox and braces. They had rejoiced at her wedding and had shared her grief, and she had turned her back on them.

They had given her love and she had repaid their devotion by running away. First to Saudi Arabia for three years and then to Islamabad, Pakistan. She had written them, and had even seen them, meeting them in impersonal places, such as her parents' apartment or a hotel. But she had not set foot in their house, the house of her childhood dreams and memories. Not until tonight.

"I'm sorry," she whispered, her voice choked with tears. "I never meant to hurt you."

"I wasn't hurt, only rather worried," Gloria reassured her. She dropped her arms and stepped back. "You're too young to bury yourself in the middle of nowhere."

"Pakistan isn't exactly the end of the world," Jessica protested mildly. To Aunt Gloria, the only civilized places on earth were Washington, New York and Miami.

"Of course not," Gloria Barton agreed, "but it's the next thing to it. I can't tell you how excited we were when you wrote that you had applied for the position at the U.N. Your uncle was all set to pull a few strings to make sure you'd get the job. I had the hardest time keeping him from interfering."

"I'm glad you did," Jessica said firmly. "I wanted to succeed on my own merits."

Gloria nodded her understanding. "I think your work with the Afghan refugees helped a lot. Plus the fact that you speak Farsi like a native. But, whatever the reason, I'm glad you're coming back. When do you start?"

"In September. My job in Islamabad ends in June. Then I'll have two months vacation. That should give me enough time to find an apartment in New York." She made a face. "I hate moving. You can't imagine the amount of stuff I've accumulated over the years."

"You always were a pack rat. You still have several boxes here in the basement."

Jessica stiffened. Those boxes were filled with Michael's belongings, personal items she hadn't wanted to give away. Even now, she didn't know if she was ready to open them. "If you don't mind, I'd like to leave them there a little bit longer."

"Jessica." Gloria Barton sighed. "I'd hoped that by now you had come to terms with Michael's death. It's been six years. You can't spend the rest of your life in mourning."

Jessica heard the anxiety in her godmother's gentle words and responded to it. "I'm all right."

"Then why haven't you found someone else? Are there no men in Islamabad?"

Jessica shrugged her shoulders. "Most of the men I work with are married. There are, of course, any number of businessmen looking for a good time during their short stay. Really, I'm quite content with my life. I have several good friends and my work."

"New York is full of attractive, eligible men," Gloria pointed out. "As soon as you've settled down, I'll round them up for your inspection," she teased.

Jessica chuckled. "Don't you start matchmaking, too. Mother's constant hints are bad enough. There isn't a letter in which she doesn't touch on that subject. If you join ranks with her I'll go overseas again."

"Your mother only wants to see you happy," Gloria defended her best friend.

"I'm not ready yet for a house in the suburbs," Jessica said, serious now. She disliked making plans that went up in smoke and commitments that caused pain. So far she hadn't met anyone she'd been particularly interested in. The men she knew were too smooth, too superficial, or too set in their ways.

"It's your life," Gloria sighed. Getting to her feet, she added, "There's more to marriage than the long-drawn-out love affair you had with Michael. You didn't have time to find out about the other aspects, the commitments, the sharing. And today, marriage needn't be a prison for a wife." Her eyes went over Jessica's dress. "I like your dress.

I wish I could still wear strapless, clinging little numbers like that.''

The ruffled bodice drew attention to Jessica's smooth, tanned shoulders and the soft swell of her breasts. The loose fit of the silky material clung to her hips when she moved. A slit revealed glimpses of slim long legs with every step.

"At my age, I have to hide my wrinkles."

"What wrinkles?" Jessica asked. Except for a few laughter lines around her eyes, her godmother's face was as smooth as her own.

"The ones I'm hiding." She patted her high collar. "Under here. What happened to your legs?"

Startled, Jessica looked down. "I almost forgot to change my nylons." She walked to her purse, searching for another pair of pantyhose. "You won't believe what happened to me," she said, laughing. Swiftly she told her godmother of her excursion into the garden—and its consequences—making light of the whole affair.

Gloria chuckled. "So that's why you were so stiff and formal when I introduced you to Damon." A look of concern crossed her face. "Did he hurt you?"

"No." She wriggled out of the torn nylons and tossed them into the wastebasket. She didn't want to talk about Damon anymore. She wanted to forget that cool, hard voice that had so unexpectedly softened in the end. She also didn't want to examine her own feelings of disappointment when she'd thought that he had handed her over to security.

"I don't understand it." Frowning, Gloria shook her head. "Despite his size and strength, Damon is quite gentle. You really must have looked suspicious."

Jessica wondered if they were talking about the same man. The impression she had of the tall dark shadow who had lunged at her didn't resemble the Damon Noble of her aunt's description. "Perhaps," she admitted doubtfully. "Remember those concrete blocks? I'd climbed on them to get a better view."

Her godmother grinned. "Oh, I remember. I once found you standing there in your nightgown. In November, and you were frozen through."

Smiling, Jessica drew on the fresh pantyhose, then stood up and smoothed down her dress. "Yes. I caught a bad cold and you made me stay in bed for three days." She took out a lipstick and applied it. Smoothing down a strand of hair, she said, "I think we better join your guests before Uncle Howard comes looking for us."

Gloria nodded. "There are several people here tonight that I'd like you to meet. Women, too," she said with a grin when she saw Jessica frown.

The living room was large. Jessica looked for her parents and for Damon. She didn't see them. If Jessica had been alone, she would have moved swiftly to the dining room and the den. Instead, while her eyes examined every tall man, Gloria's introductions forced her into stopping every so often, shaking hands, smiling and answering questions.

She cradled the glass of champagne she'd picked off a tray, warming but not drinking it. At receptions in Islamabad, foreigners rarely drank, in deference to local customs. Pakistan was a Muslim country and liquor was frowned upon.

"Gossip," Jessica muttered as she followed Gloria into the den. If she heard one more version of a certain senator's exploits, she'd scream.

Gloria grinned. "What else is there to talk about?" she asked lightly. "Politics?"

Jessica shrugged her shoulders. She knew that tonight's carelessly uttered word might cause tomorrow's political embarrassment. To avoid such accidents, everyone talked about the misfortunes of others, speculating, ridiculing. They also listened, hoping to catch someone else's unguarded words. And they watched. They were watching her now. Jessica could feel several pairs of eyes looking her over because she was new to the scene.

Patience, she told herself when her godmother introduced her to Senator Dempsey and his wife. Jessica had met the senator when he'd visited the Afghan refugee camps a few months earlier. Like others before him, he had promised to send more aid in the form of medical supplies and

food, but so far his promises had also remained unful-
filled.

"Such things take time," the senator explained after repeating his promises. "Cost proposals and approvals are
time consuming."

Just how much? The refugees were starving now. Every
day some died from malnutrition, many more from infec-
tions and open wounds. Only the day before her departure,
Dr. Brooks, a British physician in charge of the camp near
Peshawar, had complained that he was running out of syringes.

"I know that you're doing everything possible to expe-
dite the shipments." Jessica gave the man one of her brilliant smiles. "You saw for yourself how badly help is
needed. Perhaps you could impress on the other members
of your committee just how urgent the situation is?"

The senator spread his pudgy hands. "I'll try, Mrs. Stanton."

Words dripping with sarcasm hovered on her lips. She
swallowed them and thanked him with a smile. Ranting and
raving would only harm the refugees. She turned away, once
again searching the room.

Suddenly she stiffened.

Colonel Henderson! What was Army Intelligence doing
here? His path had crossed hers several times during the last
months. Too many times for her liking. She had first run
into him about eight weeks ago at one of the official government parties in Islamabad. After their first meeting, he
seemed to turn up everywhere in the small town. Her friend
Barbara had teased her about the colonel's apparent pur-
suit. Jessica, however, had found Henderson distasteful and
had been relieved when the man left.

"Isn't it terribly dangerous to live in Pakistan?" Mrs.
Dempsey asked, drawing Jessica's attention.

"I've never run into any trouble. We don't travel alone
outside the city limits though," Jessica explained, her eyes
shifting back to the colonel.

"But what about the Pushtuns? From what my husband says, they're really quite barbaric." The slim woman shuddered delicately.

Barbaric? Jessica struggled to hide her impatience. The tall mountain men were fiercely independent and very proud. The Pushtuns Senator Dempsey had visited were friendly and civilized.

"They're a proud and highly intelligent people," Jessica stated firmly. "Those who have left their tribes are very successful. Many of them hold important government jobs. But," she added, to appease Mrs. Dempsey's hunger for sensationalism, "it is true the tribesmen don't welcome strangers. Even the Pakistani government forces avoid penetrating their territory."

Mrs. Dempsey smiled, then turned to the man standing on the other side of her. "They still keep their women veiled. What an anachronism in this day and age."

Jessica could have pointed out that Pushtun women preferred the protection of the veil. But Mrs. Dempsey would not appreciate her explanations about traditions steeped in faith and about *pushtunwali*, the simple but effective law that ruled their lives. Mrs. Dempsey was a butterfly, skimming the surface of life. Besides, Jessica did not wish to upset her. Too many lives depended on the senator's goodwill.

Unobtrusively, Jessica nudged her godmother. Gloria looked at her and nodded slightly, but continued her discussion.

Impatiently, Jessica shifted her weight from one foot to the other. So far she hadn't seen her parents. And where was Damon Noble? Again she looked around the crowded room. Once more she stared at the colonel's sleek, blond head in speculation. Suddenly he turned, staring straight at her.

Goose bumps formed on her skin. Jessica felt a freezing shiver run down her spine. His cold blue-gray eyes had always had that effect on her. Even in the heat of Pakistan she'd frozen under that arctic gaze.

He smiled at her, raising his glass in a silent salute. Jessica nodded coolly, then breathed a sigh of relief when the colonel's companion, a small curvy brunette, claimed his attention. She watched the brief exchange between the two before the colonel's eyes drifted away.

Curious, she followed his stare, her eyes picking out several likely subjects, until she noticed Damon Noble's broad back in the farthest corner of the room.

Earlier, in the foyer, she'd been too upset to really study the man. Now she let her eyes rove over him. Black hair, worn slightly long, brushed the collar of his shirt. His broad shoulders pressed against the dark cloth of his tuxedo as if the confinement irked him. Or perhaps he was aware of the colonel's interest. Henderson's eyes seemed intent on burning a hole in Damon's back.

She recalled the tilt of Damon's arrogant head and the width of his shoulders. In the darkness of the garden he had seemed like a giant, too tall, too powerful, too unreal. But then the whole scene had become unreal, now that she was safe and surrounded by bright lights. Yet here he was, just as tall and just as big as she remembered.

Suddenly he turned. Their eyes clashed and held.

What a striking face. A strong face. A study of contrasts. Thick, straight brows. A slim, crooked nose. Deeply set eyes. Prominent cheekbones with hollows below. A stubborn jaw and a sensual twist to his wide, firm mouth. Then he smiled, his teeth a brilliant white against the darkness of his tan. Jessica's eyes focused on each of his features separately before combining them into a picture of uncompromising strength and humor. As she watched, laughter lines formed crescents around his eyes.

"He's laughing at me," Jessica muttered under her breath. She tried to tear her eyes away from his face but she couldn't. She stared, and heat flushed her face.

I'm behaving like a teenager, she thought. Yet even at seventeen she couldn't remember feeling so moonstruck.

That guy scared me, he frisked me and he watched me cry, she reminded herself. The recall of her humiliation had the right effect. She turned her back to him just as Gloria skillfully extracted herself from her partner.

"I'm sorry about the delay. Did you see either of your parents?"

Jessica shook her head. Involuntarily her eyes returned to Damon. He had his back turned once again.

"They must be around here somewhere. Perhaps Howard found them and sent them upstairs."

"That's possible."

Gloria looked at her sharply. Jessica seemed distracted and tense. Following her gaze, Gloria spotted Damon almost immediately. Seeing that Jessica was intrigued by Damon, a satisfied grin spread across her face. She couldn't have planned it better.

Damon Noble was one of her favorite people. He was single, very eligible and absolutely devastating. She chuckled. Trust Jessica to pick the most handsome, most elusive bachelor present. No. Another chuckle escaped her. It was Damon who had done the picking. And right off the windowsill.

At that moment Damon moved to one side. "Jessica," Gloria said, laughter bubbling in her voice, "I just spotted your father."

Jessica nodded. "I saw him, too." She was oblivious to her godmother's mirth. Her blood boiled with anger behind the icy facade of her face. How dare Damon Noble search out her father and question him. First he had spoiled her surprise—and now her reunion. Her eyes looked straight past him to a man of medium height with a shock of coppery hair streaked with gray. The handsome face was permanently tanned by years spent under the tropical sun.

"Pat, look who I've found." At Gloria's gay words, Patrick O'Connor turned.

Jessica smiled at the momentary look of stunned disbelief on her father's face. She rushed forward, pushing past her godmother while her father stepped toward her. "Jessica! What are you doing here?" Patrick O'Connor smiled broadly, drawing Jessica into a bear hug.

"Looking for you," Jessica gasped as her father's strong arms tightened around her. She tried to balance her glass of champagne, holding out her arm to avoid spilling its contents over his jacket. A firm, steadying hand covered her own; then the glass was removed from her hand.

With a grateful smile, Jessica looked up. Damon's black eyes danced with little flames of laughter. Swiftly, before she could make a fool of herself again, she looked away.

"Are you glad to see me?" she teased her father.

"What a dumb question," Pat O'Connor said gruffly, slowly releasing her. "Your mother and I wanted to come to New York. But between your schedule and mine, there just wasn't time. I tried to call you this afternoon. How did it go? Did you get it?" When Jessica nodded, he beamed. "That's great. Does your mother know yet?"

"Jessica got here only a few minutes ago," Gloria explained. "Just where is Mary? We haven't been able to find her."

"I think she's in the dining room. Jessica, why didn't you let us know you were coming? We would have met you at the airport."

"It was one of those spur of the moment decisions." Jessica grinned. "I would have been here earlier, but I had no idea that it would take me all afternoon and part of the evening to fly from New York to Washington."

"Are you always so impulsive?" Damon asked from behind her.

Jessica had wondered just how long Damon would tolerate being ignored. The polite thing would have been to retreat from this family reunion. Why couldn't he leave her alone? Slowly she turned her head. "Sometimes," she admitted coldly, looking at his bow tie, refusing to meet his eyes. "Life would be very boring otherwise, Mr. Noble."

His lips curved into a crooked smile. "I don't agree with you. I don't like surprises." The crooked smile changed to a rueful twist. "Personally, I prefer a little advance notice before my family descends on me."

I'll bet, Jessica thought.

"But then your situation is vastly different from ours," Patrick O'Connor interrupted. "At our age, Mary and I can do with some surprises to brighten our lives." His eyes moved from Damon to Jessica. "Oh, you two have met. Somehow I had the impression that you didn't know one another." He shrugged his shoulders. "Damon is a good friend of your sister and brother-in-law. Must've been something they said."

Jessica almost groaned with dismay. The Bartons, her parents and now her sister. Damon Noble seemed to have infiltrated her family in the six years she had been overseas.

"Gloria introduced us earlier," Damon explained, looking at the controlled mask of her face. For a redhead she hid her emotions well. The cool look she gave him was polite and impersonal. Too impersonal for his taste. Then he caught the green sparkle in her eyes and the slight quiver of her nose. Someday he would tease her about the specks of gold dancing across its bridge when she was angry. But now he wanted to take that mask from her face. He wanted to be warmed by her smile.

"I've heard a lot about you. From several members of your family," Damon teased, his tone suggesting that not everything had been good.

Jessica clenched her fingers into balls. Some day, Ali, she promised her sister, I'll return the favor. There was no doubt in her mind that Ali was the culprit. Her sister had never quite forgotten nor forgiven the childhood pranks Jessica had involved her in. She suggestively raised her eyes to the crooked shape of his nose. Plainly she wasn't the first one he had teased into fury.

The intensity of her feelings shocked her. She couldn't remember the last time she had been filled with bloodthirsty thoughts.

"You have the advantage, Mr. Noble," she said stiffly. "I haven't been in Washington for quite some time. I don't recognize your name."

At her stilted words, Damon's eyes filled with amusement. "There's no need to apologize," he told her almost patronizingly.

Jessica's temper flared. "I wasn't apologizing." She glared at him. "I was trying to be polite. Are you an up-and-coming light around here?"

"I hope not!" He rejected her suggestion with such a comical look of horror on his face that Jessica smiled.

"You mean you have no political ambitions at all?" she asked, wondering what he was doing here at this party, where, one way or another, most of the guests were involved in politics. Then she remembered Colonel Henderson's interest in him. Maybe Damon Noble did not seek public office. Maybe, with his tough body and swift reflexes, he was part of the darker side of politics. The world of intelligence and counterintelligence. Colonel Henderson's world. Her smile froze.

"Absolutely none." His words were firm and reassuring, but Jessica couldn't shake her doubts. Men like Henderson did not waste their time on nobodies. She turned to her father hoping he might shed some light on Damon's identity. Her father was deep in conversation with her godmother.

"Then what do you do? Apart from playing games?" She turned back to Damon.

"I enjoy myself." His voice deepened. He was caressing her bare skin with his eyes. "And you, Jessica Stanton, do you like games?"

"I love them. Puzzles are my specialty." She would love to find all the missing pieces to the puzzle that was Damon Noble. "You mean that's all you do with your life? Enjoy yourself?"

"Is there anything wrong with that?" One dark eyebrow raised in question.

"Nothing, of course," Jessica answered sweetly. "What else do you do? When you're not baiting me."

"Is that what I'm doing?" The dancing lights were back in his eyes, small sparks of fire that burned her face.

"You know it is." Her voice sounded husky, no longer cool. As his eyes slid from her face down her neck, her anger melted. She could feel her skin become flushed until it seemed to glow.

The ice was melting. Damon could feel the glowing embers spread their warmth, touching him, warming him. He wanted to move closer, to stir those embers to bright flames. But not here. Not with the rest of the world watching. He raised the glass to his lips.

Jessica watched him lift the glass he had rescued to his lips, waiting for his reaction with barely suppressed amusement. The champagne had to be warm and flat. She had cradled it in her hand for some time. As he tilted the fluted crystal to his mouth not a single bubble rose to the surface.

He swallowed. The look of disgust on his face made her laugh.

"Why didn't you warn me that the stuff was flat?"

"That is my champagne you're drinking."

"You want it back?" He offered her the glass.

She shook her head. "No, you may keep it," she said graciously.

He smiled at her, a fascinating, crooked grin. "Don't tell me you hate warm, flat champagne as much as I do." He turned to look for a waiter.

Jessica's eyes strayed to the hand holding the glass. It was tanned and strong with long fingers and short nails. She knew just how strong and how thorough those hands were. She could feel his touch even now. The memory of moments of fear, hurt and utter helplessness returned.

Unable to find a waiter, Damon turned back to her. The hurt he saw in her eyes hit him like a blow. He wanted to take her in his arms, cradle her against him and hold her until the hurt had vanished. But he could do none of those things.

Not until September.

He bent his head, his breath caressing her skin. "I'm sorry I hurt you. I wish I could do something to erase those moments from your mind."

Slowly the nightmare faded. Jessica looked at him. She saw regret in the depths of his eyes. "I guess my behavior did seem rather suspicious." But only to someone who was used to dealing with terrorists. No ordinary person would have attacked her first and asked questions later.

"Rather unusual, yes." He stared at her curiously. "Why did you go into the garden?"

Her lips twisted wryly in self-mockery. "I was reluctant to face this crowd."

He shook his head. "I watched you after you came downstairs, Jessica Stanton. I saw you long before you recognized me. You hide your feelings well. I didn't see any reluctance."

"I was afraid of—" She looked into the dark eyes filled with regret. Impulsively she covered his hand. "What happened in the garden had nothing to do with it. You actually made it easier for me to enter the house. I was more afraid of you than facing painful memories."

"And now?" His voice was harsh. "Are you still afraid of them?" The memories she had been reluctant to face must have to do with her husband's death. "Do you still mourn for your husband?" He disliked the thought.

"He died six years ago."

Damon tensed. She hadn't answered his question. Six years could mean that the time passed was too short to stop mourning or too long to sustain her grief. He tried a different question. "Was it very painful?"

"My husband's death or entering the house?" Jessica asked coolly. She disliked his probing. But something beneath the harshness of his face made her relent. "I was very much in love."

Her voice was soft, filled with sadness, but free of pain. He relaxed a little.

"In the garden I didn't have time to shed tears, because someone rudely interrupted my trip into the past."

He smiled. "Then I did you a service. Am I forgiven?" He raised her hand to his lips.

Jessica didn't know when he had reversed the position of their hands, or when he had shifted the glass. She tried to withdraw her hand now, but his hold tightened, caressing her skin with his lips.

Warmth spread through her from the tips of her fingers up her arm. Her hand had been kissed many times in greeting, but not this intimately, not with such softness and sensual expertise. She felt weak all over.

"Only if you tell me what you were doing outside," she countered.

"If you explain what else was in your purse."

"Nail polish. Makeup. A bottle of shampoo. Passport. Driver's license. Is that enough?"

Nodding, Damon groaned. "No wonder the bag weighs you down. Is that why you left it on the bench?"

She nodded. "It was too heavy to carry down memory lane." She looked at him pointedly. "Your turn."

"I needed some room. A breath of fresh spring air. This place smells like the perfume counter at Bloomingdale's—"

"Jessica," her father interrupted, coming to her side. "I think we should look for your mother."

Jessica turned swiftly, disengaging her hand. "Yes," she agreed reluctantly. She didn't want to leave yet. She wanted to find out more about this man who wore his tuxedo with self-assurance yet seemed to hate these receptions as much as she did. But there was no time.

"Perhaps we could meet tomorrow for dinner." Damon's voice held a hint of urgency.

Jessica looked back at him, shaking her head. "I'm leaving for Pakistan tomorrow."

Gloria Barton watched the exchange with satisfaction. She had purposely drawn Patrick into an involved discussion to give the two time to talk. "Pat, there's really no reason why all three of us should search for Mary," she said. She had no intention of letting Patrick end what looked like the beginning of something promising. "Why don't we leave those two to decide on a time and a place for their next meeting." She stared at Patrick, willing him to understand.

When Patrick winked, she turned back to Jessica. "Did Damon tell you that he plans to visit your part of the world soon?"

Jessica shook her head. She was too embarrassed to object.

"He's going to India," her father added with a grin. He turned to Damon. "Jessica can tell you more about Delhi than I can. She's been there several times during the last few years."

"Pat, let's go. Mary will be livid if we don't find her soon." Gloria moved away swiftly, before Jessica could find her voice. Patrick followed her, shaking his head, leaving an uncomfortable silence behind.

Damon looked at Jessica's averted face. He wasn't angry with Gloria; instead he actually felt rather grateful. But he regretted the effect her words had had on Jessica. Once again she had withdrawn behind her cool mask. "Do you want to follow them? You don't have to stay if you don't want to."

Jessica turned to face him. His mouth was twisted in wry amusement and his eyes were soft with concern. Laughter welled up and her eyes began to sparkle. "They didn't mean to—"

"Yes they did."

A giggle escaped her. Damon chuckled, his shoulders shaking.

"No finesse," Jessica added, laughing openly now. "Should I apologize for them?"

"Only if it makes you feel less embarrassed."

"And what about you? You really don't have to stay."

Abruptly he stopped laughing. "I don't want you to disappear. All my life I've searched for a woman like you. Now that I've found you, I don't want to let you go."

Speechless, Jessica stared at him. Slowly the crooked smile reappeared on his face, tugging at her heart, but his eyes were sober. This was no flattery. He wasn't joking. He meant every word. What was she going to do about it?

She didn't know.

Chapter 3

Tell me about your trip to India. Where do you plan to go?" India was a safer subject, one she was familiar with, one that didn't scare and excite her at the same time.

"Did I shock you?" he asked softly.

"Isn't that what you intended?" Jessica countered. He was rather good at shock tactics and better than she was in dealing with them. Before she had left for Saudi Arabia she had attended a course in terrorist activities. She knew the value of surprise and of keeping the adversary off balance. In this case what she didn't know how to handle was defense. So she chose to ignore his efforts to rattle her.

"Are you going to India on business or for pleasure?"

With a gleam of amusement he asked, "Changing the subject? All right, let's play the game of questions and answers. My trip is a combination of work and vacation. First I have to spend a few days in Delhi. From there I leave for the south. I'm told tigers will soon be extinct in the wild and I've always wanted to see them in their natural habitat. The rest of the time I plan to go mountain climbing."

Jessica listened to his words intently. Why didn't she believe him? Was it the tone of his voice? Maybe it was his lack of excitement and enthusiasm. He sounded bored with the prospect of a trip others would regard as the dream of a lifetime. He spoke like a man who had seen it all. Perhaps it was the fact that no sane person would plan such a trip for the beginning of the monsoon season that made her doubt his words. "Just when is this trip going to take place?" she asked slowly.

"In about six weeks."

"Perhaps you should check with your travel agent," Jessica suggested smoothly. "India is very uncomfortable during the monsoon."

Damon smiled, a smile that failed to reach his eyes. "I didn't know that the rains would come so soon."

"Didn't you?" She looked into the dark fathomless depth of his eyes. "They begin at the end of June." Something told her that he knew all about the hellish monsoon season, when it rained almost constantly and humidity reached one hundred percent. Men like Damon were rarely caught unprepared.

Why was he going to India at a time when even Indians living abroad avoided visits home? What was the real purpose behind his trip? She couldn't see him riding on elephants through dripping forests or slogging through constant mud just to catch a glimpse of some big cats. He must have another reason for going. One he didn't want to talk about.

Danger. Jessica could almost smell its acrid fumes. Warning signals went off inside her head. Her stomach tightened in response. "Who are you?" she whispered, involuntarily stepping back.

His face changed subtly, hardening until it seemed carved of stone. His body tensed. He was utterly still and deadly dangerous.

Jessica felt goose bumps roughen her skin. The fascinating companion was gone. Before her stood the stranger who had jumped her in the garden, the faceless man with deadly skills. The man who attacked first and asked questions later.

She had been unable to picture him riding elephants through rain forests. But she could easily imagine his powerful, lean body moving through the undergrowth, a silent shadow searching for terrorists.

"I don't think I want to know," she whispered.

"Jessica?" His voice was gentle, reassuring, as warm as the hands stroking her arms. His eyes had lost their flint-like hardness, smiling down at her. "I'm only a man very much attracted to you," he said soothingly.

Jessica closed her eyes, fighting the pull of attraction that drew her closer inch by inch. She could not afford to become involved with a man like Damon Noble.

She had spent eighteen months of marriage fearing for the safety of one man. Never again. No more sleepless nights with nightmares as her only companion. No more days spent frozen with fear, feeling none of the sun's warmth. And there was the waiting.

She should leave now to go in search of her mother. Flee, before she became drawn closer to this disturbing man. Run, before it was too late.

But she made no move.

Damn it, she was through with running. It felt so good to be whole again.

"Don't be afraid of me," Damon said softly, stepping closer. He looked at her averted face, wanting very much to kiss away her fears. Impatiently he looked around. As far as he could see, no one was watching them. But, if he kissed her, someone would notice, and spread the tale. For himself, he couldn't have cared less. But Jessica deserved better than having her name whispered around town.

Instead he cupped her chin. "If I promise never to hurt you again, will you look at me?" She was staring right past him.

Reluctantly, Jessica turned her head. His harsh features had softened with tenderness and he teased her gently with his crooked smile.

"What makes you think you could hurt me?" Jessica asked coldly, pulling away to dislodge his hand. "You are nothing to me."

Smiling, he shook his head. "Don't deny what is between us." He lifted his finger, touching her lips, stroking soothingly, gently, until the tight mouth relaxed.

His touch warmed her, setting her lips on fire with slow seductive strokes until all anger fled. She raised her hand to stop him until her breathing could return to normal.

As she grasped his finger to remove its touch, to stop its movement, his hand closed around her own, keeping it in a firm hold.

"There's nothing between us," Jessica insisted, fighting the warmth spreading from his touch. "How could there be? I know nothing about you."

"What do you want to know?" he asked carefully.

"Nothing you couldn't talk about," she said succinctly. "Only little things, like where you live, what you like and why you're here."

He grinned. "In other words, my vital statistics? Will knowing that I work for my father, live in New York, like good music—Bach is my favorite composer—and love pizza make you trust me?"

"No," Jessica admitted, "but it does help. You didn't answer one question, though. What are you doing here?"

"Ever heard of Buck Noble?"

"Buck Noble of International Combine?" Jessica had dealt with representatives of the farm equipment company, but she had never met its chairman. "Is he your father?"

When Damon nodded, Jessica exclaimed, "My sister Ali went to school with your sister."

He nodded. "Andrea introduced me to your family. Now she's married and living in Chicago with her husband and their two boys."

"And you're not married." It was a statement of fact. Gloria would have never left them alone if Damon had a wife.

"Divorced," Damon said, his voice flat. "What else do you want to know?"

Several questions came immediately to her mind, most of them centering on his wife. How long had he been married? Had he loved his wife? Why had they divorced? Did they have any children? But she asked none of these. Instead she said pointedly, "You didn't tell me what you're doing here."

"Selling tractors. What else?"

"What else, indeed," Jessica said dryly. "Somehow I can't imagine you selling farm equipment." But I can imagine you dodging bullets and bombs, she thought.

At every turn she was confronted with contradictions. She had never met a man like this. Hard, tough and dangerous one moment, gentle and smiling the next. An agent in her imagination, a businessman in reality. Who was the real Damon Noble?

"I don't actually sell it," Damon explained. "All I do is make the contacts, mostly with foreign governments. That's why I'm here. It's also the main purpose of my trip to India."

"Just how long do you plan to stay there?"

Damon shot her a piercing glance. "Eight to ten weeks. I'll be back in September." September suddenly seemed light-years away. "Jessica, if I came to Islamabad, would you have dinner with me?"

"No." Her answer was swift and firm. "I don't think that's a good idea. Besides, Pakistan is not on your itinerary."

"I imagine I could squeeze a short side trip into my schedule."

She shook her head. "I'm leaving Pakistan at the end of June."

Swiftly Damon counted. She would return to New York two months before him. Damn, perhaps he should cut his own trip short. But he knew he couldn't rearrange his schedule. His plans had been made a long time ago, too long ago to change any part of them now.

"Then have a drink somewhere with me now." He knew of a small, intimate place where they could talk freely without being watched. Talk? He wanted to kiss her until the warmth of those kisses melted the ice lodged deep within him, until her eyes blazed with desire and her lips promised to await his return.

But what if he didn't come back?

The thought sobered him. He had no right to make love to Jessica. He was torn between relief and frustration when she shook her head.

"I can't." Her voice was soft with regret. Dinner in Islamabad she had to turn down. After making a special trip to Pakistan, Damon would expect more than her company over a meal. Going out for a drink today, though, was different. She struggled against temptation. "I really couldn't disappoint my parents."

A sudden movement made her turn her head to look past Damon. She tensed when she saw Colonel Henderson picking his way toward her.

At any other time Jessica would have kept track of the colonel and might have avoided this distasteful meeting. But she had been too preoccupied, and now it was too late. Colonel Henderson was only a few feet away.

"We're about to have company," she whispered, the mask slipping back into place.

Damon's eyes sharpened. Slowly he turned to see who had taken the warmth from Jessica's face.

"Ah, Mrs. Stanton," Colonel Henderson said smoothly. "What a pleasure to find you here." He turned. "And Mr. Noble. It's been quite some time since our last meeting." His cold eyes moved from Damon to Jessica. "I hope I'm not interrupting anything?"

"Not at all, Colonel," Damon said smoothly. "I just hoped to keep Mrs. Stanton to myself a little longer."

Jessica watched the encounter with interest. That the two had met before was obvious. That they didn't like each other, Jessica could only guess at. Damon's sudden tension was subtle for only his eyes seemed more alert. The colonel stood seemingly relaxed. On the surface nothing was unusual. Beneath, however, Jessica sensed crosscurrents of dislike.

"Mrs. Stanton is always in great demand," the officer agreed. "In fact, I find it difficult to speak to her alone."

At his words, Jessica almost grinned with satisfaction. She had always made certain she was surrounded by friends when the colonel was around.

Damon smiled, a slow, dangerous smile that sent shivers down her spine. "I'm very glad to hear that. I don't like competition."

"That, Mr. Noble, is no surprise to me. But then I have come to know you quite well over the years."

Jessica listened as the men talked. They traded veiled insults and subtle threats while smiling. They acted like two dogs warily circling each other. Somehow Jessica had become the bone of contention between the two.

Yet she didn't feel insulted. She guessed that her involvement was purely incidental. Had she not been here, they would have disputed over anything else. The air began to sizzle. Words flew like bullets. Colonel Henderson and Damon were bitter, implacable foes.

But why? Jessica listened carefully, but none of the words revealed the reason for their hatred. Finally she decided to interrupt the duel before the fight became too intense. "You make me sound like a femme fatale," she teased. "I'm only a hardworking woman with little time for play."

"Of course you are." Damon turned to her, specks of amusement flickering in his eyes.

"Your hard work seems to have paid off," the colonel promptly agreed. "May I congratulate you on your appointment?"

Jessica barely hid the surprise she felt at his knowledge. "Thank you." Intelligence certainly moved fast. Too fast. How had the colonel heard of her appointment? Why was he keeping tabs on her? she wondered, though none of her thoughts showed when she said, "I look forward to my return to the States."

"For the next few months I, too, will be staying in New York. Perhaps we could have dinner together and take in a few shows."

Pointedly, the pale eyes moved over her face, his almost leering expression leaving Jessica in no doubt about just what kind of shows he had in mind. His gaze fastened on her lips, then slid down to her shoulders, finally lingering on the swell of her breasts.

Jessica froze. Goose bumps once again prickled her skin. She clenched her hands at her side to keep from slapping him.

Suddenly Damon moved to her side. He couldn't stand the colonel, but never before had he felt such deep hatred for the man. Never before had he burned with such rage. Over the eleven years of their acquaintance, his skin had toughened to hard leather, impervious to the colonel's barbs.

But Jessica was soft, too vulnerable to protect herself. He could feel the tenseness of her body, the slight trembling of her limbs. He moved like a shield between them. With forced casualness, he laid his arm around her shoulders. "I'm afraid, Henderson, you're too late." He had shed all pretense at politeness. His voice was cold and hard.

The eyes sharpened. The thin mouth tightened. But the colonel's voice still sounded pleasant. "Do I sense a romance? Hands off? Is that what you're trying to tell me, Noble? How long has it been going on?"

"That's none of your business." Damon's voice was a low growl. Then he compressed his lips, fighting for control. Already he had said more than he should have.

The colonel smiled. His eyes narrowed, searching, probing. "On the contrary. Everything you do is of great interest to me. And now, if you'll excuse me, I must return to my friends. I enjoyed our meeting, Mrs. Stanton." He nodded and turned. Almost as an afterthought he said over his shoulder, "Can you hear fate laughing at you, Noble?"

Puzzled, Jessica watched him wind his way back to his group. His last words didn't make any sense. Unless . . . She looked at Damon curiously, her earlier suspicions resurfacing. Was Damon Noble involved in more than just business deals? Did he work in some capacity for the Central Intelligence Agency? Jessica had heard more than once about the rivalry existing between Army Intelligence and the CIA.

"I think I just found another piece of the puzzle," she said slowly.

Jessica knew all about political machinations, about the wheeling and dealing that went on behind the scenes. She also admitted that intelligence was a necessary part of politics. But she hated the violence associated with it. Searching his face, Jessica detected no wariness, nothing that would strengthen her suspicions. His eyes were clear, with just a hint of amusement in their depth. She bit her lip in puzzlement.

"How long have you known Henderson?" Damon asked casually while looking hungrily at her perfect white teeth. He wanted to outline their shape with his tongue, tease her mouth apart and taste her lips. The arm around her shoulder tightened, drawing her body closer to him. For a moment he felt the soft curves yield in response. Then she stepped aside.

"Too long. I try to avoid him as much as possible," Jessica said.

"Exactly my sentiments." Damon grinned easily.

She smiled in response. Her imagination was playing overtime tonight. The idea that a man like Damon Noble was mixed up with the Agency seemed ludicrous.

"Obviously Colonel Henderson doesn't share our feelings," Jessica pointed out dryly, still not wholly convinced. She knew she had not imagined the undercurrents of hate.

Damon looked at her steadily. "His breed never does. Men like Henderson are trained to suspect everything and anything." It was a poor description for a man without human decency. "Jessica, avoid the man."

She looked at him, sparks of green anger flickering in her eyes. "Until you came along, I was actually quite successful in dodging him. Now, thanks to your charade, he's going to keep close watch on both of us."

"Look, I'm sorry I intervened. I could have stood by, letting him undress you in front of everybody with his eyes."

"Of all the—" She stopped the angry words and closed her eyes, counting to ten.

"You were literally shaking," Damon coolly pointed out.

"I was not shaking. My skin was crawling," Jessica corrected. "He gives me the creeps. But until now I've always managed to handle him. Damon," her face softened, "I'm not some helpless maid in distress. I've been fighting my own battles quite successfully for years."

"The colonel is—" Damon said harshly.

Jessica leaned forward and whispered in his ear, "—is Army Intelligence. I've known that for quite some time. What puzzles me is why he shows such interest in my movements. I have nothing to do with the military."

Damon's face was as smooth as his voice when he asked, "What exactly is your job at the embassy?"

"I'm in charge of the relief program for the Afghan refugees. I deal with pharmaceutical companies."

Damon's eyes sharpened with interest. "You order medical supplies and food. How much? And how is it distributed?"

"The allotment depends on the number of refugees in each camp. We distribute the supplies by trucks."

"We?" Damon asked her quietly, a chill running down his spine. He knew enough about the area to understand the danger of those trips, especially for a beautiful young woman like Jessica.

"My assistant and I," Jessica explained lightly, as if the trip was little more than a delivery to a neighborhood grocery store.

Suddenly her face brightened. "There's my mother."

Swearing silently, Damon turned his head and watched a slim blond woman dressed in a gown of black moiré move toward them. "Change your mind about that drink?" he asked softly.

Jessica looked at him, regret roughing her voice. "I can't. I haven't seen my mother in almost a year." Slowly she held out her hand. "I guess this is goodbye."

Damon grasped her hand tightly. "Not goodbye, Jessica." His deep voice flowed like black velvet over her. He bent his head until his lips touched her palm. "We'll meet again in September."

Warmth once again flooded through her. *"Insh'Allah,"* she whispered, freeing her hand.

"Kismet?" Damon asked, the crooked smile back on his face. "Don't tell me you believe in fate?"

Jessica had no time to answer. Her mother was there, hugging her. Then her father appeared and the Bartons, too.

Soon they were in the foyer, ready to return to the O'Connors' spacious Washington apartment. Jessica ran upstairs to retrieve her coat and purse. When she came down the sweeping staircase, Damon was waiting for her.

"Take care of yourself," he said, helping her into her coat.

He was so close that Jessica could feel his breath caress her neck. Slowly she nodded. She turned her head. "Be careful," she whispered. "Our friend hates you."

Damon smiled.

More words of caution hovered on her lips, but in the flurry of goodbyes they were never said.

Damon followed Jessica and her parents to their waiting car. Politely he helped Mary O'Connor. Then he turned to Jessica, opening the rear door for her. She smiled weakly. Why had she turned down his offer for a drink? Suddenly his lips closed over hers, warm, firm, searching. Before she could respond, he raised his head and gently pushed her into the back seat. "September," he murmured for her ears alone. "Good night. Have a safe ride home," he added, addressing her parents, too.

Then he closed the door. As they drove off, Jessica craned her neck to catch a last glimpse of him.

But the shadows had swallowed him up.

The apartment was large: three bedrooms, a living and dining room, and a study. Patrick O'Connor had bought it when his children had first been sent back to the States. After years of spending their vacations in hotels and rented rooms, this was their first permanent residence.

There were treasures everywhere, bought in the many foreign countries where Patrick O'Connor had worked. In the foyer stood an old saddle. Jessica had bargained for it in the bazaars of Kabul, Afghanistan's capital. In the living room, the parquet floor was covered with Oriental rugs:

Saruyks, Bucharas, a camel Mauri—all bought in that wild mountainous state.

A big copper tray from India, resting on a stand carved in the shapes of elephant's heads, served as a table. Leather hassocks from Morocco dotted the room. Several ebony statues from the Congo graced a beautifully carved chest from Thailand. There were silver bowls from Iran, brass trays from India and copper vases from Mexico. Jessica looked around with pleasure. Each item had a story attached to it.

For example, it had taken her father days to come to some agreement about a price for that rare old prayer rug from Afghanistan. The old Afghan he had bargained with had been as reluctant to sell it as her father had been eager to buy it.

Smiling, Jessica looked out of the huge window that covered almost one full wall of the big room. For years they'd had an unobstructed view of the capital city. Now the ivy hanging from the ceiling and the masses of begonias, African violets and jade plants partially obscured the view. Like Aunt Gloria, her mother loved plants. The lack of them had been a constant source of complaint whenever they'd met here.

"Well, Mary, are you happy that our daughter is returning stateside?" Patrick O'Connor looked at his wife with affection.

Mary nodded. "Just think, we'll all be together this Thanksgiving and Christmas. Except for Douglas, of course." Douglas was Jessica's brother. Like Jessica, he had joined the foreign service. At the moment he was attached to the embassy in Bogota, Colombia.

"Where are you going to put us all, Mother?" Jessica teased. "Are you planning to build a house?" The apartment had never been a real home to any of them. Jessica had often compared it to Grand Central Station. The family members would join there briefly, then part again to different parts of the world.

"We're thinking about it, now that your father has decided to stay here in Washington," her mother said.

"You'll have to do something," Jessica agreed. "I refuse to share a room with Ali's Terrible Twins. I love them, but they're little horrors to live with."

"They're just normal little boys," her mother protested.

Grinning, Jessica shook her head. "That depends on your definition of normal. Personally, I prefer my bed without dead snakes or cold fish." When her mother defended her grandchildren, Jessica laughed. "Why don't you let them sleep in your room? There's room enough there to put up two cots."

Her father raised his hand in mock threat. "The day they move into my bedroom is the day I move out. Mary, why can't we spend the holidays at Ali's house in Westchester County? She certainly has enough room. It seems rather stupid to build a big place just for our children and their families."

Mary smiled tightly, her beautiful face set. "We'll see."

"You're going to lose this argument," Jessica teased her father. For years her mother had placed her father's career before her own wishes. Jessica knew how she had hated to leave her children in the States. Douglas had been eighteen and Ali three years younger when her father had gone to Africa, to a place too small for American schools and too dangerous to live in. Even the two years Jessica had stayed with them in Afghanistan, when she'd been fourteen, had not satisfied her mother. Now she seemed determined to build a home for them all.

Suddenly Mary chuckled. "It's not that your father minds building a large house. He just dislikes the commitment that comes with it. As long as we live here, he'll feel free to accept a new post somewhere. He knows that once we've built the house, I won't go overseas again." Hugging her daughter, she added, "I would've preferred for you to work right here, but New York isn't too bad. Until you find an apartment, you can move in with Ali. Then Fred can give you a ride into the city every morning."

Grimacing, Jessica looked at her father for help. She had no intention of moving in with her sister. Like her mother,

Ali tended to run people's lives. Her father only shrugged his shoulders and grinned.

She turned back to her mother. "We'll see what happens." She didn't want to begin an argument. "How about that champagne you promised us on our way home? Do you want me to get it?"

"No. You stay here and talk to your father. I'll be right back."

Patrick O'Connor settled into one of the comfortable cream velvet chairs. "I think, Jessica, you'd be better off staying in Manhattan," he said when they were alone. "If you need funds—"

"Thanks. I'm all right for money," Jessica interrupted, sitting down on the big couch. "I've been saving a fair amount every month. And I still have the money from Michael's life insurance, plus the sum I got from the sale of our house."

"Then I think you should spend some of it." Returning with a tray of glasses and the bottle of champagne, her mother had caught her last words. "That dress you're wearing has seen better days. And why haven't you bought yourself some jewelry? I suggest you invest in some good stones before you leave Pakistan. They are so much cheaper over there. In fact," she continued, handing out the glasses, "I wanted to ask you to find me a star sapphire. Or a good emerald."

"You don't need any more jewelry, Mary," her husband objected, pouring the champagne. "You have a star sapphire already. I bought it for you last year when we visited Jessica."

"But I want a matching pendant," Mary argued.

"I'll see what I can find," Jessica promised, sipping her champagne and watching her parents with a smile.

"Before I forget, Jessica," her father said, "Gloria would like another rug. If you find any good Afghan carpets, buy me one, too."

In Afghanistan, her father had developed a passion for carpets and his collection was quite impressive. "You wouldn't settle for a Pakistani one, would you?" Jessica asked hopefully. "To tell you the truth, I haven't seen a good Afghan Buchara or King's Mauri in months. Sometimes refugees manage to smuggle a few rugs across the border, but the demand for them is so high that they are sold the minute they get to Pakistan."

"I'd prefer an Afghan one."

Pakistanis used synthetic aniline dyes that extracted the natural oils from wool and left the yarn dull. The Afghan rugs, on the other hand, had a silky sheen that became more lustrous with wear.

"I'd love to own another King's Mauri. Bigger than this one." He pointed at a small rug with a wide ruby red border and a light beige center. The border contained eight different patterns, each outlined sparingly in dark green, the holy color. The beige center had been knotted from baby camel hair, a very expensive and rare material. Hence the name King's Mauri.

"That's preposterous," Jessica's mother protested. "Just where would we put another carpet?"

"On the wall. Afghan style," her father teased. "Until we build that house you want."

Her mother sighed. "I guess we'll have room for one more then."

Patrick winked at his daughter.

Jessica leaned back against the couch, watching them spar. How she'd missed having her family around. Life overseas could be rather lonely.

Her mother looked at her. "This is rather nice, isn't it, the three of us together? Do you really have to leave tomorrow? Couldn't you stay just one more day?"

Jessica shook her head. "I leave on the seven o'clock flight to Frankfurt. But I'll be back soon."

"Will you mind leaving Islamabad?"

"I'll miss my friends," Jessica said, already guessing her mother's next question.

"Is there someone special?"

Damon's dark face rose, unbidden and unwelcome, before Jessica's eyes. "No," she said firmly. Hearing her mother sigh, she added, "Mother, I'm not like Ali. I'd get claustrophobia staying at home."

"You heard her, Mary," Jessica's father intervened. "Jessica will settle down when she's ready."

Mary shot her husband an impatient look. Couldn't he tell that Jessica lacked stability in her life? Her daughter needed roots. A husband with a nine to five job. Not a man like Damon Noble. Mary had missed none of the smiles that had passed between her daughter and that man. Restlessly, she stood up. "I don't know about you two, but I'm hungry. I hardly had time to try any of Gloria's delicious buffet."

"I could do with a sandwich or two," her husband agreed.

"Do you want me to help?" Jessica smiled her agreement.

"No, darling, I don't need any help. I know you want to talk shop with your father. You can do it while I'm busy in the kitchen."

"How's Hugh Cantrell?" Patrick asked his daughter when they were alone. "Is he treating you well?"

"His Excellency is fine. He sends his regards," Jessica replied with a smile. Her father knew most of the veteran diplomats. "He's thinking of retirement."

"He is?" Her father's eyes began to sparkle with wanderlust. "I wouldn't mind going to Pakistan for a few years." Then he shook his head. "No, I can't do that to your mother. I guess it's the lawnmower for me."

"You can always hire someone to mow the lawn," Jessica pointed out.

"Yeah. Somehow, though, I have the feeling that your mother won't be happy until I do the job myself. So, tell me, what's the latest news from Afghanistan?"

Jessica was startled. The swift change of topics caught her by surprise. "Little has changed. A few reports of fighting. More refugees than ever. The Russians seem to lose ground steadily." She looked at her father pointedly. "I'm sure you know more about the situation than I do. I don't have your level of security clearance."

Her father shook his head. "But you're right at the
source. You must hear quite a bit when you visit the refugee camps."

"I've been too busy appealing to government agencies for
food supplies and medical attention to spend much time at
the camps. We were sent only six crates last month. Six
crates for almost three million refugees. It's disgusting."

"There's talk about some form of legislation to help your
refugees."

"Talk we always get plenty of. Supplies are what we
need," Jessica grumbled.

"The situation is rather difficult," her father pointed out
reasonably. "Officially, there's no war going on in Afghanistan. If our government interferes, we step on Russian toes."

"It's a mess, all right," Jessica agreed angrily. "And
you're sounding just like Senator Dempsey. He doesn't
know any better, but you should. You lived in Kabul for
three years. Do you remember what you used to call the
Afghans? Kings of the mountains. Well, now they're beggars, blinded by nerve gas and crawling in dirt. Perhaps the
State Department should send you over for a visit."

"I haven't forgotten," her father said quietly. "You're
too close to the Afghan question to consider the other
problems involved. Besides, your beggars are doing a damn
good job of cutting the Russian army down to size."

"They're absolutely amazing," she agreed. "With only
a few antiquated guns, the *mujahidins* are winning."

Mujahidins were the freedom fighters, proud men with
hard faces and dark, expressionless eyes that surprisingly
softened with laughter when they looked at a small child.
These eyes were like Damon's eyes.

"What do you know about Damon Noble?" she asked
abruptly.

"Interesting fellow."

"Very," she agreed restlessly, reaching for her glass.
Somewhere there was a connection that kept eluding her.

"I don't know him that well," her father said, looking at her closely. "Ali could tell you a lot more about him—at least the things you might be interested in."

"I want facts," Jessica stated firmly. "Not Ali's type of gossip."

"He's thirty-nine. Divorced. President of the international division of International Combine. Travels a lot overseas, and has a knack in dealing with foreign governments. He'd make a great diplomat."

"That sounds like an FBI file." Jessica grinned.

Her father looked a little sheepish. "I want to know who's playing with my grandkids. And you, my girl, are too sharp."

"If you didn't want me to know that you looked up his file, you shouldn't have sounded like you were reading from it."

Her father gazed at her steadily. "Is there anything else you want to know?"

Jessica nodded. "What is the connection between Damon and Colonel Henderson?"

"Where did you find out about that?"

"I'm smart. Remember?" Jessica teased. Then she briefly described the meeting, leaving out her personal involvement.

Her father's eyes sharpened with interest. "I've heard quite a bit about Henderson. Unpleasant fellow. But very effective. He and Noble are involved in a personal vendetta. From what I could get out of the report, they first met eleven years ago at the Industrial Fair in Leipzig. Noble apparently had a brief affair with one of the East German hostesses, Tanya Rebrow. Damned foolish and risky, but Noble was something of a playboy. And she was—still is—an exceptionally beautiful woman. Unfortunately, at the time, she also happened to be Henderson's mistress. He was there as a liaison officer."

"Where is she now?" Jessica asked tersely.

"Right here in Washington. For a poor orphan girl, she's done quite well. I don't know why she switched partners in Leipzig. Perhaps she saw her chance to escape from behind the iron curtain. Noble returned to the States without her, but a few months later he went back and took her out right from under the colonel's nose."

Or out of his bed, Jessica thought grimly.

"He married her shortly after."

Jessica's eyes widened with shock.

"Who married whom?" Coming into the room, Mary had caught her husband's last words.

"We were talking about Damon Noble."

"I should've guessed," Mary sighed in exasperation. She handed out plates and napkins in silence and placed the tray of sandwiches on the table. "I'm really upset with Gloria. She shouldn't have introduced you two."

Jessica's mouth tightened with impatience. What did her mother know about Damon?

"Actually, Mary, I rather like the man," her father protested.

"You wouldn't if you heard some of the things his wife says about him."

"They're divorced, Mary. Few women speak well of their ex-husbands."

Impatiently, Jessica watched her mother reach for one of the tastefully arranged sandwiches. Damon's voice had been flat, expressionless and cool when he'd mentioned his divorce. She wished she knew how he really felt about his wife.

"Tanya doesn't exactly complain about him," her mother went on. "All she says is that she couldn't stand the loneliness. He used to spend months overseas, traveling for his company. But even when he was in the States, she apparently saw little of him. It must have been a solitary life for her. I think she's better off now." She took a bite of the food. "She has the most marvelous little boutique here. I'll have to take you there, Jessica, when you come back."

"What does she look like?" Jessica asked, ignoring her mother's offer. She had no intention of visiting Tanya's shop. The more she heard about the woman, the less she liked her.

"Blond, with blue eyes. Vivacious. Her accent is very charming."

To Jessica she sounded like a bitch.

Later, in bed, Jessica went over the conversation. Had Damon loved his wife? Somehow she couldn't see Damon falling for a cold calculating woman. Yet why else had he smuggled Tanya Rebrow out of East Germany? She punched her pillow with vexation.

At least the reason for the colonel's hatred had been explained. No man liked to lose his mistress to another man, especially not someone as vain as Henderson. Jessica was certain that Tanya's rejection and escape to the West had bruised the colonel's ego. Still, to hold a grudge for eleven years was rather ridiculous and unhealthy. Hate was like cancer. If it wasn't controlled early enough, it destroyed.

The colonel wanted revenge. He was a predator, lurking in the dark, patiently watching for Damon to make a fatal move.

Impatiently, Jessica tossed from side to side. Something bothered her. She had missed a clue. Again she looked back.

Suddenly she sat up. Mountain climbing! Her heart missed a beat. She had forgotten about that little bit of information, the last leg of Damon's trip.

Which mountains? Kashmir?

No, Afghanistan.

Damon was planning to go into Afghanistan. But why? Surely not, she thought grimly, to sell farm implements. The *mujahidins* had no use for them. They needed guns, tanks, ammunition. Was Damon involved in arms deals?

She rejected the thought almost immediately. Somehow she could not imagine Damon selling implements of death. Yet what other reason could he have for going into a war zone?

She slid off the bed and walked to the window, opening the blinds. The more she thought about it the more she became convinced that Damon did work for the Agency. Dealing mostly with governments of Third World nations would provide him with the perfect cover.

She tensed when she thought of the colonel's recent trip to Pakistan. Was it coincidence that Henderson had visited that part of the world only a few months before Damon's scheduled trip? She didn't think so.

The trip need not be dangerous. She tried to calm her fears. Several news crews had returned home unscathed.

But others had not.

Chapter 4

The next morning Jessica said goodbye to her parents. As always, her mother remembered last minute items and asked her to write the moment she arrived in Islamabad. Her father's hug and kiss held more than warmth. "In case you need something special," he whispered and closed her hand over a wad of bills.

Jessica waved until the car had disappeared. Long ago, the family had decided not to wait around until boarding time. Long-drawn-out goodbyes made the inevitable parting only more painful.

Jessica looked at her watch. She had almost an hour until boarding time. Browsing through the bookstore, she picked up a *Vogue* magazine for her friend Barbara and a chocolate bar for herself.

Outside the store, she added the magazine to her tote bag, then opened the candy wrapper.

"So we meet again."

Jessica froze as she recognized the colonel's voice. Reluctantly she raised her head and stared at the man standing in front of her. As always, he was impeccably groomed, wearing a gray suit, snow white shirt and matching tie. Not a single blond hair was out of place.

"Good morning, Colonel." Coolly, Jessica inclined her head, fighting an irrational urge to run.

"I didn't know you had a sweet tooth." The colonel ignored her demeanor.

"I've just lost my appetite," she muttered beneath her breath, eyeing the swiftly melting candy bar in her hand. If she wasn't careful it would stain the white linen of her suit. "Have you seen a trashcan?" she asked the colonel.

His gray eyes narrowed with suspicion. "Why?"

Jessica didn't answer. They were standing in the middle of the big hall. People were passing them right and left. But no trashcan. And no escape, either. Damn!

"You constantly surprise me," Colonel Henderson said, raking her slender form.

Jessica felt the familiar prickle erupt on her skin. Angrily, she tossed her head. "Oh? I think I've been rather obvious."

"I've been interested in you from the moment I saw you," he said smoothly, his eyes lingering on the V of her green blouse where just the hint of a cleavage showed.

Jessica wished she was wearing her trench coat. The slim white linen suit hugged her figure, and the V-neck of her blouse was rather low cut. It wasn't an indecent exposure, but his cold gray eyes made her feel as if she was topless.

"Colonel, the only thing I'm interested in is finding a trashcan as quickly as possible." The candy bar was oozing in her hand. "Perhaps you could do me a favor and look around for one." She reached for his hand and placed the bar into his palm before he could withdraw. "Dump this for me. I have a plane to catch."

She started to move past him, but his next words stopped her. "And where is your friend, Mr. Noble?" he asked, casting a dubious look at his gingerly extended hand. "I expected him to accompany you back to New York, especially since you're leaving this afternoon."

Jessica saw the stains on his flat palm, brown against the white softness of his skin. She bit back a giggle. "You mean you don't know his whereabouts? Did your men lose him last night?"

"You read too many spy novels, Mrs. Stanton." He shrugged his shoulders, smiling openly. "Noble's influence, I guess. He, too, has a vivid imagination. Noble's movements don't interest me, but yours do. I find you very attractive." A sudden gleam lit his eyes.

For the first time Jessica could see why women were drawn to him. The contrast between his threatening coldness and the sudden warmth was startling and alarming. Never before had he exerted such an effort in trying to charm her.

A flicker of alarm, swiftly controlled, widened her eyes. She didn't want to be drawn into the web of hatred between Damon and the colonel. "I'm not interested in you or your activities, as long as they don't involve me," she said with cold finality.

"But you interest me a great deal, Mrs. Stanton. It's personal, not professional."

Personal, like his vendetta with Damon? Cold flutters of fear crept up her spine. "I'm not flattered," she snapped. "Find someone else to play your games with." With a downward sweep of her eyes, she looked at his hand. The candy bar was oozing more and more. "Enjoy the candy."

She tried to move past him. He stepped into her way. He was a man of medium height and slight of build, yet, standing in front of her, he seemed as tall and solid as the Berlin Wall. Shivers of fear licked her skin. Slimy tentacles seemed to curl around her feet. Her eyes flared with sudden fear, then became expressionless. Within moments she had her fear under control.

"I have a flight to catch," she said.

"There's plenty of time." His cool eyes mocked her. "I'm taking the same flight."

"I'm not flying to New York." Not on the next shuttle anyway. Just the thought of sharing the same plane with him made her sick. "I have to go now."

She turned, determined to take the following flight or the one after that. His hand closed around her arm, holding her, stopping her retreat.

Panic hit her like a tidal wave, sucking solid ground from under her feet. "Let go of me." She struggled and twisted.

She was free.

Run, a voice inside her screamed. But she didn't. If she fled now, he would become the hunter, a menace in her life, a constant fear.

Taking slow deep breaths, she controlled her panic. She looked around. This was an airport, not some back street alley.

A stocky young man in security uniform stood no more than ten feet away. At the moment he was watching the entrance. But Jessica knew she had just to shout to draw his attention.

What a fool she was.

The colonel had wanted to frighten her—and she'd let him. It galled her to admit it. Furious with herself, she spun around. "I warn you. Never touch me again."

"And if I do, Mrs. Stanton?" His satisfied smile mocked her. "What will you do then?"

She met his eyes without flinching. "Then I'll call for help. And certain people will listen to me, Colonel. I'm not without connections."

She stepped past him, forcing herself to walk away from him with her head held high. Silently she cursed her weak knees and the high-heeled sandals that prevented her from striding out to widen the distance between them.

She knew he was following her. Her fear-sharpened senses screamed that he was right behind her. He was closing in on her . . . reaching for her.

A steely hand gripped her shoulder. She stumbled off balance. With a hiss she turned on him. Muscles, rock hard, and tanned skin met her assault. No gray suit, instead bare flesh.

"Jessica?" The velvet softness of the deep voice was soothing and questioning at once.

Jessica tilted her head back. "Damon."

She leaned against him, shaking with relief. His arms closed around her, hard and protective. For a few moments she drank of his strength. Then she lifted her face. "How did you get here?"

"By taxi." He smiled at the absurdity of her question.

Jessica grinned weakly. "That's not what I meant. What are you doing here?"

"Same as you, I imagine. Catching the shuttle to New York."

Was it coincidence or design? Jessica didn't care. Silently she thanked fate for Damon's presence. Then she remembered how she had turned on him.

"I'm sorry I tried to hit you. Are you okay?" Raising her hands, she pushed against his chest.

"I'm all right." Puzzled, he searched her face. She was smiling now, her eyes holding a mixture of relief and embarrassment. And fear.

His eyes sharpened. Why fear? What or who had frightened her? His arms tightened around her slim body while he scanned the crowd. "Who scared you?"

Jessica swiftly looked back. The colonel had disappeared. "No one," she lied, then asked with a twisted smile, "Do you always sneak up from behind?"

"Impulsive and a bad liar." Damon shook his head. "I didn't sneak up on you. I guess you didn't hear me, but I did call your name." Again his eyes searched the hall. Why wasn't she telling the truth?

"There's so much noise in the hall." Jessica shrugged her shoulders.

"Jessica?" he prompted her, a hint of exasperation in his voice.

"I hate being attacked from behind." She refused to tell him about her meeting with the colonel. She was not going to add fuel to the flames of hatred already burning between the two men.

I know I can handle that snake, she thought grimly. And I am going to do it my way, without interference from Damon. His involvement was worse than no help. Without Damon's intervention last night, her meeting with Henderson, like all previous ones, would have passed with a polite exchange of greetings and some cool smiles. Damon's statement had changed the game. No longer was she simply an object for conquest to the colonel. Now she was a means of revenge.

A second Tanya Rebrow.

She was not concerned. Within hours of checking, Henderson would uncover Damon's lie. And even if he did not, he would find it difficult to frighten her again. Earlier the sudden change had taken her by surprise. Now she was forewarned.

Damon cursed silently, sensing that, once again, he had been the cause of her fear. "What about being attacked from the front?" Perhaps, if he joked about it, last night's incident would fade.

"I like it much better." She grinned. "I hate talking to shadows."

"I can see your point." His eyes softened, lights dancing in their depth. "I prefer watching your face." He pressed her closer, folding her body into hard muscle and sinew. Yet his hands were softly caressing.

Unconsciously, she moved into the caress. Pleasure darkened the hazel of her eyes until they shone like brown velvet. Her hands began moving over his chest.

"You're very beautiful," he whispered, bending his head, his lips brushing over hers. With an involuntary sound of pleasure, she opened her mouth to his probing tongue.

He couldn't resist temptation and drank deeply of her sweetness.

The loudspeaker hummed.

Damon lifted his head, his thumb replacing the pressure of his lips, stroking her lips softly. "We have a plane to catch," he said, his voice filled with regret. "Unless you want to give this flight a miss."

Jessica's fingers curled around his thumb, stilling its movement. "And the next one? Then the one after that?" Smiling, she shook her head. "No, I have to get back to New York." She looked around and read the time on the big clock. She gasped. "We'll have to run."

He stared at her sandals. "In those shoes?" He reached for her purse, sliding the strap off her shoulder with his free hand. "Let's go, then," he said.

Swiftly they crossed the crowded hall. Once they had reached the long corridor with its red carpet, they increased their speed. Jessica wished she had worn sneakers. For each of his steps she had to take two.

"You're out of condition," he teased.

"I am not. Your legs are twice as long as mine."

"Want to compare their lengths later?" When Jessica lowered her eyes, he laughed softly.

She stumbled again. With a sigh, she stopped and slid the sandals off her feet, swinging them in her hand. Her stride lengthened. "Damn." She heard the tight lining of her skirt rip slightly.

"Planning to take the skirt off, too?" he asked expectantly.

"Do you prefer your women to run around naked?" Jessica grinned.

"Yeah. Or hidden behind veils."

"You're contradicting yourself. You can't have it both ways," Jessica pointed out dryly.

"Why not? Some sheikhs do." He slowed as they neared their gate.

"Even they're having to choose these days," Jessica joked. "Besides, you're no sheikh. Although dressed in a burnoose you might pass for one." She grinned, her eyes sparkling. "I can just see you, riding through the desert on a camel—"

"No camel," Damon protested. His laughter was deep and warm. "Have you ever ridden on one?"

"Yes. I got seasick. When I climbed down, I tried to apologize, because the camel looked so offended. The beast spit right into my face."

Damon smiled crookedly. "Mine wouldn't get up. It kneeled in the dust until I finally climbed down to pull it to its feet by the reins. As soon as I touched the ground, it rose and calmly walked off. I tried to catch it but it always stayed just out of my reach."

Jessica laughed. She could not remember the last time she had enjoyed herself so much.

Smiling politely, the flight attendant looked at them. "There was no need to run," she said coolly, looking at Jessica's flushed face, then at the sandals in her hand. "You had plenty of time."

Was the woman telling her that she looked a fright? She probably did. Strands of hair curled around her heated face, and her feet were filthy. She looked at Damon. Did he mind?

He was handing his boarding pass to the flight attendant. His hair, too, was disheveled, falling over his forehead into his eyes. She chuckled.

He looked up at the sound. His eyes filled with tender amusement, holding messages of shared laughter and something else. Something disturbingly new.

Jessica was the first to lower her eyes. She fumbled for her own boarding pass in the pocket of her jacket, finally handing it to the patiently waiting woman.

With another smile they were waved through.

A few steps further, Jessica stopped to slide back into her sandals.

"Let me help you." Damon held out his tanned, hairroughened arm. Jessica held on to it, slipping the straps over her heels.

"Thank you." With both feet back on solid ground, she released her hold. The tip of her fingers slid down his warm skin in a gentle caress.

With a twist of his hand he caught her own. "Those ramps are always a little uneven."

Jessica curled her fingers around his without comment. She had never stumbled on a ramp, but it was a good excuse to touch him.

He took her hand and raised it to his lips. His mouth burned into her skin.

"You're not playing fair." Her protest was weak and husky. She didn't want him to stop.

"I don't have time to play fair." Damon raised his head. "If I had my way, I'd whisk you away and make love to you all day until your plane had left without you." His voice was rough with desire.

Jessica smiled weakly, fighting against temptation. "All day?" she tried to tease him. She turned away. "I think we had better board the plane."

He nodded. The disappointment in his eyes mirrored her own regret. The hold on her hand tightened as they stepped into the plane. He did not release her even as they squeezed through the narrow aisle.

People were staring at them. Jessica smiled. Suddenly she paused, stiffened, then went on. It was an almost imperceptible sequence of movements, a reaction to the colonel's cold stare. She hoped that Damon had not noticed the brief hesitation.

But he had.

His eyes went from her to the colonel. Cold, hard, speculative.

And knowing.

Damn! She should have agreed to miss the flight. She should have known that Damon would discover the truth.

Silently, she followed Damon to the seats in the last row. He helped her out of her jacket without a word.

Jessica slid into the seat, watching him stow her jacket in the overhead compartment. His lean body stretched, his light cream shirt tugging at the belt of his khaki pants. She folded her hands in her lap to keep them from reaching out to touch him. Five minutes earlier she would have done so without thought. Now their light mood was gone.

Damon sat down in the seat next to hers. "What did he do?"

"Who? Henderson? Nothing," Jessica denied, calmly meeting the quiet rage in Damon's eyes, giving him no encouragement to pursue the matter further. "He just said hello and goodbye."

His firm mouth twisted. "And that's what sent you running?"

"I didn't run." Her eyes flashed at the sarcasm in his voice. "I was simply walking away from the man. I told you last night, I can't stand him."

He shook his head. She sounded so convincing he almost, but not quite, believed her. The fear in her eyes had been too real, and the way she had turned on him in blind panic strengthened his suspicions. His dark eyes hardened. He barely controlled the rage burning within him. His hands itched to close around Henderson's neck, to slowly choke the life out of him. Patience, he told himself. One wrong move and eleven years of work would go down the drain.

"I have a feeling that from now on he's going to ignore me," Jessica added with a grin on her face.

Damon's grim face softened. "Little hellcat." He fastened his seatbelt. "What did you do to him before you, ah, walked away from him?"

Jessica smiled with relief, sparks of mischief dancing in her eyes. "I shoved a melting candy bar into his hand." Briefly she described the scene, omitting anything that might refuel Damon's rage. "I wonder what he did with it?"

"Who cares? I hope he choked on it." Damon wasn't deceived. The man had frightened her badly. And soon he was going to even the score. "I'm not going to waste more time on the colonel. I have better things to do."

Startled, Jessica searched his face. "Like what?"

"This." He cupped her chin, and kissed her nose. "Your freckles dance when you laugh. When you're angry, too," he told her between tantalizing pecks. He touched each sunspot with the tip of his finger. "There are seven of them," he told her. Then he gently outlined her mouth, teasing her until her lips moved with impatience.

His warm breath kissed her skin. She could feel herself flush under that almost real caress. Heat welled up in her. The desire to draw his mouth closer became so strong that she turned her face into his hand away from temptation.

The plane began moving. She raised her head, her eyes dark with longing.

Damon stared at her soft mouth and lowered his head. For one brief moment his lips brushed against hers.

Suddenly she was pushed backward against her seat. The roar of engines became a high scream of power as the plane shot forward, leaving the ground, climbing into the sky.

Jessica realized that she had missed the taxiing to the runway. What else had happened while she'd been wrapped in a cocoon of pleasure? Swiftly she looked across the aisle, then breathed with relief. The seats were still empty.

She met Damon's eyes. They were soft, their centers so wide as to make them appear black.

"We almost missed the takeoff," she said, thinking that this was the first time she hadn't clenched her hands around the armrests in a swift surge of apprehension. She was not afraid of flying—she had hopped on too many planes to be scared—but the sudden surge of power at takeoff and the throttling restraint prior to landing had always made her stomach feel queasy.

Damon smiled, his eyes questioning. "Is there something special about takeoffs?"

"No. Nothing special." Except that for the first time she could remember she hadn't needed a whole pack of gum to keep her stomach from churning and her ears from buzzing. Her whole life seemed to be changing, and suddenly she was afraid again.

"Are you afraid of flying?" Damon asked, seeing the tightening of her lips.

She shook her head, wishing that it was fear of flying that tightened her throat. There were pills one could swallow to numb that fright.

"If you're not afraid of flying, why are your hands clenched?" He reached across and covered her fingers. "And cold." Frowning, he looked at her. "Are you afraid of me?" he asked, unable to think of another explanation. He straightened her fingers and warmed them between his palms. "Don't you know that I would never hurt you intentionally?"

Jessica turned her head from side to side. "I'm not afraid of you. It's what you do that scares me."

"Selling farm equipment?" Damon asked, raising one brow.

She took a deep breath. "No. As you pointed out last night, you don't sell equipment. You make the contacts." And what else are you involved in? She wished she could come right out and ask him if her suspicions were correct, but she knew Damon would deny any other activities. Then the mood between them might become tense.

Abruptly she said, "My husband was killed in a bomb explosion. He was working as a geological consultant for one of the big oil companies. Michael always denied that his work was dangerous. He wouldn't have recognized danger if it hit him smack in the face."

"Just what are you trying to tell me?" Damon asked, his face expressionless.

Jessica took a deep breath. Without looking at him, she said, "I don't want to get involved with you. I don't want to constantly live with fear for your safety. I want more than nightmares as my only companion in the dead of night." She stopped, then added, "I don't want to fall in love with you."

Damon sat very quietly. No muscle moved in his face. Her hand, still clasped between his own, felt suddenly hot. Or was it that he was freezing cold?

It was nothing new, this lump of ice in his chest. He had lived with it for so long that he had forgotten what being warm felt like.

Until last night.

Last night he had felt alive for the first time in years. After Jessica left he had felt the chill inside him more acutely. It was then that he had decided to meet her at the airport and take the same flight. A simple phone call had given him the information he needed. He had been determined to spend the rest of the day with her.

He still was.

"If I promise not to touch you again, will you spend the day with me?"

Jessica looked at him, sensing his loneliness, his pain. A small smile tugged at the corners of her mouth. "If you can keep that promise, you're a stronger person than I am."

Warmth filled his eyes. Slowly he let pent-up air escape his lungs. Smiling crookedly, he shook his head. "I'd promise anything to keep you with me. Even if I died of frustration. I'm glad you won't hold me to it, though."

"My plane leaves at seven," Jessica warned. "I still have a few things to buy before I leave." She had about three hours to spare. What could possibly happen in three hours that hadn't happened already?

"I'll take you out to lunch. What food do you prefer?"

"Real hot dogs. Coney Island style. I'm tired of the canned or frozen variety."

"Hot dogs?" He laughed softly, shaking his head. "I had something a little more romantic in mind. There's a little French restaurant—"

"I stopped over in Paris on my flight to New York."

He shrugged his shoulders. "Hot dogs it is." Gently he touched her lips. Sparks of amusement danced in his eyes. "I think I'll enjoy feeding you hot dogs."

Suddenly the flight attendant appeared with her beverage cart. "What would you like to drink?" she asked.

"Nothing. Thank you," Jessica said. She wasn't thirsty, at least not for anything on the cart. She wanted to drink of Damon's mouth. If she couldn't have that she wanted nothing else.

"Orange juice," Damon ordered. He quickly drank it down. It helped, he decided, and asked for more.

When he'd finished his second glass, he turned to Jessica. She was watching him, her wide-spaced hazel eyes clear, if slightly troubled. "What do you have to buy before you leave for Islamabad?" he asked abruptly.

"Little things. Magazines, some film." Suddenly she smiled. "And some gum."

He grinned. "Gum?"

"I always need gum at takeoffs and landings. A whole pack of it." She raised her fingers to his lips. "You taste better than gum."

Smiling, he caught her hand. "I'm glad to hear that," he said, his voice deep with laughter. "How would you like to drive to the beach? I'll get you that Coney Island hot dog there."

"Great." Her eyes sparkled with pleasure. "It's been months since I've seen anything but mountains and dust."

Chapter 5

Damon had parked his Porsche Targa in the overnight parking lot. The black interior had the rich smell of leather. Damon helped Jessica inside, then stowed their luggage before joining her.

Jessica watched him fold his tall body into the compact interior with smooth coordination. He fastened his seat belt. "Ready?" he asked. When Jessica nodded, he turned on the engine. The powerful car roared to life.

"Do you want the windows open, or do you prefer air conditioning?"

Outside the day was warm and sunny. As they'd walked the short distance from the airport building to the parking garage, Jessica had felt the fresh sea breeze on her face. "Let's open the windows," Jessica said. "I like the smell of the sea."

Smiling, Damon pushed a button. The windows slid silently down. "We'll be driving through Queens and Brooklyn," he warned. "If the fumes get to you, let me know."

Swiftly they left the airport and joined the traffic on the parkway. Jessica watched Damon drive, his long fingers curving around the black steering wheel. His muscles moved smoothly under the dark-haired, bronzed skin.

He looked at her sparkling eyes, at her smiling mouth. His eyes darkened with desire. "Move closer."

Jessica shook her head. "Too dangerous," she said, struggling with temptation. "Tell me about your childhood."

He raised one eyebrow. "It was perfectly normal," he assured her. "Local schools, Cub Scouts, Little League. And a kid sister with as little respect for her elders as you seem to have shown."

She grinned. "You sound like my father. You know, I asked my father about you last night."

"What did he have to say?"

Jessica shrugged her shoulders. "This and that," she teased. "Mostly he repeated what I already knew."

He looked at her sharply. "But it isn't enough," he guessed flatly.

"I just want to catch up," she said slowly. "You know so much more about me than I do about you."

Jessica wanted to know about his wife. She wanted to find out why a young man with a perfectly normal background moved among terrorists with the well-trained and highly coordinated movements of an agent.

She had seen men move like that at every embassy. Men with ordinary jobs, sometimes dull and unimportant jobs; jobs they could leave at a moment's notice without interrupting the smooth flow of embassy business. No one inquired after their whereabouts. No one asked how smooth hands had suddenly turned rough and pale faces had become dark. For the last three years Jessica had watched a large number of them come and go. On the surface they were ordinary employees. They joked and laughed and went to parties. Only sometimes their eyes were hard. Like Damon's eyes, when he wasn't smiling. She shuddered.

Damon had steeled himself for more questions. When none came he looked over at her. He saw the convulsive movement. "What are you afraid of?"

Jessica smiled weakly. "Ghosts." She had learned early in life to ignore certain discrepancies. "Tell me about your wife." Asking about Tanya Rebrow showed only a natural curiosity about his life, Jessica decided. It was unlike prying into possible security affairs. "My mother mentioned that she lives in Washington and owns a boutique there."

He did not move a muscle. His face looked distant, cold. His eyes were hard as granite. His voice sounded like a recording, without life. "If your mother has met Tanya, you know everything there is to know about my ex-wife."

"I doubt it," Jessica said dryly, then she unconsciously repeated her father's words. "Divorced spouses rarely speak well of their former partners."

"What Tanya says is true," Damon assured her quietly. "I did neglect her. I spent as little time at home as I possibly could."

Jessica sat quietly watching him, waiting for him to continue.

"I went to Leipzig when I was twenty-seven. It was my first business trip overseas and my father figured I couldn't do much damage at the industrial fair." He smiled grimly. "He was wrong.

"Tanya was a hostess at the fair. She invited me to her apartment and I went. I was curious. And, also, Tanya is a very attractive woman." He did not smile.

"We began seeing each other. The last night of the fair, one of the other businessmen threw a party. I got so drunk I almost missed my plane the next day.

"Two months later, I received a note that Tanya was pregnant. It must have happened that last night, a night I still can't remember. I wasn't going to let my child grow up behind the iron curtain, so I flew to West Germany and found someone to help me plan an escape for Tanya. I got her out and married her two weeks later. Then, on our honeymoon, she lost the child."

Jessica made a sound of distress. "I'm sorry."

Damon turned to her briefly, showing no regret. "No need. She'd been pregnant almost five months. It wasn't mine."

Henderson's child, Jessica guessed grimly. When had Damon found out that he had not been Tanya's only lover? Had Tanya told him? Or had the colonel presented Damon with the news later on?

"When she could travel again," Damon continued, "we went to New York. I stayed around until she'd made some friends, then left her alone."

"Why didn't you divorce her?" Jessica asked, looking out the window.

Damon glanced at her sharply, but all he could see was the back of her head. "She needed my protection. As long as she was my wife no one dared to harm her. I waited until Tanya had become a citizen, then I asked for a divorce."

There were things he had not mentioned, like the fact that the father of the child had most likely been Henderson. She felt an aching sadness for the carefree, trusting young man he had once been, with a bright future suddenly dimmed.

"I'm sorry," she said, facing him with her anger controlled.

"Don't feel sorry for me," he said softly. "It's all in the past."

Maybe Tanya was, Jessica thought, but Colonel Henderson certainly was not. She recognized the wounds those two had inflicted, wounds that hadn't healed and were still festering.

When Jessica did not respond, Damon looked at her sharply. His face was hard as rock, hiding his fear that Jessica would withdraw from him. He could not blame her for shying away from the dark side of his life; most women would.

"I'm a fool to make you upset," he said roughly. "I want you to remember this day with pleasure, not with tears."

"How much farther is it?" she asked with forced brightness.

"Another five minutes." He pointed toward a sign. Moments later they left the parkway. Traffic became dense. Ten minutes later they drew into the parking lot next to the New York Aquarium.

"The hot dogs won't be first class," Damon warned as they walked barefoot toward the boardwalk.

They weren't even third class, Jessica agreed a little while later. But she had never enjoyed a meal more. They fed each other, his fingertip lingering on her mouth, touching her face with little tender strokes. Jessica kissed the mustard from the corner of his lips, brushed her face against his hand as he handed her a drink.

"How about some ice cream?" Damon asked when they had gathered their paper plates, cups and napkins.

Jessica glanced at her watch. "It's already two o'clock."

"Plenty of time for an ice cream and a walk along the beach." Damon smiled.

Jessica nodded. They were surrounded by people in various states of undress, stretched out on gaily colored beach towels to absorb the sun. She saw couples holding hands, children digging in the sand, teenagers tossing Frisbees and moving to the private rhythms of their Walkmans. Such ordinary sights. Scenes Jessica had not wanted to be a part of—until now.

"Let's get that ice cream," she said with a slightly forced smile.

Damon looked at her mouth. Dimples teased the corners, little spots that deepened and flattened as she tried to smile. His eyes darkened with desire. Slowly he caressed the smooth graceful line of her neck. He wanted to kiss her, make love to her. Harshly he said, "Let's go."

They bought the cones, chocolate for Damon and raspberry for Jessica. Then they walked to the railing of the boardwalk and looked out to the sea.

"What did you do after the Little League?" Jessica asked, licking a drop of purple from her lower lip. Swiftly, Damon lowered his head, licking another spot off her chin. Their tongues met. Jessica retracted. Damon followed. For a moment their mouths clung.

A teenager passed, a ghetto blaster perched on his shoulder, its blaring music announcing his presence to the neighborhood. He shouted encouragement at Damon.

They broke apart. Turning their backs on the youth, they stared across the beach, their ice creams dripping to the sand below while they tried to control their wildly flaring passions.

"I went to high school. Then came college and a lot of parties. And after college more parties, until my father began breathing down my neck. That's when he sent me to New York."

"How old were you when you came here?"

"Twenty-five. An old friend of Dad's ran the office here then. He was a tyrant." He smiled. "He kept me working day and night. Then he got sick, just before the Leipzig Industrial Fair." His face sobered. "I went over there alone and made a mess of it. International Combine hasn't been allowed to exhibit there since."

"When Dad's friend retired a few months later, I took his place. I hired a classmate of mine from college days. It was the best thing I ever did. Bert Haggart doesn't like to travel. He runs the office while I'm away."

In a way his job resembled that of certain embassy personnel. He, too, could leave without disturbing the smooth running of the company. "So that's how you can take off months to go traveling," she said dryly.

His eyes sharpened at the bland look in her eyes. Jessica was too perceptive by far. Swiftly he changed the subject. "Your ice cream is melting."

Jessica looked at her cone. It was almost empty. Rivulets of purple ran down her fingers. She made a face. "Yours, too," she pointed out. "How did you manage to keep your hands clean?"

Damon laughed softly. "Practice." Tilting his head he let his eyes run over her slender form. "You look like an urchin."

The wind had tugged at her hair until tendrils curled everywhere. Her blouse had slipped free of the waistband of her skirt. Her bare feet were coated with sand. She had never looked more beautiful to him.

"Kiss me," he said, his voice rough with desire.

Jessica had been trying to clean her hands. Startled, she looked up. She saw hunger and need in his eyes. The same need and hunger that pulsed through her blood.

"Not here," she whispered.

He stepped closer. Jessica's hand tightened on her purse strap. Another step and she dashed past him, lightly running toward the steps leading to the beach.

Jessica had no intention of turning this into a race. At the bottom of the steps she waited for him. But one look at his determined face as he appeared at the top made her run on. She dodged children, circled couples. She flew over the sand, leaving people behind. Pins dropped from her hair. The heavy locks came tumbling down, flowing behind her. Jessica felt so light on her feet, so free. She heard Damon's steps behind her, coming closer, catching up. Suddenly she stumbled over a small sand hill and fell to her knees. Suppressing a giggle, she stretched out.

Damon kneeled beside her, asking urgently, "Are you hurt?"

Silently she shook her head. She couldn't talk.

Firm yet gentle hands fastened on her shoulders and turned her over. One strong arm raised her up.

"I'm all right." She couldn't hold back the laughter any longer. It burst from her throat, convulsing her, making her more breathless than before.

Damon covered her lips, punishing her for scaring him. He kissed her slowly, deeply, drinking from her mouth like a man long deprived of water. "Little tease," he muttered.

"I am not. All I wanted was some privacy," Jessica responded, kissing him back as if there was no tomorrow. And there wasn't. Not for them. They could not watch the sunset together, nor make love in the light of the moon. They had only a few hours, a few tens of minutes. Like the waves rolling to shore, time did not stop. Like the sand she could feel running through her toes, time passed. Seconds ticked by.

Jessica stopped counting. She stopped thinking. She stopped listening to caution, too. All she did was feel Damon's lips tasting hers. Her lips tasting Damon's. Damon's hands on her body, caressing her. Her own hands on Damon's skin, caressing him. The past didn't matter. What mattered was that tomorrow would take care of itself.

Damon left her mouth, sliding his lips across the hollow beneath her cheekbones, following the line to her ear. "You taste of sun and salt and sand. Earthy. Real. No dream." Gently he traced the curves of her ear with his tongue.

Jessica shuddered. "Stop teasing," she muttered, her hands moving restlessly, sliding under his shirt. She stroked the heated skin, rubbing the tips of her fingers against his dark curls.

"Is this what you want?" His mouth returned to her lips, plunging deep within.

She nodded. She could not talk. She clung to him until she was breathless.

Damon raised his head first and gathered her close, his face buried in the jasmine-scented silk of her hair. Then he lowered her to the sand, one arm protectively placed under her head. He followed her down until his body covered hers.

"You look like a houri, one of Mohammed's nymphs." The coppery cloud of her hair spilled into his hand.

"They were sloe-eyed and dark-skinned," Jessica protested.

"Some day I'll stop that saucy mouth of yours," Damon vowed huskily.

"Some day you'll forget to talk," Jessica promised him in return. She smiled as his thumb silenced her mouth. Slowly he trailed a path down her neck, his lips following wherever he touched. "Beautiful, you're so very beautiful."

Jessica felt an ache burn through her body. She arched her back, silently begging for more. Her arms went around his back, tugging at the tail of his shirt.

Damon longed to uncover her silken flesh. He wanted to merge his body with hers. But he was aware of their surroundings. Right now this small stretch of beach was deserted. But how long would that last?

Slowly he resisted the temptation of her clinging arms. He leaned over her on one elbow, his free hand cupping her chin.

Jessica opened her eyes, searching his face. His hair looked unruly, ruffled by her hands. His skin seemed to have darkened in the hour spent in the sun. His mouth, too, looked different, more tender than she had seen it before. The look in his dark eyes made her feel weak.

Yet, he was gently holding her off.

With a question in her eyes, she examined his face. She could feel the tension in him, as if he was fighting for control.

"What is it?" she asked. "Did I do something wrong?" She bit her lip in embarrassment. Had she been too forward?

He shook his head, turning his mouth into her hand. "No," he said softly. "You're simply beautiful. It's this place. The beach. The sand. The lack of privacy. How can I make love to you here?" He reached for her purse and substituted it for his arm under her head. Then he rose swiftly to his feet and faced the sea, turning his back to Jessica before he gave in to temptation and made love to her anyway.

He breathed in deeply, controlling the throbbing in his loins. What had come over him? This urgency to make love no matter where he was was new to him. Never before had he felt such gripping need, such consuming desire to touch, taste and feel. Tanya had taught him to control his sexuality long ago. At times he had sought oblivion in some woman's arms. The affairs had never lasted. Overseas he had buried himself in willing arms, trying to forget the heaving seas of blood that had once been men, women and children.

Since his divorce, there had been a few women, though not quite the number everyone credited him with. He chose his companions carefully. Intelligent, interesting women with whom he enjoyed talking over dinner. Brainless nymphs to sleep with. None of the latter would have placed any importance on whatever he might say in his sleep. That was another lesson he'd learned from his wife. He talked in his sleep, and Tanya had had the brains to use the information.

Jessica watched him, mixed emotions churning inside her. Why had he really stopped? Sea gulls were the only possible observers. Silently she cursed her inexperience. Her friend Barbara had told her often enough that men preferred experienced women. Jessica had felt that if she cared for a man, and he for her, then her lack of experience would not be held against her. Perhaps she had been wrong. Perhaps feelings were not that important. Perhaps actions counted more after all.

She shrugged her shoulders. All these years she had done the rejecting. Now, apparently, it was her turn to be rejected.

Jessica sat up and reached for her purse. Taking out her brush, she began pulling it through her hair. She carefully brushed out the sand, combing the thick mane forward so that it fell in a shimmering curtain over her face. With a deft movement, she finally tossed her hair back, smoothing it down. As always, brushing her hair had a soothing effect. She closed her eyes and raised her face to the sun.

Damon turned back to her, and watched her with narrowed eyes. Her hair shone, catching the rays of the sun. His body tensed, fighting the lure of her warmth. He placed his hands in his pockets to keep them from reaching out, from taking the brush from her hands, and....

"Stop tempting me," he growled, his voice harsh with restraint.

Startled, Jessica opened her eyes, pain still lurking in their brown depth. Moments later she had herself under control and her mask slipped back into place. The hand holding the brush continued its soothing motion. "You don't have to pretend with me. Stop being kind," she said quietly.

Damon swore under his breath. Swiftly he crossed the space separating them to kneel beside her. He took the brush from her hand, then placed her fingers inside his shirt to cover his heart, letting her feel its thundering beat.

"Now tell me I'm pretending. That I'm just being kind."
His voice was rough. "Jessica, I want to make love with
you. I want to bury myself in your warmth and forget about
tomorrow."

Whatever his reason had been for turning away from her,
it didn't exist now. His heart thudded against the wall of his
chest, vibrating with need. "I'm not stopping you," she said
softly.

My conscience—or whatever's left of it—is, he thought
grimly. "Jessica," he said, then stopped. How was he going
to explain his conflicting emotions without revealing secrets that were not his to confide? He gathered her closer.
The gold of his watch caught the rays of the sun. He looked
at it. It was three o'clock already.

"Come on. We have to be quick. You don't want to miss
your flight."

Jessica snatched her hand away, struggled out of his arms
and got to her feet in one fluid motion, her face devoid of
color beneath her tan.

"Thanks for the warning," she snarled, "but I don't go
in for quickies." Jerkily, she bent and picked up her brush,
stuffing it into her purse with a violent shove.

Slowly, Damon got to his feet. "You have quite a vocab-
ulary," he said, smiling.

Jessica glared at him. "Just leave me alone."

"And a suspicious mind, too," Damon continued calmly.
"You misunderstood my words."

Jessica renewed her struggle. "I know what I heard."

"When I make love to you, it won't be here on the sand,
and it won't be quick. Have you looked at the time lately?"

Jessica stared at her watch and gasped.

"That's how I felt. And that feeling has nothing to do
with the other one." Slowly he reached for her wind-tossed
hair, stroking it back from her face. His hand speared
through the rippling silk, finally catching the ends and
curling them around his finger.

Jessica watched his dark, almost brooding face. "I'm
sorry," she said softly. "I misunderstood. I am—" She

swallowed and started over again. "This has happened so fast. It doesn't seem quite real."

He nodded, a tender smile spreading across his face. "It's real," he assured her. Raising her hair to his face, he said, "I won't forget the scent of jasmine mingling with salt air. Nor the flecks of sunlight sparkling in your hair. Some tribes consider red hair good luck." He hesitated, then asked roughly, "Would you let me cut a curl?"

Jessica knew that Pushtuns used henna to ward off evil, like people here wore charms and preserved four leaf clovers. She didn't believe in superstitions, but she wanted to give Damon something of herself. Not pausing to think, she opened her bag and took a pair of scissors from the small sewing kit she carried. Without a word, she handed them to him. Carefully he cut off a small lock, wrapping it around a finger.

She watched him reach into his back pocket and take out his wallet, extracting a white piece of paper. He gathered the fine hairs into one curl in his palm, folded the paper around it and returned the paper to his wallet.

The gesture was so tender, so impossibly, ridiculously romantic. He did care for her! The caressing way he'd shaped the curl spoke louder than words. "You should've made love with me." Her voice was shaky. "It isn't fair."

He smiled faintly. "Few things in life are. Or haven't you noticed?" He drew her against him, cradling her in his strong arms, his face harshly defiant as he raised it into the wind. Then he kissed her—once—before he gently pushed her away.

The roar of jet engines made them look up. All afternoon, planes had been landing and taking off at Kennedy Airport in the distance, but they had ignored the sound. Now they watched one big silver bird rise gracefully from across the bay, following its path until it faded into the blue sky.

"September is just around the corner, Jessica."

September was almost four months away. Four months of waiting. Four months of fear. What had she gotten herself into? "Why can't you give up that trip to the mountains?'' Jessica's voice reflected the bitterness welling up inside her.

Damon's eyes sharpened. She had guessed his destination. He was almost sure of it. "I can't. My friend would be very disappointed if I canceled my trip," he said calmly. "We've planned this meeting for quite some time."

"You're just visiting a friend?" she asked, a ray of hope brightening her eyes. Perhaps her imagination had run wild, she thought, willing to clutch at even a straw.

"Ahmed and I were roommates in college. He went to medical school here. For a while he even practiced on Long Island."

She tilted her head and searched his face. He was smiling. He must be telling the truth. "Was he as wild as you were?" she teased, feeling oddly relieved.

"We weren't wild," Damon protested with a grin. "We never got into trouble."

"That," Jessica chuckled, "doesn't prove a thing. It only shows that you were too smart to get caught." Suddenly she remembered that his imprudence had caught up with him and his punishment had been much more severe than his crime. He was still paying for it. Her smile vanished.

"We have to go." Damon's reminder interrupted her thoughts.

Jessica nodded. "It's getting cool." She rubbed her arms against the sudden chill.

They walked swiftly back to the car. The trip back to Manhattan was made in record time. In the lobby of her hotel, Jessica asked, "Do you want to come up to my room or wait down here?"

Damon smiled faintly. "I think I'd better wait right here."

"Then I'll leave my suitcase with you." She almost ran to the elevators. If she had hesitated, she might have tried to change his mind.

They had only minutes left. She didn't waste any time. Swiftly she showered. Dressed in her underwear, she packed the big suitcase, leaving out a white and mint green striped shirt and matching skirt.

She was closing the zipper when a knock sounded on her door.

"Just a minute," she called, guessing it was the bellboy. She took the clothes and ran into the bathroom. "You can come in now." When the door opened, she said, "I've only the one suitcase. Please take it downstairs. I'll meet you there."

Damon closed the door. "Do you always leave your door unlocked?"

"I was in a hurry." Swiftly she shrugged into her blouse. "What did you do with my other suitcase?" Why had he come upstairs?

"I left it at the reception desk. I thought you might need help with the rest of your things."

Jessica's hands were trembling. Suddenly the buttons were too big for the holes. She swore softly.

"Need any help?"

"I'm all right." Holding the blouse together, she peered around the corner. Damon was bending over the suitcase, buckling the leather straps, his muscles rippling beneath his shirt. Jessica caught her breath.

Damon lifted the case from the bed. Turning, he said, "Before we leave we can have a drink together at—" His eyes darkened at the sight of her. For a moment he stood still, staring at the thick fall of her hair, at her blouse clutched together in front of her. One slender bare leg was clearly visible. Then he moved forward, drawn by the look of desire on her face, propelled by his own burning need.

Jessica reached out to him, the front of her shirt hanging open, revealing her soft form. Damon's hands curved around her waist, touching skin instead of cloth, heated flesh instead of cool cotton.

With a groan, he drew her into his arms. His kiss was bruising, filled with need. The lobby downstairs had been cold, a freezing contrast to the afternoon heat. Damon had come upstairs in search of her warmth.

He covered her mouth, bending her backward over his arm, pressing her hips against him. The heat of her skin washed over him. He took her closer into his embrace.

Jessica clung to him, her arms roving over his back, tugging at his shirttail. She moaned under the onslaught of sensations as skin touched skin.

Suddenly Damon was touching her breasts through filmy lace, moving the fabric back and forth, fanning the fire in her loins until she clung weakly to him. He carried her to the bed, following her down upon it.

Jessica's arms closed around him. With a groan he buried his head in her silken mane. Jasmine and the scent of the sea surrounded him.

"Jessica." He breathed her name before once again drinking of her mouth.

Jessica clutched at his shoulders, restlessly seeking smooth skin. Her hands found buttons. She almost tore the fabric in her need. She pushed at his shoulders. "Help me take off your shirt."

Damon raised his head, his eyes blazing with fire. Swiftly he rose from the bed. The shirt fell to the floor. His other garments followed. He straightened, meeting her wide-eyed stare.

Jessica had known about his strength. She had felt the subtle movements of skin over muscles of steel. But she hadn't known just how beautiful he was. Broad shoulders tapered down to slim hips. Dark hair curled over his broad chest, forming a thin line down a tightly ridged stomach. Like the ancient statue of Apollo, he radiated tightly leashed power. His skin gleamed like bronze in the afternoon sun casting shadows and catching light as he moved.

She wanted to whisper his name, but no sound escaped her tight throat. Silently she held out her arms to him.

Damon stood staring at her soft, smooth curves, at the warm welcome of her arms. Hunger and need burned within, almost shaking him. "Can you get pregnant?" he asked, his voice harsh, fighting for control. "I have nothing with me."

Jessica did not take contraceptives. But she shook her head anyway. "Are you always so careful?" she asked. His words had struck a discordant note.

Swiftly he bent over her and gathered her in his arms. "I got caught once," he said with harsh bitterness.

Jessica froze, stunned, as if he had slapped her. Then she twisted and turned, trying to get away from him. "Just get the hell out of here," she snarled. "You're so tainted with bitterness, that you can't tell the difference between Tanya and me."

Swearing softly, Damon easily subdued her with his strength, holding her without bruising her. "Listen to me, little hellcat." He covered her body with his own, cupping her chin. "I was thinking of you, Jessica. I wasn't trying to protect myself."

Jessica turned on him with a hissed, "Let me go."

Damon shook his head, his crooked smile back in place. "I want you and you want me as much as I do."

Jessica stared at him mutely, eyes narrowed and bright green with hurt and frustration. Her body was tingling from his touch, desire mingled with anger.

Slowly Damon bent his head and kissed her tight lips, teasing them with gentle heat until they relaxed under his persistent caress. His tongue filled her mouth, velvet texture and moist heat soothing her anger still further.

Jessica admitted to herself that he had reasons to be hard and suspicious. She had known about the still present sores of bitterness. Even with gentle care sores did not heal overnight. In time Jessica hoped he would come to trust her. With aching gentleness, she smiled. Her hands moved to his shoulders, slid up the smooth, strong column of his neck, tangling her fingers in his crisp, black hair. "Yes," she admitted, her surrender a whispered caress. "I want you."

Then she kissed him with a hunger she had learned from him, the hands in his hair drawing him closer to her.

His mouth roamed over her face, licking and biting her ear gently, his breath fanning the heat he created deep inside her. Smoothly, powerfully, he slid down, his lips closing over one silk-covered breast. "I can think of nothing more beautiful than seeing my child suckle here," he said, his voice gritty with emotion. His mouth trailed fire across her stomach. "But I want to be right beside you and watch you swell with my child. I want to touch you and feel it move.'' He covered her once again. Cupping her face, he looked deep into her eyes. ''I have no right to ask you to wait for me. I shouldn't even make love to you now. But I need to touch you. I need your warmth.''

Tears shimmered in her eyes. With trembling lips she said, ''Damn your way with words.''

''No more words then,'' he promised, his voice low. Bending his head, he stilled her trembling mouth with his own. Cupping the fullness of her breast with one hand, he undid the clasp of her bra with the other and smoothed the straps off her shoulders. Then he caught one nipple between his teeth, nipping it gently, then soothing it with his tongue moments later. He shifted to the other one, circling the sensitive skin with soft, moist strokes until her nipples stood hard and erect with longing.

Jessica shivered and arched against him with feline movements, her fingernails digging into his shoulders. She clung to him as wave after wave of excitement broke over her, moaning as he caressed the soft skin below.

Consciousness retreated under the onslaught of the feelings his fingers and lips created. She had never been touched like this before. Eagerly she moved into his caresses. Tiny shudders began racing through her body, increasing in strength, until she was shaking with the need to feel him inside her. She moved against him blindly, her hands sliding down his back.

Slowly his hand stroked over her hips, following their gentle curves, then caressing her stomach until she burned. His hand teased the dark triangle of her hair, drawing closer and closer to her liquid warmth. A gasp of pleasure broke from her lips when he touched her woman's center. Her hips moved in mindless need, soft cries urging him on until she shuddered and released her warmth. With a groan Damon slid between her legs and entered her. She felt tight and he waited until she had become accustomed to his strength. Then he moved slowly, powerfully, his body hard with restraint.

Jessica looked at him, eyes wide and dazed with emotions. Her arms slid over him, bringing him closer to her. Her hips moved in unconscious surrender and silent invitation.

Hoarsely crying her name, Damon moved inside her, his rhythm increasing in ever-growing waves of pleasure. They flowed together. Cresting wave after wave, Jessica moaned softly, her moans changing, becoming harsh and abrupt.

The final wave broke. They clung together, crying out. Tossed high by the force of their feelings, they held their breaths, savoring the rapture of the moment.

For a long time afterward Damon held Jessica in his arms, storing up warmth. He would need it. The mountains were cold, he thought as he stroked her fiery hair, and the valleys were dark. He watched her open her eyes in wonder. They were shimmering with tears.

He felt torn between the longing to kiss away the tears and the knowledge where such action would lead. "Thank you, my love," he murmured, his dark eyes sliding over her possessively, savoring the shimmering eyes, the glorious tousled flame of her hair, the soft, golden skin and the soft, vulnerable mouth, memorizing her. Then he swiftly rolled off the bed.

Tears spilling over, Jessica watched him gather his clothes and disappear into the bathroom. She wiped them away. This was no time to cry. She got to her feet and began to dress. When Damon returned from the bathroom, Jessica went in to clean up.

They hardly spoke during their crazy drive to the airport. They arrived with no time to spare.

"This is fast becoming a habit," Damon said as they raced to the gate. At the security check, they stopped, black and hazel eyes locking for moments in time.

"September." This time it was Jessica who uttered the word.

Damon kissed her hard, then he turned her, pushed her gently through the gate and waited until he could no longer see the fiery sheen of her hair.

Then he moved swiftly to the nearest phone. Inserting a coin, he punched in the numbers and waited impatiently while his hard eyes searched the crowds.

"Eagle insurance."

"I want to insure a shipment to Paris," Damon gave the code.

"Sea or air freight?" the voice asked politely.

"Sea," Damon answered.

There was a chuckle. "I'm glad you called. What's up?"

"I want you to search all shipments to Pakistan," Damon said. "Especially those to Islamabad."

A whistle came from the other end. "How'd you get that bit of news? I don't know how you do it."

"Pure luck. Oh, there's something else. I want a check run on Jessica O'Connor Stanton."

Another whistle. "Pat O'Connor's daughter? Sure hope she's clean."

"So do I," Damon muttered. "I'm almost certain of it."

Chapter 6

Evening hung over Islamabad, hot and humid and threatening rain. The fading light of dusk seeped through the windows into the room where Jessica sat on the floor surrounded by disaster, the result of three years' accumulation of papers, letters and magazines.

"Why did I save this?" She squinted at the *Vogue* magazine, September issue, 1982. Shrugging, she added it to the steadily growing pile of garbage. She was not going to ship anything but the most important stuff back to the States. With space in New York at a premium, her apartment would probably be less than half the size of this house.

She worked steadily, the blue linen of her shirt clinging to her body, her jeans shadowed with perspiration. From the nearby mosque, the mullah's call for evening prayer broke the silence.

Jessica leaned against her desk and reached for the tall glass of iced mango juice. Sipping slowly, she looked toward the open windows.

The room was filled with the hearty scent of roses growing beneath the window. A gecko clung to the screen, its small body clearly visible against the lights flooding the garden.

Night fell swiftly. The gecko caught his prey. Jessica stirred, reluctant to get up and turn on the light. The humidity was making her lethargic. But she didn't want to turn on the air conditioner until the rains came. She hated to be shut tightly inside.

A car door slammed. Moments later someone rang the bell at the gate in the high wall surrounding the house. The whisper of Aya's sandals sliding on the tiled floor told her that her maid was answering the call. She listened to the murmured exchange of voices, recognizing Peter's exasperated hiss and Barbara's chuckled response. Those two were always squabbling with the ease of longtime friends.

"Jessica. Where are you?" Barbara's voice called out to her from the living room across the hall.

"In the study."

Barbara groped through the semidarkness. "Where's the light?"

"To your left, behind the door."

Footsteps. Stumbling. Another curse. "What is this? An obstacle course? What a dumb place to put a switch."

Suddenly the room flooded with light. Jessica closed her eyes against the sudden brightness.

"What a mess!" Barbara started laughing. "Jessica, do you ever throw anything away?"

Slowly, Jessica opened her eyes, grinning at her tall, slender, dark-haired friend. "Not often," she admitted ruefully. "Can I interest you in some old magazines?"

Barbara shook her head, her black curls dancing. "No thanks. Most of those were mine to begin with."

"You can have them back now," Jessica muttered. "Where's Peter? I thought I heard the two of you fighting as you came in."

"He's making himself useful by fixing us a drink," Barbara said. "And we weren't fighting, just arguing as usual."

"Did I get any mail?" Jessica asked. She had left her office early in the afternoon, before the diplomatic pouch had arrived.

Barbara took a bundle from her purse, waving it in the air. "You got a few letters. One is from your sister. I'll bet you a dollar she changed her mind again about the color of the sari she wants."

"Tough. I'm not going to exchange it a third time. If she doesn't want the blue and silver sari, I'll give it to my mother. It would go beautifully with the star sapphire I bought for her birthday." Jessica wiped her damp face with her sleeve. "What else is there?" She held out her hand for the mail.

"Not what you're looking for," Barbara warned, handing her the bundle. She hadn't missed the bright flash of hope in Jessica's eyes. "If I'd seen another one of those envelopes with the big black letters scrawled all over it, I would've delivered it right after work."

Wearily, Jessica got to her feet. Two weeks without a word from Damon. She kicked a pile of magazines with her bare foot, muttering under her breath while she sorted through the mail. She saw a letter from Aunt Gloria, Ali's note, bank statements and an insurance bill. Nothing that required her immediate attention. Smiling tightly, she pocketed the mail, wiping her hands on her jeans. "I feel sticky all over. If you don't mind, I'll take a swift shower before I join you two."

"Go right ahead," Barbara agreed quietly, understanding that Jessica needed a few moments of privacy.

"What happened here?" Holding a glass in each hand, Peter Hallam stood in the doorway, a stunned look on his face. "Don't tell me you were looking for the missing invoices in this mess?"

Peter was Jessica's assistant, at least that was what his job description said. He was rarely in the office, though. Most of his time was spent visiting refugee camps. Jessica never asked where he disappeared to on those often lengthy trips. She accepted his reports without question.

"What invoices are missing?" Barbara's brown eyes flew questioningly from Jessica to Peter's craggy face. "How come I didn't hear anything about it?" As the ambassador's secretary she was always well informed.

With a grin Peter shoved the glass into her hand. "None of your business."

Seeing the flare of anger in Barbara's eyes, Jessica swiftly explained, "When we went to customs this afternoon to pick up our medical supplies, we found three extra crates waiting for us. No invoices, though, and no bills of lading. Peter had to open one of the boxes to make sure they were for us."

"Are you certain they belong to you? Someone else might have ordered medical supplies," Barbara pointed out.

"They were addressed to our department. I paid quite a bit of baksheesh to get them out of customs. Dr. Brooks will jump with joy when we deliver them to his camp tomorrow."

"You and your Afghans." Barbara shook her head. "Are you both accompanying the convoy in the morning?"

"Of course. We're not going to risk losing another truckload like the last time," Peter said with firm chin and hard eyes.

"How could you prevent it?" Barbara teased him. "Don't tell me you're going to stop the thieves with a gun?"

Before another squabble got started, Jessica intervened. "Of course not. We've taken other precautions. For one, we hired only drivers we know personally. And we're supposed to have an armed escort until Peshawar. Barbara, why don't you make yourself comfortable. Peter, do you think you could do me a favor by looking at my fan in the dining room? I think it's leaking oil. Aya will give you the tools."

Closing the study door behind them, she added, "I'll join you in a few minutes."

Swiftly she went to her bedroom, taking the bundle of letters from her pocket and laying them on the nightstand before she peeled off her jeans. Why had Damon stopped writing? For eight weeks he had bridged the distance with his notes. Two weeks ago they had stopped as unexpectedly as they had started.

Since they had not discussed writing on that magical day in May, his first letter had surprised her. Sitting in her office she had held the envelope postmarked in New York in her hand. With a mixture of excitement and anxiety she'd turned it over and over, afraid to open it.

His handwriting was like Damon himself, uncompromising, strong—a big black scrawl. When Jessica had finally opened the letter, a small piece of paper had fluttered out. A weekly calendar with the days marked off in red. Across it he had written "17 weeks." She had sat holding the scrap of paper, laughing and crying at the same time.

The following week another envelope had arrived. Same calendar—"16 weeks." The countdown had continued until it reached ten. For two weeks now there had been nothing. Time had stopped, filling her days with waiting and her nights with fear. What if something had happened to him?

Shedding the rest of her clothes with trembling hands, Jessica stepped under the shower, raising her face to the tepid spray.

The house had its own well. Water was pumped electrically to a container on top of the roof where the sun heated it. At intervals, Jessica had it tested for safety. She was one of the few people in the community who could drink her tap water from the faucet without boiling it first. The only disadvantage was that during the summer months the water was never refreshingly cold.

Swiftly, Jessica washed herself. Stepping out of the shower, she dried off before blow-drying her hair. It was shorter than before. Upon her return to Islamabad she'd had it trimmed.

Each time she looked into the mirror, she remembered Damon's hand carefully shaping the cut-off ends of her hair into a curl. That vision would recall other memories: the touch of his long tanned fingers on her skin, the taste of his mouth.

Abruptly she turned off the dryer, shivering despite the heat. After the first week she had given up fighting his constant intrusion in her life. The memory of every touch, every word was always with her. Like Damon, she had begun to count the weeks until September.

She guessed what his silence meant. Damon had begun his trip. Was he in New Delhi now, sweating over contracts? Or had he already left India, destination unknown?

Once again, waiting and fear had become a part of her life, her anxiety more intense than ever before. With Michael she had feared the uncertainty of a defective fuse or miscalculations in the placement of charges and inexperienced help. But at least he hadn't worked in a war zone.

She didn't know if Damon's friend Ahmed lived in Afghanistan or on the Pakistani side. Not that it made any difference. Lately, Soviet planes had even bombed Pushtun camps within Pakistani soil. There wasn't a place in the mountains that was safe.

Sometimes she wondered if she could live with nightmares for the rest of her life.

Muttering an oath, Jessica reached for a fresh pair of jeans and a yellow cotton top and slipped into them. Sitting down on the charpoy that served as her bed, she picked up her sneakers, turning them upside down and shaking them before putting them on. After years of living in countries with scorpions and snakes, the gesture was an automatic protective reflex.

Barbara sat alone in the *gulhana*, a small semicircular garden room, Jessica's favorite place. The tall French windows stood wide open, allowing for cross ventilation of cooling night air. Gulmahmad, her gardener, had placed containers filled with geraniums and zinnias against the screens and whitewashed walls. One rug, an old Saruyk, was spread over the flagstone floor. The furniture had been crafted from Jessica's own design. Sturdy wooden frame chairs with untanned leather cushions, grouped around a rectangular table, stood in the center of the room.

Barbara looked up from a magazine. "I was just going to go after you."

"I had to wash my hair. Is Peter still working on the fan?" When Barbara nodded, Jessica added, "Perhaps I should see if I can help him."

"Sit down. If he needs help he'll call. I fixed you a Scotch."

"Thanks." Jessica sank into a chair and reached for her glass. The drink was tepid, reminding her of the flat champagne Damon had rescued so long ago. For a moment she stared despondently into space. Damon was everywhere: when she combed her hair; when she opened her purse; in the morning; and especially at night. "I need more ice."

"I'll get it. You stay and rest," Barbara said, getting to her feet. Returning with a small ice bucket moments later, she added, "You look bushed."

"I am." Jessica held out her glass for ice cubes. "The heat in the customs buildings was suffocating. At one moment I thought I'd pass out."

Barbara's eyes sharpened. "Are you pregnant?" she asked bluntly.

Startled, Jessica stared. With a ghost of a smile she said, "No." She could hear Damon talking about their child. She could see his dark head pressed against her skin. She almost felt the touch of his lips. "No," she repeated abruptly. "It's nothing like that."

"Thank God." Leaning back in her chair, Barbara smiled with relief. "I kept on telling myself that you're too sensible to take such risks. But you've been upset lately. I couldn't think of anything else."

Sensible? Was that how she appeared to her friends? What would Barbara think if she told her that she hadn't given a thought to possible consequences, that it had been Damon who had cared. Most likely, she would think her a fool.

Barbara could be right. After the notes had stopped coming, doubts had cropped up again. Was Damon letting her down lightly? Was that why he had not added any personal words? Or did his continued silence have an entirely different reason? Damn it, she wished she knew.

"If you don't mind, let's change the subject," Jessica suggested tersely. "Let's talk about something else. Like what you were doing this afternoon with those old files." Before she had left the embassy, she had looked into Barbara's office and had found her swearing at old photos and newspaper clippings.

"His Excellency wanted some pictures of Ahmed Khan. Don't ask me why. The man's been dead for at least two years."

Ahmed. The name of the friend Damon was planning to visit. Another coincidence? Another puzzle piece? Slowly she asked, "Who is Ahmed Khan?"

"He *was* an Afghan. A Pushtun, really, but from the Afghan side."

The Pushtuns were the largest Afghan tribe, their territory stretching from southern Afghanistan across the Himalayan Mountains to the north of Pakistan. The tall mountain men considered themselves Pushtuns first, Afghans second. Most of them rejected both Pakistani citizenship and the national boundaries dividing their tribal territory.

"He was a prince, a cousin to the last king," Barbara explained further. "At the time of the Russian invasion, he lived in the States. If he'd stayed there, he might still be alive. But, of course, he came back and joined the Holy Warriors. He was killed in a skirmish two years ago."

The name Holy Warrior was a translation of the word *mujahidin*. To the rest of the world the resistance group was commonly known as freedom fighters.

Jessica swallowed, trying to dislodge the lump of fear in her throat. An Afghan named Ahmed. A man who lived in the mountains, but had spent some time in the States. It was too much for mere coincidence. What if the reports were false? "Are you sure he's dead?" she asked.

"That's what the report said. It's a shame, really. He was some good-looking man. There was a picture of him from Harvard. He looked handsome in his cap and gown, but the scar on his left cheek gave him a wild look." Barbara shuddered. "They identified his body by that scar. There wasn't much else left of his face."

"We were roommates at Harvard" Damon had said. Could Ahmed Khan still be alive? There must be any number of Afghans with scars on their cheeks. Someone could have made a mistake identifying the body. And if he was alive, did that mean Damon was becoming embroiled in the war?

"Who are you two talking about?" Strands of brown hair falling into his forehead, Peter stood in the doorway, wiping his hands on a rag. "I sort of fixed the leak. But the fan is on its way out."

"Thanks. As long as it survives the next two weeks."

"Say a prayer every time you turn it on," Peter suggested, sitting down. "Who died?"

"A Pushtun named Ahmed Khan," Barbara said.

If Jessica hadn't known Peter so well, she might have missed the sudden tension in his eyes. But working with him for more than two years had given her a keen awareness of her friend. Peter knew something. Perhaps he had heard rumors that the man was not dead.

"That was two years ago," Peter said. "I only remember it because it happened shortly after I arrived in Islamabad."

"Then how come I didn't know about it? I, too, was here at the time," Barbara asked.

"Perhaps you were on vacation. Or you simply missed it. It wasn't exactly headline news. The khan was killed in a raid on some prison camp in Kabul." Peter paused, then added, "I met him once at a party in D.C."

Leaning forward, Barbara asked eagerly, "What was he like?"

"Like other Pushtuns. Tall and dark. Except that he had piercing blue eyes."

Jessica listened closely, her heart in her throat. If Ahmed Khan indeed was Damon's friend, then Damon might've been with him at that party. "How long ago was that?"

"Don't tell me you're interested in him, too." Peter shook his head. "About five, six years ago, I'd say."

"Do you remember if he was alone?"

Peter looked at her strangely. "Funny you should ask. There was another guy with him. To this day I still remember the entrance they made. I thought they were brothers because they were both tall, both dark and both arrogant.

They walked into the room and the girls just melted. None of us other guys ever had a chance."

Jessica didn't need to ask the other man's name. She already knew it was Damon. The puzzle pieces were locking into place.

She could guess why the Pushtun prince had hidden in the mountains, letting everyone believe he was dead. Dead men were no threat. Dead men didn't fight. Jessica felt sure that Ahmed had used his time wisely to gather a small army of *mujahidins*. Damon had told her only the partial truth. Ahmed Khan was not only a physician quietly caring for the people of his tribe, but a leader of the resistance, actively fighting the invasion.

And now the prince's cover had been blown. Whether by accident or design, Jessica didn't know. Even with her minuscule understanding of tactics, she knew that he would have to strike soon to keep some element of surprise.

And where did Damon fit into all of this? How deeply was he involved? Had the khan waited for Damon's arrival to rise from the dead? Or was this just another coincidence?

Fear settled like a block of ice in her stomach. Despite the heat, goose bumps crawled on her skin. The sawing of the cicadas outside the windows sounded like a song of doom, the low roll of drums as more puzzle pieces fell into place with frightening clarity.

She was grateful when Peter turned to her with last minute questions about the forthcoming trip. It drew her attention away from shadow figures and mountain crevices and the sound of guns.

But when her friends left a short while later, the visions returned more vividly. Doubt, too, reared its ugly head. How could she love a man whose life was divided into separate files marked Business and Top Secret? Would their meeting in September be overshadowed by other partings, other secrets? Would she ever know the whole man?

The sawing of the cicadas stopped abruptly. An uncanny silence filled the room. Ghostlike fingers reached for Jessica's legs, keeping her chained to the chair. Her skin crawled from the touch of invisible eyes peering through the screen.

Fighting free of the frightening sensations, she got jerkily to her feet. No one was out there. It was only her imagination playing tricks. She gathered the glasses to take them to the kitchen.

Suddenly she stopped.

Was that a soft knock on the screen? She turned back. Her hand was trembling, making the glasses ring like warning bells. The screens were like black curtains, hiding the outside.

Perhaps Aya had made the sound on her way to her room. Jessica spun back and walked swiftly to the kitchen. The room was deserted, its neatness telling her that Aya had retired for the night. The maid's quarters were separated from the main house by a short walk. The sound she had heard could have been the closing of the door or the opening of the window in Aya's room.

Quickly she locked the back door and rinsed out the glasses. Returning to the *gulhana*, she closed the windows and turned off the lights. Standing well back, she searched the silent garden because the cicadas still had not resumed their song. The floodlights outside revealed nothing, no moving shadows, no unusual forms.

The eerie silence continued as she entered her study to begin sorting again. With a sigh of exasperation, Jessica went to the front door. There was no one out there, she felt sure. It was only her imagination playing tricks on her already overactive mind. She threw open the door.

A dark shadow rose up in front of her. The shadow of a man.

Biting back a scream, Jessica stepped back, trying to slam the door in his face.

"Jessica."

The sound froze her. Now she knew she was imagining things. She thought she'd heard Damon's voice.

"Aren't you going to invite me in?" The shadow loomed closer, towering over her.

Blinking her eyes, she whispered hoarsely, "Damon?"

"I'm not a ghost. Touch me. I'm flesh and blood," he said with a smile in his voice.

"What are you doing here?" Shock kept her feet glued to the floor, her hands bonded to her sides.

"I know you turned down my dinner invitation when we first met. Could I change your mind?"

"No. Yes. Damn it, how did you get in? Why didn't you ring the bell?"

"I didn't want to wake your servants. Are you going to invite me in?"

His gentle teasing brought warmth to her frozen limbs. Jessica could feel her legs buckle. She sagged with relief. Suddenly she was in his arms, clinging to his broad shoulders, her heart pounding against her ribs.

"You scared me. Did you scale the wall?" She was bubbling over with excitement and happiness and the release from fear. Her hands reached up to touch his face, needing the contact to hold on to reality as a proof that this wasn't some cruel dream.

A soft brush of hair moved against the palm of her hand as he answered, "Your door was unlatched. I just let myself in."

He turned his head to place a kiss into her palm. "I'm sorry I frightened you."

He had carefully planned his sudden appearance, deliberately throwing her off balance to give her no chance to hide her feelings behind a mask of polite welcome. But now, holding her in his arms, feeling the irregular thuds of her heart beating against his chest, he cursed himself for having frightened her. His arms tightened protectively around her slender form.

Jessica laughed softly. "But you do. Each time we meet." She let her hands slide over his beard, testing its sensual softness. "Come inside." Even now, with her fingertips caressing his face, he felt unreal, like a figment of her dreams.

In the foyer she looked at him for quite some time. The short clipped beard hugging his chin emphasized his harsh features, changing his appearance drastically. He looked like a Pushtun warrior, tough and dangerous. But her momentary fear was forgotten when she met the familiar laughter in his eyes.

Happiness rushed through her, bringing a sparkle to her eyes. Her mouth softened, her breath quickened with longing. She threw her arms around him.

Damon drew her against him, bending his head. His mouth descended in hunger, crushing her lips in his need. "I missed you," he said huskily, showing her how much with every kiss. His lips roved from her mouth to her cheekbones, before once again descending to her mouth.

"I missed you, too. I still can't believe you're here," Jessica whispered, letting her fingers run through his soft dark hair. Testing, she closed her eyes, then opened them again.

Damon looked at her with a mixture of amusement and tenderness. "I won't fade into the walls."

But hours, at most days, from now he would fade into the mountains with Ahmed Khan. Her hands clenched into his broad khaki-clad shoulders as if she could hold him by force and prevent him from leaving her.

"Can I get you anything? Are you hungry? Thirsty?" She looked into his face. For the first time she noticed the tired lines, the deeper set of his eyes.

"Coffee, if you have it." His arms moved over her harshly, pressing her against the hard lines of his body. He groaned deep in his throat. "But not just yet." He took her lips in a long kiss, drinking of her as if he had been thirsting for her.

Jessica softened, taking and giving, her arms holding him as fiercely as his held her. They kissed without reservation, holding nothing back, their hunger for each other shaking them both.

When they finally broke apart, they stared at each other with naked desire.

"Damon," Jessica finally whispered. "I'm so glad you came."

"I couldn't stay away," he said roughly, pressing her head into his strong shoulder, stroking her silky hair. "How about that coffee?"

"Come with me into the kitchen while I make it." She wasn't going to be separated from him for one moment of their time.

"Still afraid I'm going to disappear?" Damon teased gently.

"No." She led the way to Aya's domain. "But I like your company."

"But not my beard." His words held no question.

Startled, Jessica looked at him. Even now, after weeks of separation, he could still read her thoughts. "The beard suits you." She did not dislike its looks. But she hated the reason for its existence. Most Pushtuns wore beards. She imagined him with a turban wrapped around his head. Damon would become one of the tribesmen, indistinguishable in appearance from the *mujahidins*. Damon settled himself into a chair at the kitchen table, his long legs stretched out in front of him. "I'll shave it off in September," he promised her softly.

"In September I won't care." Jessica turned away, opening cupboards, taking out coffee, filter and cups. Her hand clenched around the pot as she poured water into the coffeemaker. Would September ever come?

When the coffee machine began gurgling, Jessica asked, "Do you take sugar? Cream?" The question reminded her just how little she knew about him. He liked pizza, hot dogs and chocolate ice cream. He disliked official receptions and tepid champagne. And he cared for her. Enough to make this special trip to see her.

For now that had to be enough.

"I like it black."

Jessica grinned, the freckles on her nose dancing. "I should have guessed."

"And you like the bitter taste softened with cream." His deep voice flowed over her, caressing her skin. His dark eyes were watchful, however. He saw the fear and uncertainty behind her facade of easy banter.

"When I drink coffee, I do. But mostly I prefer tea." She put the non-dairy creamer on the table. "I'm afraid it's a little late for a dinner date. I could heat something up." She wanted to prolong the domesticity of the situation. Here in the kitchen she could make believe that they were like other couples. Ordinary people, meeting after a day's work. As long as she asked questions about how he liked his coffee and if he liked to eat, she could not ask the one uppermost in her mind.

How much time did they have?

Damon rose in one smooth, powerful movement and drew her into his arms. "I'm hungry for you." Turning her face up, he kissed her gently until he could feel her body relax against him. Then his kiss changed, becoming hard and searching, possessing her with a force that drove every conscious thought from her but her longing for him. She forgot about the nights filled with dread. She forgot the nightmares to come.

Her hands sought the warmth beneath his shirt, brushing aside buttons when the material wouldn't stretch. Fingers splayed against the wall of his chest.

Damon's eyes narrowed with desire. His hands slid up beneath her yellow top, seeking her soft skin. He drew circles, tightly drawn at first then expanding, until he covered her back with long strokes.

She wore nothing beneath the top. He had dreamed of touching her since that long-ago day in May. He had imagined burying his face in her thick, fragrant hair. Reality was much sweeter, more potent than any dream. She moved against him with liquid fire, burning to cinders some of his fears. "You didn't change your mind about September." The words were half-question, half-statement.

Jessica raised her head. "No," she said softly. "But when your notes stopped, I thought that perhaps you had changed yours."

He kissed her, hard, proving to her the falsity of her thoughts. "I knew I was going to see you when I left New York. Why did you never answer them?"

The harshness of his voice startled her as much as the question itself. "It never occurred to me," she said slowly. There had been nothing personal in his notes. They struck her as needing no response. "I don't think you would've appreciated letters filled with gossip."

"Is that the only kind you write?"

"I do when there's nothing else to talk about," Jessica said, her voice flat. "Or when I can't write that I am scared."

Abruptly Damon released her, turning toward the coffee machine. Her frank words only confirmed what he already knew. Jessica was afraid. Afraid for him and of the life he led.

He shouldn't have written anything at all. He shouldn't have visited her tonight. He should have trusted in fate. He should have trusted Jessica to keep her promise.

But, although life had taught him many things, it had not taught him how to trust.

He poured the coffee into the cups, his face hard with resolve. "It's late. I have to go back to my hotel."

Abruptly she sat down, stunned by his decision and her pain. "But I thought—" She'd thought that he would stay with her, that they would have more than these few minutes, that she would spend the night wrapped in his arms. She watched him replace the coffeepot with careful movements before he turned around.

"What did you think?" His voice sounded distant. He had seen a hunger equal to his own in her wide, hazel eyes and soft mouth. How easy it would be to forget about her vulnerability and reach for her. And how hard it would be to leave.

"That you would stay here."

Slowly, Damon walked toward her, looking down at the haunted expression tightening her face. He didn't reach out to stroke the taut cords in her neck, waiting instead for her to make the next move. "Even if I stay here, I still have to go into the mountains."

"But not tonight," Jessica said huskily, moving against him with need.

His arms closed around her. Pressing her body tightly against him, he spoke against her lips. "No, not tonight." It was all the assurance he could give her.

For the moment, it was all she asked.

Jessica wound her arms around his neck, clinging to him, weak with relief. Despite her earlier vows, she had almost pushed him away from her. Damon had looked right through her smiles, recognizing her fears. She wasn't used to anyone being able to read her like an open book. His dark eyes missed nothing, not the slightest tension, not the moment's hesitation. He saw all the way to her soul. Recognizing the fear tearing her apart, he had decided to leave her, to spare her further pain. He hadn't known that his leaving would be even more devastating.

"I'm glad." Drawing his head down, she kissed him, teasing his bottom lip with her teeth.

His tongue came out swiftly, sliding into her mouth. Filling her to the deepest recesses, he crushed her against his tense body.

His urgent response told Jessica how much he wanted to stay, and how much the decision to leave her had tested his self-control.

"Not half as glad as I am," he whispered, leaving her mouth to slide his lips across her cheekbones, raining kisses on her nose. "Your freckles have haunted me in my dreams. Sometimes I'd wake up in the middle of the night and wonder if I had imagined it all. Then I would reach for your curl. I fantasized about what I would do to you in September. And I knew I couldn't endure four months of loneliness and uncertainty, and changed my plans. I went early to New Delhi and rescheduled the meetings. If the Sikhs hadn't stirred up more trouble and disrupted the talks, I would've been here two days ago."

"At least I had your notes," Jessica said, sliding her hands beneath his shirt. "They were a weekly reminder." Her fingertips brushed his dark, silky curls. "Do you still want your coffee?"

"You're all the stimulant I need." His mouth descended, closing over her lips, his tongue entering her moist sweetness, tasting fine old whiskey and a flavor that was particularly her own.

A stab of pleasure ran through her, shaking her slender frame. Her tongue twined around his, drawing him deeper within. The sensual caress of his beard heightened her pleasure. For the moment the meaning of its existence was forgotten in the torrents of emotions, becoming an integral part of him. Her fingers grasped his thick hair, drawing him closer and closer, never wanting to let him go.

Without breaking the kiss, Damon lifted her against him, cradling her against his chest. Then, pulling back, he unerringly found his way through the dark passageway to her bedroom and switched on the light.

Pressing her face into the strong column of his throat, he looked around the room.

Warm earth tones welcomed him, a palette ranging from the dark brown of the dresser to the creamy white of the sheepskin rug. Native fabrics draped the windows with bright orange, beige and yellow stripes. Her furniture was a mixture of different periods and styles, bought, he guessed, at garage sales, from departing friends and in the bazaars. Rice bowls made from bamboo leaves and pottery mingled with high-gloss finishes of mahogany and rosewood. A balance of sophistication, simplicity and warmth. Beautiful, as was the woman in his arms.

He crossed the room to the bed, laying her down on the soft spread made from the wools of fat-tailed sheep. He followed her down, leaning over her, drinking in the sight nestled among the soft skins. His long fingers raked her hair, spreading it into a circle around her head. "I love your hair. It's strong and vital and has a will of its own. Like you."

"It must look an absolute mess," Jessica protested huskily.

Smiling, Damon shook his head. "It sparkles with fire, reminding me of glowing embers that give warmth on a cold winter night." He threaded his fingers through the mass, watching golden highlights flowing sensuously over his tanned skin. With a groan he lay down beside her and buried his face in the fragrant cloud.

"Damon." Jessica whispered his name, her voice filled with longing and protest that he could seduce her with words alone. Her arms closed around him, stroking his back. She wanted more than words and kisses. Her body burned with desire to feel his skin sliding over her as it had on that sunny afternoon in May.

He pushed himself up on one elbow, leaning over her, dark eyes blazing in a tightly controlled face. "I've dreamed of this for weeks. You and me, together, making love. Slowly, without haste." His fingers lightly circled her mouth again and again, until her lips were trembling with longing.

"We have all night." Jessica curled one hand around his neck, drawing his mouth closer to hers until it hovered only a breath away from her own. Then she raised her head and kissed him, not wanting to waste a minute of that time.

The touch of her lips wiped away the restraint he'd put upon himself. Thinking that she deserved more than fleeting pleasure, he had planned to go slowly. But the lure of her taste was too strong. He kissed with driving need, until they broke apart, both breathing hard.

Then his mouth trailed a path down her slim neck to the shadowy cleft of her breasts. His hands stroked the flesh beneath the fabric until the nipples stood erect, before moving down to the edge of the fabric, rolling it up. His hand trembled with desire to remove the top in one swift pull. But he forced himself to go slowly, uncovering inch by inch of her soft skin. "You're more beautiful than I remember," he groaned. He touched her lovingly.

Jessica's eyes darkened with the onslaught of sensations. Her hands moved restlessly, pushing the shirt off his shoulders, seeking the warmth of his flesh. Strong muscles rippled under the tips of her fingers as she slid them over his heated skin. Damon shrugged out of his sleeves, letting the shirt drop to the floor. Reaching for the snap of her jeans, he smoothed the fabric down her hips. His lips followed, kissing each part of her as he uncovered it, until she was revealed in all her warm beauty.

With fluid movements, he got to his feet. Reaching for the bedside lamp, he turned it on before flicking off the overhead light. And then he stood by the bed, staring down at Jessica with blazing eyes.

She lay in a pool of warmth, her slender curves framed by the soft creamy wool. Her hair was a cloud of fiery fire, wild

tangles created by his hands. Her eyes glowed with desire
and her arms were reaching for him. "I'm almost afraid to
touch you. You're more perfect than my dreams," he said
roughly, gazing hungrily at her. He stood outside the pool
of light, a dark shadow tight with restraint, as if he feared
to touch her.

"I don't want to be stared at," she protested huskily. She
was no statue, but a woman in love. Made of flesh that
burned for his touch. Her blood flowed with desire, stirred
by him. "Touch me, Damon," she pleaded hoarsely.
"Come to me."

"I will." His hands went to the buckle of his belt.

"Let me do that." Jessica rolled off the bed and came to
him, her fingers pushing his aside. Kneeling before him, she
stroked the pants down the strong columns of his legs.
Lights and shadows sculpted his muscles to bronze perfection.

And then she saw the scar on his left side, curving from
his waist to his hip. She sucked in her breath, her finger
gently tracing about four inches of old puckered tissue. "I
missed this before."

That day, in New York, she had thought him beautiful.
A magnificent statue of Apollo, a god of light. Now dark
shadows changed her perception. His muscles moved
smoothly. Long sinewy bundles of strength and power. A
warrior's body. The beard suddenly fit. "Where did you get
this?" Her lips touched the jagged scar tenderly.

Damon shuddered under her touch, his desire swelling to
breaking point. He lifted her in his arms and returned her
to the bed of soft skins. "In San Salvador," he said, stopping further questions with his lips as he followed her down.

He moved over her with the same smooth power with
which he had lifted her. Jessica welcomed his weight with a
sigh. Her arms closed about him, raking his back with her
nails.

He groaned with pleasure, the sound reminding her of the
contented purr of a cat. He arched his back into her, breaking the kiss. He nibbled at her nipples with his teeth, then
soothed them down with soft strokes of his tongue. Cup-

ping her swelling mounds, he said, "I love the way your breasts fit into my hands."

Her eyes clouding with desire, she watched his dark head bend again to her light skin, kissing and caressing her until she cried out. "I can't take much more."

Her voice held a note of fear. She had never felt so wild, so abandoned, so out of control.

Damon responded to that sound, firmly framing her face with his hands. "Don't be afraid of me." His voice was gritty with desire. "There is nothing to fear. You're my woman." And then he kissed her again, sweetly, soothing her fears. And his hands began moving up and down her body, drawn to the warm center of her.

Jessica arched against his caresses, opening herself to him. Fear receded, reality receded. Only Damon existed and the pleasure he gave with his touch. His voice came to her, his murmured words encouraging her, steadying her when the first shudders shook her. Before he moved above her, he reached for a small package. Then he slid into her warmth, moving deep within, filling her so completely that a cry of pleasure broke from her lips.

Jessica's eyes widened with surprise as she reached for his shoulders to steady her rocking world.

Damon smiled down at her, his face tight with passion and control. Then he moved slowly, powerfully, inside her, fanning her pleasure gradually. Flames flickered, burning brightly until they finally leaped out of control and her fire flowed over him. With a final thrust he melted into her, calling out her name.

Jessica clung to his strength. His arms were the only solid place in the spinning universe.

"Rest, my love." With strong, easy movements he shifted her to his side. Her strength and vitality were so deceiving. He tended to forget just how small and vulnerable she was.

With her head nestled in the hollow of his shoulder, she smiled, her eyes filled with wonder. "Who are you? A demon with magic powers, drawing me into his web of sorcery?"

Silent laughter shook his chest. "If I am the sorcerer, you are my red-haired witch."

Smiling, Jessica's lids swept down, the lashes fanning her cheek. Magic, she thought, giving in to weariness. Her last thought was that magic wasn't real, that spells didn't last. But she was too tired to care about tomorrow. Her arms slid around his waist to hold on to the now.

Damon held Jessica tightly, watching as her breathing deepened into sleep. Sometime later he lifted her gently, sliding her between the sheets. Even in sleep she clung to him as if she was afraid that he might vanish into the night. Tenderness softened his hard features as he joined her, flicking off the light.

What a marvel she was. So full of life. Strong, yet soft. And incredibly warm. He moved closer until there wasn't a space separating their bodies. He closed his eyes, not afraid of talking in his sleep. He trusted Jessica with his life.

He dreamed of a small house, bright with sunshine, echoing with laughter. And loving Jessica in front of the fireplace, embers glowing, the color of her hair. He dreamed that he had found the end of the rainbow.

It was the first dream in years free of nightmares.

Chapter 7

W ake up, Jessica. Someone's knocking at your door."
Damon shook her gently.

Reluctantly, Jessica opened her eyes. "What time is it?"
Her voice was slurred, husky with sleep.

"Three in the morning," he said, looking at his watch.

Jessica groaned. Three o'clock. The convoy was scheduled to leave at six. She had asked Aya to wake her early
because she still had to pack her suitcase. Then she remembered that she had locked Aya out.

"Damn!" She had forgotten about the trip to the refugee camps. For a moment she was tempted to ignore Aya, to
ignore duty and remain here in Damon's arms.

"Peter's going to blow his top," she muttered, and,
twisting away from temptation, jumped out of bed. "I'll be
right back," she promised hastily, reaching for the robe
hanging behind the door. In her rush she didn't notice the
sudden tension stiffening Damon's body and his utter lack
of response.

When she returned a few minutes later, Damon had
switched on the light. She hesitated inside the room, stopped

by the cold harsh look on his face and the fact that he was already partially dressed.

"You're leaving?" She stared at him, her eyes wide with shock. Her face still looked flustered. It hadn't been easy to explain to a stunned Aya to prepare breakfast for two. She shouldn't have felt uncomfortable explaining to the old Pushtun woman that she had spent the night with a man. She was twenty-nine years old, without ties and in love. But she had never faced such a situation before.

And now the man she thought felt the same about her, looked at her as though she meant no more to him than a good time. And having gotten what he'd come for, he was leaving.

"Who is Peter?" His voice was a low, dangerous growl. He folded his powerful arms across his chest, restraining himself to reach out for her and shake her. She looked guilty as hell.

Jessica blinked in confusion. "Peter is a friend. What does he have to do with this?" She looked pointedly at his clothes.

"That's what I'm trying to find out. Just how friendly are you? Are you—" Abruptly he stopped, realizing that he had no right to ask her if she was sleeping with her friend. But why else would the man knock on her door at three in the morning?

Her eyes narrowed in confusion. What was Damon getting at? Then the meaning of his words hit her like a blow. Confusion turned to anger and hurt. How could Damon ask her such a question, even think along those lines?

"Damn you," she spat at him, spinning around and groping in her closet for the suitcase she still had to pack. Her fingers closed convulsively around the handle of the overnight bag. How dare he insult her as if she were nothing but a cheap tramp.

Damon watched her fling the case on the charpoy where he had given her his soul. "Are you leaving with him?" he demanded, stepping forward.

"Yes," Jessica snapped, reaching into her closet to take out a dress for dinner at the hotel in Peshawar where she and Peter planned to spend the night.

Hard hands bit into her shoulders, spinning her around. The dress slid through her suddenly nerveless hands and dropped to the floor.

Damon stared down into her angry face with a mixture of rage and disbelief while his dreams turned to nightmares. History was repeating itself.

"I see." His hands slid off her shoulders. He stepped back, his powerful muscles bulging under the strains of letting her go when he wanted to sling her over his shoulder and carry her into the mountains to force her to his will. But he knew, better than most men, that violence breeds more violence. He knew that he could never hurt her, even if she destroyed his dreams. He moved away.

Jessica watched his back bend as he reached for the shirt he had dropped on the floor only hours earlier. Before he had made such beautiful, tender love to her. Before he had called her his woman. Before she had given herself to him in complete trust.

Was she going to let him walk away from her because life had taught him to be suspicious? She wanted to show him that the world was not filled with Tanya Rebrows, bullets and hate. Tenderness welled up in her, softening the lines of anger and hurt on her face.

"Peter and I are going to Peshawar this morning," she said slowly, watching him shrug into his shirt. He did not reach for the buttons. He stood utterly still. Waiting. And, thank God, listening.

She drew a deep breath and continued. "We are spending the night there. But in separate rooms. We've shared rooms before though, and on rare occasions even a bed, when nothing else was available. Each wrapped in our individual sleeping bags. We're friends."

Slowly he turned, staring at her across the room, his narrowed eyes searching her face. Her eyes were steady and clear, not veiled by lies. "It seems I owe you an apology," he said stiffly.

She shrugged her shoulders. "I led you on." A slow smile warmed her face. "I have a terrible temper when I'm hurt."

He moved closer, cupping her chin, tilting her head back. "Why did you explain yourself, Jessica? You could've let me imagine the worst."

"I did," she pointed out softly.

"Only until your temper cooled." His harsh features relaxed into the ghost of a smile. "I should've known you don't play those kinds of games. You wouldn't enjoy seeing men fight over you. You'd hate for anyone to get hurt."

"I'm no saint," Jessica said succinctly. "But I hate cruelty."

He lowered his head. "To me you're perfect. Temper and all." Then he kissed her with sweetness.

"I don't want to leave," she whispered against his lips. She knew Damon would be gone when she returned. Her arms tightened around him convulsively.

Damon rained kisses over her face. "Then stay."

"I can't. I have to accompany a convoy of medical supplies to the refugee camps. All the arrangements have been made. We leave at six this morning. There's no way I can cancel it now."

Abruptly, Damon's kisses stopped. Jessica could feel the muscles under her hands stiffen with sudden tension. "You and one man?" he asked harshly. "That's too damn dangerous."

"We have an armed guard, too, although that's a first. On the last shipment, we lost a whole truckload of supplies. I don't even know when it happened, or where. The truck with the crates just disappeared. But no one has ever threatened us personally."

"There's always a first time," Damon growled. He pushed her away and began buttoning his shirt. His face looked grim and hard. "Hugh Cantrell is getting careless in his old age. Does he know about this trip?"

"Of course he does," Jessica said, exasperation in her voice. It didn't surprise her that Damon knew the ambassador personally. "He knows I'm capable. I've visited the camps for years." Today's trip would be safer than any she had made before, unless... She watched him push the shirttail into his pants with guarded eyes.

Unless Damon knew something she did not.

Tiny prickles formed at the back of her neck, warning signals she wanted to ignore.

"Unfortunately capability has little to do with it," Damon said harshly, buckling his belt with controlled movements. "You're young and beautiful. And you're an American diplomat."

"I've enough sense not to go dressed up like visiting royalty," Jessica pointed out dryly, almost slumping with relief. His reaction had been prompted by concern for her safety, nothing else. "And after visiting the first two camps, I look as if I've been in a mud fight."

A gleam lit his dark eyes. "Still fond of that stuff?" he asked.

"What—?" Jessica stared at him in confusion. Then she grinned. "You've been looking through my family albums," she accused him.

"Ali was very obliging." He grinned.

"I'll bet she was." In every photo, her sister had looked like a little doll. Jessica had preferred to make mud pies, without a stitch of clothes.

"You were beautiful, even then." Tenderness softened his face. "Mud and dirt cannot hide your kind of beauty, my love, the kind that comes from within. The kind that radiates warmth and makes men forget about perfection of face and body." He reached for her, letting his hands slide over her breasts, following the gentle curves down to her waist.

"I'd hate to see that warmth frozen by fear." He rested his hands on her hips and drew her against him. His arms closed around her slender frame, as if he would keep her safe.

Blinking moisture from her eyes, Jessica framed his face. "If there was a way, I would cancel the trip. For you. But too many people depend on the supplies. I have to go." Her eyes pleaded with him to understand. Not to pressure her further. To accept her decision as she had accepted his last night.

He agreed with a shrug of his shoulders and a curious twist to his mouth. But his lips closed over hers with a fierceness that gave lie to his gestures and words. His hand slid under her robe, caressing her silky skin.

For a few moments Jessica clung to him, meeting his strength with equal fierceness. Then she gently pushed him away.

"I have to get ready. Will you share breakfast with me? Aya, my maid, is preparing it now."

"I'll stay," Damon promised her huskily. "If you can find me a spare toothbrush."

"In the medicine cabinet." Jessica turned the light on in the bathroom, then opened the shower faucets. Stepping out of her robe, she moved behind the glass of the stall. She fastened her hair on the top of her head with a barrette and reached for the soap, watching Damon as he opened and closed the cabinet. She observed each of his gestures, recording each movement for the time when memories were once again her only companions. God, how she hated partings.

Ten minutes later Jessica was dressed in jeans, boots and a long-sleeved, blue linen shirt. With deft movements she coiled her hair at the back of her head, then studied her reflection in the mirror. No glamour. Serviceable clothes, plain hairstyle and no makeup. Good. She filled her suitcase with more jeans, more long-sleeved shirts. During these trips, she often changed clothes three or four times. On top, she laid the dress she had taken out earlier, and added wisps of underwear, a nightgown and several pairs of socks.

Damon sat in the *gulhana*, a cup of coffee in front of him. "All set?" he asked, his dark eyes sliding over her.

"I'm packed," Jessica answered, reaching for the cup he had filled for her, "but I still have to check my papers."

Aya shuffled into the room, bearing a tray of omelets, biscuits and freshly pressed grape juice. "No bacon," Jessica explained with a smile. "Aya is a Muslim and won't touch pork."

"This looks great," Damon assured her, then turned to Aya and thanked her in fluent Pushtu. The old woman's face wrinkled into a grin, and she giggled like a young girl as she left.

"You speak Pushtu like a native." Jessica was surprised.

"I learned from a native." Damon reached for the eggs.

"Your friend Ahmed," Jessica said flatly.

"My friend Ahmed," Damon confirmed coolly, his eyes opaque.

"Are you going to meet him today?" Jessica knew she was changing the rules, asking sensitive questions. But rules changed when situations changed. Damon had changed their relationship from friends to lovers, giving her the right to ask about his plans. She met his eyes with a stubborn tilt of her chin.

"Maybe," Damon said softly, raising one brow. But his eyes were watchful, guarded.

"Where? In Peshawar?" Jessica took a bite of her omelet while silence ticked away. "You can tell me to shut up," she said in exasperation when she could talk again. "But until you do, I will pound you with questions."

Damon leaned back in his chair, a tight grin on his face. "Pound away. You may hit the jackpot yet."

"I don't want the jackpot. Just to put together a few more puzzle pieces," Jessica sighed. "Did you know Prince Ahmed Khan when he studied medicine at Harvard?"

"Yes." Damon sat very still. He didn't move a muscle yet his face changed subtly, his body tensed. The easy grin turned feral. His lips barely moved.

"Are your friend Ahmed and the prince the same person?" Jessica stubbornly pressed on.

"Jackpot. First time around."

A cold breeze seemed to run up Jessica's spine. Prince Ahmed Khan was alive. She froze, staring at Damon while premonitions and fears battled within. For a moment the air seemed to vibrate with the thunder of guns and cries of pain.

"I still have to go into the mountains," Damon had warned.

Last night she had accepted that fact. Last night she would have lied to keep him with her. But this morning, with dawn painting the sky in shades of pink, umber and blue, she wanted to reach out to Damon and beg him not to go.

"How did you find out?" Damon asked, his eyes sharp and penetrating.

"I like solving puzzles, remember?" Jessica picked at her eggs, her hand trembling.

"You should've joined the CIA."

I should have done many things. Like not becoming involved with you, Jessica thought. But she had. She didn't regret one kiss, one smile. "Too rough," she said lightly, eating another bite of the omelet.

"No rougher than your trip today," Damon said sharply. "I still wish you weren't going."

"That makes two of us." Jessica swallowed. "The solution is simple. Come with me. If you're going to Peshawar anyway, why can't we travel together? I'd be perfectly safe with you."

Damon's face hardened. "Jessica." His voice was rough, as if the idea was tempting. "I have some arrangements to make before I can leave."

"You could take my car, and meet us later. The convoy travels slowly. You could meet us at the second camp." She slid from her chair and almost skipped from the room, returning moments later with a map in her hand.

"The camps are circled in blue," she explained, handing him the map with the route the convoy would travel outlined in red.

While Damon studied the map, Jessica looked down at his dark head. Her fingernails bit into the palms of her hands. Abruptly she moved to the window, staring out into the dawn.

Damon watched her walk away, frowning at the sight of her. The loose blouse only emphasized the small size of her waist. The jeans still drew attention to the enticing curves of her hips and long legs. By American standards she was adequately covered. The Pushtuns, however, had different ideas. Their women wore loose garments, even beneath the veils. They did not ordinarily expect western women to conform to their own style, usually they accepted jeans and blouses as sufficient cover. But these were not usual times.

The camps were filled with discontented men who had already lost everything. They could be insistent on their moral code, and not hesitate to kidnap a disrespectful American diplomat if they thought that the capture would better their lot.

He rose to his feet and walked across the room. Circling her waist from behind, he drew her against him. "I'll meet you at the second camp."

Jessica leaned her head back against his shoulder. She'd gained a whole day. She wanted to shout with joy, but her voice was level when she said, "I'm glad."

Damon chuckled at the understatement. "I assume you have a road pass for your car?"

"I always ask for two, one for Peter's and one for mine. Just in case one car doesn't start."

"Very efficient." He dropped a kiss in her hair. "Let's finish breakfast. Somehow I have the impression that we won't eat again for some time."

Jessica turned within the circle of his arms. "I'm taking a picnic lunch." The tips of her fingers brushed across his lips. "Will this change of plans cause problems for you?"

Smiling, Damon shook his head. "Don't worry about it."

As they finished their breakfast Jessica wondered just what business Damon had to see to in Islamabad. She looked at him speculatively.

Damon leaned across the table and kissed her lips. "No more questions and answers," he warned her, smiling. But his eyes were serious.

"It's a deal. For now," she added with a grin. "Tell me about Aunt Gloria and Uncle Howard. Did you see my parents?"

In between kisses and caresses Damon told her about her family while dawn broke over the nearby mountains.

Just before five, Damon left in the Mercedes Jessica had bought from a German diplomat when she had first arrived in Islamabad. A few minutes later, when Peter arrived in his big Ford, Jessica was ready for him, waiting with two coolers and her overnight case.

First they went to the embassy compound to supervise the loading of the trucks. The lorries were unlike any seen in the western world. Their bodies had been painted in bright yellows, reds and blues with tigers, peacocks and other animals decorating the hoods. Inside, with their velvet throw rugs, pillows and tassels fringing the windshields, the cabs looked like last century's boudoirs. One blue lorry displayed the voluptuous charms of a famous Indian actress on its hood. It belonged to a friendly Pushtun, Asadullah, one of their most reliable drivers. He would drive the extra crates to Dr. Brooks's camp near Peshawar.

With only a thirty minute delay, the convoy finally left the compound. Peter and Jessica followed the long line of trucks and military jeeps northwest along narrow but well paved roads.

"You look happy," Peter commented, looking at Jessica.

"Everything went without a hitch," Jessica said lightly, wondering how to explain Damon to her friend.

"In fact you're positively glowing," Peter added. "If I didn't know you better, I'd say you had a very lively night."

Startled, Jessica blushed. "What makes you say that?"

"Your cheeks are rosy. As if a man's beard had chafed your skin."

Jessica grinned, her eyes dancing. "It did. I had company last night."

Peter smiled. This was a new side to Jessica. As far as he knew she had slept alone every night during the last three years. "Who is the lucky guy?" he teased.

"Damon Noble," Jessica answered, trying to keep a straight face. "You're going to meet him later on. He's following us to the second camp in my car."

"You're kidding." Peter shot her a wry look, not sure whether to believe her or not.

"I'm perfectly serious," Jessica assured him. "He flew in from New Delhi last night. Since he's going to Peshawar today, I thought we might spend some time together. I hope you won't mind if I abandon you when he arrives."

Peter stared straight ahead. "That explains the two coolers," he said quietly. "Have you known him long?"

Jessica shrugged her shoulders. "He's a long-time friend of my family." She had mentioned Damon to Barbara but not to anyone else.

Frowning, Peter said, "Do I know him? I think I've heard that name before."

Grinning, Jessica said, "You've met him. He was the man you mentioned last night, Ahmed Khan's companion at that party in D.C."

His frown deepened. "What's he doing here?" He was a realist. He didn't believe in fate and coincidence.

"Visiting me," Jessica said lightly.

Peter didn't answer. Instead he muttered a curse and pointed toward the slowing column ahead. "I wonder why they're stopping." Pressing on the gas pedal, he raced ahead, passing the other trucks and the military jeeps.

One of the trucks had developed a flat tire and, as usual, there was no spare. Jessica watched the driver skillfully repair the flat. Within minutes, they were moving again.

They reached the first refugee camp an hour later. While Peter supervised the unloading of the supplies, Jessica talked to the medical director, a Swede, and several of the multinational staff, making a list of their most pressing needs.

After the paperwork had been disposed of, they walked around the tent city of a hundred thousand refugees. Daily cloudbursts, added to the bowls of water emptied into the roads between the rows of tents, had softened the hard ground and turned the roads into avenues of mud.

Women busied together beneath the canvas planes, washing and mending clothes, kneading bread, nursing babies. Children played around the communal faucets, spraying water and throwing mud. Men squatted in circles, gesticulating and arguing. From time to time they would face toward the distant cloud-capped mountains, their eyes hard, their gestures threatening.

The depression, anger and desolation of the Afghans tore at Jessica's heart. There was so little she could do to lighten their loss. Whatever help relief workers could render would never be enough. They could never compensate for the loss of families, homes and country.

"I feel so helpless," Jessica said to the British nurse walking beside her.

The young woman nodded. "I felt the same when I first came here. Now, I'm scared. The mood here is changing from bitter to ugly, especially among the men. They stare at us with hatred, watching every move we make with expressionless eyes. And they fight among each other. Two days ago, one was killed in a brawl."

Jessica shivered. For the first time since she'd begun visiting the camps, she could sense a mood of hate and violence barely held in check. Few of the women greeted her as she passed. The children no longer crowded around her. She had known some of the families for years, and they had always responded to her greetings with smiles, waves and a few words. Some had even approached her and spilled out their stories of death and loss. Now there was only thick and threatening silence.

She felt relief when the convoy left a few minutes later.

"I hope the morale is better at the next camp," she commented after she had discussed the situation with Peter.

Peter muttered something beneath his breath, then added, "Perhaps it would be safer for you to stay at the administration office."

"If the mood is nasty, I won't go far," Jessica agreed, hoping that Damon was already waiting for her. He might agree to accompany her through the tent city.

When they arrived at the second camp, Damon had not yet arrived. After dealing with the paperwork, Jessica asked about trouble in the camp.

"Nothing we can't handle," Dr. Hansen, the tall German medical director, assured her. "At least, not yet." Like many Germans he spoke excellent English.

"You mean it's safe to look at that old section that's falling down?"

Dr. Hansen shrugged. "I don't see why not. I'll walk with you, if you like."

"I can manage," Jessica assured him. "Don't let me keep you from your work."

"I could do with a break." The tall German reached for his bag. "I wanted to have a look at one of the children anyway."

The scenes in this camp were almost identical to the ones Jessica had just left behind. Except here there was occasional laughter. A group of children accompanied them, asking for baksheesh, then stood back good-naturedly when told to stop. But the circles of men radiated the same kind of charged silence as before.

They stopped outside one of the tents. "The old section is just a block ahead. Why don't you have a look at it, while I check the infant?"

"Ten minutes?" Jessica checked her watch.

"Fine," the doctor agreed, raising the flap of the tent.

Slowly, Jessica slogged through the mud, her eyes noticing frayed canvases and the need for additional shelter. The number of refugees grew daily. Already more than a third of the total Afghan population lived in camps like this. An estimated four to five million refugees had fled their country, patiently waiting for peace.

"Hey, lady. Are you American?" A group of young Afghans, dressed in traditional wide trousers and big flowing shirts, stepped in her way. Beneath their turbans their faces were broad, their Mongolian features marking them as members of one of the northern tribes.

"Yes." With narrowed eyes, Jessica focused on the leader, a man in his mid-twenties and of medium height. A scar flamed on his right cheek. His dark eyes glowed with hate.

"You get us visas for America." Threateningly, he stepped closer, his four companions forming a half circle around her.

Jessica straightened her shoulders, betraying not a flicker of fear. "Let's go to the administration building to talk about it," she suggested calmly.

"No! You promise now!"

This wasn't the first time her influence had been sought for a visa. She had been pleaded with, even offered bribes, to obtain visas. But never had she faced a situation like this, with five young men, tense with anger, caging her in. "Your English is very good," Jessica said slowly, playing for time. "Where did you go to university?"

"In Kabul. I am third year medical student. My friends also are students. One lawyer, two teachers. Hamil was police officer. He speak German. We all want to get to America."

You and the rest of the camp, Jessica thought soberly. As more and more people crowded the camps, the conditions were deteriorating rapidly. For these bright young men the ghettolike conditions must be impossible to bear. They had not only lost their families, homes and country, they had lost their futures, too. Who could blame them for reaching to the sky for help? Jessica understood their need and their fears, but she was powerless to change the conditions. Only an end to the war could bring relief.

"You will have to fill out the necessary forms," Jessica explained. Pity roughened her voice, but her vigilance didn't relax. Desperate men sought desperate measures to better their lot.

The leader laughed. A bitter sound that tore at Jessica's heart. "We filled out papers a year ago. Nothing happened." He moved closer, his eyes glittering with determination. "You stay with us, until visas come." Muttering their support, the other four closed in until they formed one solid wall of flesh, effectively hiding Jessica.

Jessica couldn't see past their bodies. Sweat trickled down her neck and beaded her brow. Her fingers clenched around her purse strap in her effort to calm her fears. "Taking me hostage won't get you your visas." She hoped they didn't hear the slight quiver in her voice. She had to keep a cool head. Nothing would be more detrimental to her safety than showing fear.

"We will see. You come with us now." The wall of men moved as one. No one laid a hand on her. But they prodded her forward with the weight of their bodies.

"Don't do anything foolish," Jessica warned. "There is a troop of Pakistani soldiers waiting with our trucks. If I don't return soon, they will come looking for me."

The leader shrugged his shoulders. "We have many tents to hide in."

They trudged on, the sucking noise of the mud the only sound. No one came to inquire what was going on. No one wanted to become involved.

Jessica bit her lip to keep from yelling for help. Screaming would be useless, a futile depletion of her strength. Instead she concentrated on the direction they were taking, counting the right and left turns and watching for a space to open in the wall around her. She was determined to escape.

They turned right and then left. They squeezed between tents until they joined another quagmire track. With each step, the mud splattered higher, until Jessica's jeans were covered to her thighs. With each step she argued with the leader to let her go. But the men ignored her, slogging on.

Clay clung to her boots in clumps, making each step heavier and more difficult than the last. She caught a glimpse of new canvas, tents recently erected. Jessica knew the location of the new section. It was close to the hospital housing the severely injured and the handicapped.

This was the time to make her move. Jessica suddenly dug the heels of her boots into the mud. Her unexpected stop took the two men flanking her by surprise and they walked a few steps ahead, leaving an opening in their human wall. Jessica darted through the break, shouting for help.

"Jessica? Where are you?"

Damon! At the sound of his voice she slowed her pace. "Here!" she yelled loudly. Then rough hands clamped over her mouth, stifling further sound.

Half-dragging, half-leading her, they drew her forward. But this time Jessica fought. She bit the hand covering her mouth. She kicked with her pointed boots. The men's muttered curses increased her strength and her determination to be free of them. She scratched and punched and snarled. She acted like a wildcat.

"Let her go."

At the clipped, chilling command, the Afghans dropped their hands. Slowly they turned around and faced the tall, powerfully built man.

Jessica wasted no time. She backed away from the men, circled them at a distance and dashed toward Damon.

"Get behind me," Damon said, his eyes never leaving the group of young men. Jessica obeyed swiftly, stopping about ten feet on the other side of him.

"Are you afraid of one American man?" the leader jeered in Farsi to his friends. Slowly the phalanx moved forward, then began to fan out.

Damon stood silently, every muscle tense, more deadly in his immobility than the five men stalking toward him.

Suddenly the leader dove to the ground, intent on knocking Damon off his feet. Damon's body uncoiled, leaping into the air, one booted foot catching the leader in his stomach. With a twist of his body, he kicked again. The man sprawled in the mud. Two of his friends flew from the side. With shocking speed, Damon caught one man with a sideways chop right in the face. He sidestepped the other with a dancer's grace, booting him from behind, propelling him face-down into the mud. The remaining two stood frozen, their faces awed. As if undecided whether to join or give up the uneven fight, their eyes alternated from the tall man to their groaning companions.

They hesitated too long. A jeep roared around the corner behind them, blocking off their escape. Moments later all five men were rounded up and handcuffed by camp security.

"Did they hurt you?" Damon crossed the space toward her with long strides.

Jessica shook her head. She couldn't talk. Her teeth were chattering as she recovered from her shock.

His arms closed around her, supporting her, as he whispered words of comfort into her hair.

Weakly, Jessica leaned against his strength, her legs like rubber snakes. "I'm sorry," she said after a moment. "I'm behaving like a fool."

"You fought five men off and kept them busy so security and I could get close to you," Damon said gently. "There's nothing foolish in that."

"But now I'm pure jelly. And you're so calm."

"After my first few fights I felt sick, too."

"And how long ago was that?" Jessica asked with a shaky smile. "Thirty years?" Damon had fought with a deadly skill, a skill honed to a fine art over a number of years. Each movement had been swift and clean. No flailing, no wasted energy. Only deadly strength and lightning speed. The Afghans never had a chance against such a master of the martial arts.

It was a bit of information she could have done without. She didn't need more knowledge about the dark side of his life. What little she knew was frightening enough.

"I rarely fought at ten." Damon shook his head. "I was already tall for my age and my classmates respected my size. But size is of little importance when you fight with guns instead of bare hands. Weapons are a great equalizer," he added harshly.

Weapons would even turn his size into a disadvantage, Jessica thought, shivering.

Damon's arms tightened protectively around her slender form. His face was grim. "I should've killed those bastards."

"They're not bad men," Jessica objected. "Just desperate. None of them laid a hand on me until I tried to escape. They thought that by holding me hostage they could force the embassy to give them visas. Wouldn't you try to escape from this?" She made a sweeping motion with her hand. "I wonder what's going to happen to them now."

"They deserve to be punished," Damon said firmly.

Jessica bit her lip, knowing Damon was right. But she still felt sorry and guilty for them. She shouldn't have ignored Damon's and Peter's warnings.

Wearily, Jessica pushed herself out of his arms. "I need to change." She looked at Damon. Some of her mud had rubbed off on his jeans. His denim shirt was as splattered and stained as her own. "I hope you came prepared."

Damon nodded. "We're attracting quite a bit of attention, too. I'll feel a lot safer when we're back at the administration building."

For the first time, Jessica noticed their surroundings. They stood among puddles, surrounded by tents. Refugees stood in the openings. Many of the men, women and children were on crutches and canes, wearing bandages and fresh scars. Their eyes were curiously blank, as if they had forgotten how to weep or smile.

"Let's go," she agreed, her voice rough with tears.

Chapter 8

Peter was waiting for Jessica when she returned to the car.

"I told you to stay put," Peter said harshly, leaning against his Ford.

Recognizing the concern hidden beneath the display of anger, Jessica answered gently, "I wish I had. But everything seemed calm in the camp. Did you run into problems?"

Peter hesitated briefly. "All went smoothly. The crates are stored and the trucks are on their way back to Islamabad."

"Good." Only three more camps to visit, two before they reached Peshawar. Briefly she closed her eyes.

"You feel all right? Those guys didn't hurt you, did they?"

"No. I'm fine." She searched her purse for the keys to her car. Opening the trunk, she put the bundle of dirty clothes into one corner. The cavern was filled with Damon's duffel bags, a leather briefcase and a camera case, leaving barely enough space to add her overnight bag.

"So your friend came," Peter observed slowly. "The nurses seem to think he's Superman. They said he single-handedly took care of five Afghans."

"Not quite. He only knocked down three before security came," Jessica said dryly, closing the trunk lid. "I have to go in and file a report."

"I'm coming with you," Peter said, falling into step beside her, determination written all over his face. "Just want to make sure you're not pleading for those men."

But, despite Peter's disapproval, she did plead the Afghans' case.

Damon had already filled out his part of the report. He stood silently, watching her argue with the Pakistani officer until the man agreed to a charge of assault instead of attempted kidnapping.

"That was a dumb thing to do," Peter muttered when they were once again outside, walking toward their cars.

Damon stiffened. "It was Jessica's choice," he said coldly.

Compressing his lips, Peter shot him a look of dislike. "They're getting off too easy."

"It's already done," Jessica said firmly, giving Peter an exasperated look. From the moment she had introduced the two men to each other in the office, Peter had treated Damon with barely veiled hostility.

So far Damon had ignored Peter's abrupt behavior. But Jessica let out a sigh of relief when they separated in the parking lot.

"I don't know what's got into Peter," she said when Damon slid into the driver's seat. "He's usually so easygoing."

Damon looked at her with a gleam in his eyes. "It's nothing personal. He's merely jealous."

"That's ridiculous. There's never been anything between us. Besides, he's in love with my friend Barbara."

Damon started the car and slowly followed Peter's Ford. "Then perhaps he doesn't like my beard." Damon shrugged his shoulders.

Jessica reached out and touched it gently. "I'm getting used to it," she said with a smile.

Damon chuckled. "Always the diplomat."

Jessica responded with a grin of her own. Then her face became serious once again. "I wasn't very successful this morning. At one moment I thought I had them listening to me. The next thing I knew—"

Damon reached out and covered her hands. "It wasn't your fault. And they did get away lighter than they deserved."

Jessica looked at him soberly. "Then you agree with Peter that I shouldn't have interfered?"

They were approaching the camp's gate. Damon slowed down behind Peter. "You are in a better position to judge than I am. You talked to them."

Jessica's fingers curled around his hand, squeezing it. "Thank you," she said softly. Damon understood that she couldn't have lived easily with the knowledge that she had sent five young men to prison for years. They had been blinded by anger. But they did not belong with the dregs of society, without hope of reform.

Outside the gates a group of Afghans squatted, watching the trucks pass. One man had his head turned toward the mountains. But as Damon sped up, the man turned around.

Jessica's eyes widened with shock and disbelief. It was Colonel Henderson, dressed in Afghan clothes. Beneath the turban his beardless face was smooth, in strong contrast to the weathered complexions of the other men.

For one instant their eyes met. Goose bumps formed on her skin despite the heat. Abruptly he turned away. The car shot through the gate.

"I just saw Colonel Henderson." Jessica's voice was quietly restrained, no more than a whisper above the purr of the engine as they gathered speed.

Damon turned his head. "I doubt it," he said smoothly. "Henderson is still in the States."

"He was crouched among a group of Afghans, just outside the gate," Jessica insisted.

"I saw that man, too. There is a superficial likeness between the two men," Damon agreed smoothly, staring straight ahead. "Can you imagine the immaculate Henderson squatting in a refugee camp?"

A few months ago Jessica might have answered with a definite no. Since then her perception of the man had changed. She glared at Damon's strong profile, the harsh line of his mouth. "Denying his existence won't make him fade into thin air," she said, her voice filled with exasperation.

Damon looked at her with a gleam in his eyes. "But it may stop you from asking questions I can't answer."

"Can't or won't?" she challenged, her eyes glittering.

Damon caught his breath. Even angry, she was beautiful. His blood stirred, arousing his desire to kiss her until her tight lips softened. "Come here. You're sitting too far away from me."

"Don't change the subject," Jessica sighed. She didn't move.

He reached for her, his long arm curling around her shoulders. "I won't change this subject," he promised softly, drawing her against his side. His kiss was brief and hard, wiping all protests from Jessica's mind. With a sigh of pleasure she leaned against him.

The two-lane highway wound through small, dusty villages, emerald-green rice fields and tall sugarcane. Walking behind ploughs drawn by water buffalo, men worked the fields, much as had their ancestors before them. Their faces hidden by veils, the women walked behind them, raking the freshly tilled earth.

In the distance the mountains rose stark and forbidding, reaching into the clouds.

"This road seems to form the border between government controlled land and Pushtun territory," Damon commented. He had noticed that several crossroads led south, but few led north toward the mountains.

"For a while," Jessica agreed, not surprised at Damon's familiarity with the political situation. Though officially citizens of Pakistan, the Pushtuns rejected government interference. Their lives were ruled by *pushtunwali*, an uncompromising code of honor that, among other things, required blood vengeance for insults. The Guardians of the Western Frontier defended their territory with their lives.

She stared at the stretch of Pushtun land even armed Pakistani soldiers hesitated to invade. Nothing stirred, not even dust devils suggested the presence of man. Yet Jessica knew that the moment strangers set foot on Pushtun land they would be met by men carrying rifles with ammunition belts slung across their chests.

"Ever been in these mountains?" His eyes shifted from the road to the brown cliffs and crevices with a brooding look.

"When we lived in Kabul, I crossed the Khyber Pass several times. Even then, it was too dangerous to leave the road. I've always wanted to visit a Pushtun village."

"The tribes along the pass are unpredictable. They earn their living robbing and smuggling and are suspicious of strangers. But the majority of the Pushtuns are peaceful farmers—or were, before the war. Some day I'll take you into the mountains," Damon promised. Some day, when the bombs had stopped falling and men and women could live openly and not have to huddle among rocks and hide in caves.

Jessica lowered her eyes. She did not want to think of the future with its vague promises, its uncertain loneliness and fear. She pressed her body closer into Damon's until she felt the movement of his ribs with each breath he took. With forced brightness she said, "I always wanted to travel from Baluchistan in the west to the high plains of Pushtunistan in the east."

Damon's hand tightened on her shoulder. "A man would have to be very clever and very familiar with the customs of the different tribes to survive such a trip. A woman could end her life in purdah, especially a woman as beautiful as you."

"Some western women are treated as honorary men," Jessica objected, remembering a camera team that had visited a tribe not too far from here.

Damon grinned. "Women with skin like leather and no curves." His eyes swerved to her breast with intimate knowledge. "That definitely leaves you out."

"But what about *pushtunwali*? As I understand it their code of honor forces them to give protection even to an enemy."

"That's true. If you ask for protection, they won't deny you help as long as you adhere to their code. But interpretation of *pushtunwali* varies from tribe to tribe. For a stranger it would be almost impossible to make no mistakes. If you insult their honor, nothing will save you from certain death."

The column of trucks and jeeps slowed down. In the distance Jessica could see another tent city, built like the last one they had visited.

Damon stayed close to her during their stay there, a dark silent shadow, following her everywhere.

Their caravan of goodwill shrank as truck after truck was unloaded and sent back to Islamabad. Finally only three remained.

As they neared Peshawar, Jessica found it more and more difficult to talk and hide her pain. In the city at the foot of the Khyber Pass their ways would part once again. This time there would be no notes to shorten the time. She'd have nothing but complete silence until September.

Damon wove his way through the now dense traffic, dodging bicycles and cattle. His face was grim. He hated to see the mask back on Jessica's face. All warmth seemed to have seeped out of her, leaving nothing but pain.

"Are you coming with me to Dr. Brooks's camp?" Jessica stared at a donkey almost invisible under the baskets of fruit on its back. Her voice was rough as she tried to keep any sound of pleading from it.

Damon swore softly, hitting the brake as several goats strayed into the traffic. Two young boys ran after them, yelling and waving sticks, shoving and pulling the stubborn beasts back into the herd.

Jessica and Damon smiled at the antics, curses and threats. Their eyes met, laughter mingling with the pain.

"Please," Jessica whispered and then wished she hadn't as his smile disappeared, leaving his face hard, cold and unyielding as rock. "I'm sorry."

Jessica averted her face. "I understand. I promised myself that I wouldn't try to stop you. I know you have to go." She turned her head away, biting back pleading words.

She didn't want to send him off regretting that he had interrupted his trip and had changed his schedule to spend a few more hours with her.

"Jessica." Damon reached for her. He tried to be gentle, but his hand tightened over her slim shoulder with the force of repressed emotions. "If I don't leave now, I won't be able to tear myself away from you."

Jessica nodded, drawing on all her strength. "You gave me as much of your time as you could." Her lips moved stiffly in her desperately controlled face.

"Promise that you'll take care. If you have to walk through another camp, take some of the soldiers to guard you."

For a moment Jessica was tempted to tell him that the army would only escort them through Peshawar. If Damon knew that they would be without protection for the last ten miles, he would insist on making that trip to the camp. But she immediately abandoned the thought. "I'll be careful," she promised softly. "Everything will be fine."

Cars honked behind them. Cursing, Damon looked at the road and saw that the trucks had moved. He was blocking the traffic. He hit the gas pedal without his usual ease. Protesting, the motor growled and the car shot forward, swiftly closing the gap.

As they entered the outskirts of Peshawar, he said, "September is only two months away."

Jessica nodded, her eyes blind with suppressed tears. Two months of fighting with Ahmed Khan, and with Henderson waiting behind his back for his revenge.

"Why are we stopping here?" The trucks turned in a circle in front of a guarded entrance.

Jessica blinked. With dismay she noticed that the trucks had pulled up in front of what looked like a military compound. "This is wrong. Our escort is supposed to bring us all the way to Peshawar."

Major Hamid Osman left his jeep and walked toward her car. She opened the door, and went to meet him. "Why are we stopping here?" she asked tersely.

"We had orders only to accompany you to Peshawar. But my men and I would be willing to escort you to the camp. Against a small payment, of course. The men have to be paid for overtime." The officer smiled apologetically.

As in other Third World countries, the soldiers here were paid low salaries. They supplemented their income by promising extra protection in return for food, clothing and money. Jessica knew that the embassy had already paid for the services of their escort when the arrangements had been made, but the major's demand for additional money at this point came as a surprise. He was to have seen them safely through the city, not just to it. Swallowing her anger, Jessica politely shook her head. "That won't be necessary. Three of my most reliable men are driving those trucks. I thank you for the offer though." Smiling politely, she shook his hand. Peter had joined her and thanked him, handing him a carton of cigarettes.

With a shrug of his shoulders, the major turned back to his jeep. As they watched the jeeps drive past the guard-house, Peter said, "Perhaps we should've paid him."

"How much would you've been willing to pay? Two, three hundred dollars?" Jessica asked dryly. She had never been able to find out why the Pakistani ministry had only given them an escort to Peshawar and not the whole way. Now she suspected that the arrangement had been made on the expectation of extra pay. Somehow she doubted that even three hundred dollars would have been enough for the twenty men.

Peter stared through the mesh wire fence. "Not out of my own pocket," he agreed.

"I think we're perfectly safe. Only a few people knew that our escort would stop in Peshawar. Anyone with thoughts of stealing our supplies would have changed his mind when he saw the military jeeps."

"I hope you're right," Peter grumbled. "How shall we arrange the convoy? In which order are we going to drive?"

"I thought you might lead the way, then the trucks, with Asadullah at the rear." Jessica trusted the Pushtun with her life. No one would steal a truck right from under Asadullah's nose. "I'll follow you the moment I've dropped Damon off."

"You're not dropping me off," Damon said grimly from behind her, anger simmering beneath harsh features. Looking at Peter, he added, "We'll be behind you all the way." The thought of Jessica forming the rear guard of the convoy made his blood freeze. Five foot three of softness against rifles and thieves.

Then he thought of the way she had fought the men this morning and was reminded of their introduction last May and of the bruises she had left on his shins. She was not all softness, he corrected himself. Still, she was not tough enough to protect herself in case of an emergency.

"We can manage without you," Peter protested stiffly.

"I'm sure you can. But I'd rather spend the hours with Jessica than wasting them at the airport."

"You're leaving?" Peter softened slightly, curiosity replacing his stiffness.

Damon nodded. "On the six o'clock flight to Karachi."

Looking at his watch, Peter said, "You'll be cutting it damn close. It's two-thirty now."

"Then let's get going," Jessica said briskly, before Peter could ask more questions. "And don't drive too fast through Peshawar," she warned before turning back to her own car.

Despite the grim look on Damon's face, Jessica could feel her tensions seep away. Until now she had not realized how apprehensive she had been about making this last leg of the trip without an escort. The incident at the second camp must have shaken her more than she had thought.

Once inside the car, Damon looked at her angrily. "Why didn't you tell me that your escort would stop here?"

"Because I didn't know," Jessica snapped back. "As I understood it, they were to see us safely *through* Peshawar."

"And what about the rest of the trip?"

"It's only about ten miles of open fields." She stared at the guard in front of the gate. "Maybe I should've paid the major. Sometimes, though, I see red at their blatant extortion schemes."

Damon smiled faintly, remembering similar situations and his own response. He, too, had frequently walked away. His face hardened again. He had been able to take care of himself.

"You need a keeper," he growled.

"Are you applying for the job?" Jessica's voice was husky, her eyes searching his face.

"Ask me again in September." His mouth brushed across her lips in a light caress. He had no right to make promises he might not be able to keep.

When Damon would have slid back into his seat, Jessica wound her arms around his neck. With a groan he lowered his head and kissed her, showing her what he dared not put into words.

The sound of the truckdrivers starting their engines caused them to break apart. With a muttered curse, Damon turned the key in the ignition and followed Asadullah's blue truck.

When they once again joined the main road, Jessica asked anxiously, "What about your plans? Are you sure you can spare the time?"

Damon looked at her, suspicion hardening his face. But her eyes held only concern, not questions he couldn't answer. His glance softened while his lips curved into his crooked smile. "Don't worry about it. I won't miss my flight."

"I know," Jessica said softly. If Damon had made a reservation for a flight south to Karachi, it was a blind. She doubted that he planned to fly at all. Horses and mules were the most likely transport he would use. What pilot would fly north into the mountains where the air space was crowded with Russian helicopters and MIGs?

"You should have told me that the jeeps would turn back at the city limits. How do you think I would have felt if I'd heard later on that the convoy had been attacked?'' he asked quietly.

The same way I feel now, knowing where you're going, she thought. Stiff with fear. Nightmares haunting your sleep. She had known where he was going and what he was before they had made love, but she had not known how hard it would be to let him go with a smile. She said quietly, ''It didn't seem fair to use the situation to make you change your plans.'' She paused, then added, ''We've never been stopped before. The truck we lost on our last trip just vanished, driver and all.''

''Then why the tension earlier?''

''Guilty conscience,'' she flipped.

Damon shot her a glance filled with amusement. ''Guilty conscience? About what?''

Swiftly, Jessica told him about the surplus medical supplies, grinning when she described how Peter had to open one of the crates to convince the customs official that they belonged to them. ''They bore the department's name. But we didn't have the bill of lading. It cost us some baksheesh but it was worth it.''

Pointing at the truck that carried the surplus supplies, she missed the hardening of Damon's features.

''Didn't you wonder if the shipment belonged to someone else?'' Damon asked harshly. ''Is that why you wanted an escort? To keep the stuff safe in your grasp?''

Jessica's head snapped around, the smile slipping into a frown. Her eyes were wide with hurt and confusion. ''I don't think I understand. Just what is it you're accusing me of?''

''Nothing.'' His expression was a mixture of frustration, anger and sadness. ''Nothing but carelessness. Didn't it ever occur to you that someone might've used the embassy's address to get the shipment through customs without delay, duty-free, and then steal it back once you're on the road?''

''No,'' said Jessica, her voice very quiet and very controlled. ''That idea never crossed my mind.'' Only someone with little faith in human decency could imagine such deceit. Even Peter had not mentioned that possibility.

But Damon moved in a world of darkness, among murderers and terrorists, a world totally alien to her. Only by assuming the worst in people had he survived so long. She tried to envision what it must be like to trust no one, to suspect everyone. She couldn't.

"I prefer to believe that the pharmaceutical company made a mistake. It's more likely. And much more appealing."

Damon's eyes lost some of their hardness. "Dreamer."

The word touched her tenderly. Yet Jessica sensed his frustration, as if he resented that she had retained enough innocence to dream. He took his hand off the steering wheel and caressed the softness of her skin. His voice was rough with regret. "I wish I could fence your world and keep it a bright place. Warm and loving, like you."

Jessica covered his hand, keeping it pressed against her cheek. Turning her head, she kissed the palm with trembling lips. Damon, too, had once lived in her world. He, too, had dreamed. Until one morning he awoke and found darkness instead of sunshine, hate instead of love, cold instead of warmth.

Her heart ached for this strong man, hard, yet gentle, tough, yet tender. The man who had taught her the sweetness of desire and love.

She wanted to hold on to him. She wanted to draw him into the sunshine.

"There's room for you in that bright, sunny place," Jessica said, her voice husky with aching tears. "For as long as you need it."

He had called her a dreamer, but she didn't cling to a fantasy world. She knew that Damon would be drawn again and again to the trouble spots of the world. What she didn't know was how long she could smile and let him go. How could she continue to live with the seesaw emotions of happiness and despair, hope and fear?

For a moment Damon's hand tightened, and the look he shot her held such yearning, such tenderness, that tears spilled over her cheeks. Then he broke the contact.

Jessica dried her cheeks with swift movements. She hadn't cried so often for years. Damon must think her a water fountain.

But Damon didn't mind. He couldn't remember the last time someone had cried for him. Perhaps it had been his mother at his hastily arranged wedding. No, he remembered his mother sitting through the brief civil ceremony with tight-lipped disapproval. She hadn't liked Tanya and because of that dislike he had distanced himself from his family, keeping the two women apart. But his mother would love Jessica.

"Damn it. What's Peter doing?" Jessica's sharp voice interrupted his pleasant thoughts. They had been driving over wide boulevards with palm trees dividing the lanes.

"He's turning the wrong way," Jessica said, her face tight with worry. "That street leads to the old part of town."

Damon saw the detour sign before Jessica did. "The other street is blocked off."

"We'll never be able to keep the convoy together," Jessica muttered. "In the old part of town the streets are very narrow and crowded."

Damon didn't answer. His mouth was set in a grim line as he drove as fast as he dared, trying to keep up with the truck in front of him.

Jessica had always enjoyed visiting the old part of town with its high narrow buildings and dusty shops. But now her eyes were blind to the Indian women in bright saris and the emancipated Pushtun wives, wearing western-style scarves and raincoats instead of the traditional *chadris*.

Her eyes were glued to the flapping beige canvas of Asadullah's truck. When a *ghadi* moved between it and their car, she groaned and then could have laughed as, a moment later, the horse-drawn gig pulled out again to stop in front of a shop.

"Relax," Damon said. "I doubt that anyone is going to rob a truck in the middle of the street. Too many witnesses."

Jessica forced the fingers in her lap to uncurl. "But there are also too many alleys that open up like black holes to swallow a truck, cargo and all," she pointed out tightly.

Two young men, dressed in jeans and brightly colored shirts, jumped on Asadullah's truck, hitching a ride. At the next traffic light, they jumped off again and vanished in the crowd. Asadullah honked his horn, scattering the pedestrians in the intersection. Damon braked sharply to avoid hitting a woman veiled in her *chadris*. The voluminous garment covered her from head to toe, its embroidered panel across her eyes hampering her vision. She must not have seen the car until Damon had come to a full stop, tires screeching. Then she scampered off, veils flapping. They caught up with Asadullah at the next traffic light.

"I'm sure Peter's waiting on the other side of the intersection at some place where he can park," Jessica said with more confidence than she felt. The streets were too crowded and narrow to halt the convoy without blocking the flow of traffic.

"It's also risky to stop," Damon reminded her grimly. His eyes were focused on a group of tall, lean mountain men, rounding the corner. Pedestrians shrank against the houses or stepped off the curb to make room for the fierce-looking group.

Before the arrival of the group, the air had been filled with honking, shouting and the call of vendors. Now a strange silence hung over them all, not a threatening silence, but a cautiously waiting one.

Seemingly unaware of the stir they were causing, the men crossed the road in front of Jessica's car. Their tanned faces were partially hidden by beards and black turbans.

"Pushtuns." Jessica was fascinated with their proud appearance. "They're carrying rifles," she gasped. No one was allowed to bear arms on government controlled land. Not even the Pushtuns. Yet here they walked, openly defying the law, ammunition belts slung across their chests and rifles in their hands.

"Do you know which tribe they belong to?" Jessica asked Damon, not taking her eyes off the men. The colors of the skull caps around which the turbans were wrapped distinguished the various tribes. These caps were dark and too small for her to identify.

Suddenly Damon swore. Jessica turned her head just in time to see two armed Pushtuns climb into the back of Asadullah's truck. Two others were opening the doors to the cab.

Damon flung the car door open and ran toward their truck. When he was almost upon it, it tore down the street with a roar, its speed increasing too fast for Damon to catch the edge of the flapping canvas.

For a moment Jessica was frozen with shock. Then she slid into the driver's seat, giving gas and closing the door. Her hand pushed the horn, keeping it there. Her lips were tightly shut, her throat locked with fear, praying that Damon didn't reach the truck before she caught up with him.

The vehicle slowed down and the two Pushtuns in the back brandished their rifles at him. Damon swerved, but kept on running with lightning speed. Then the truck shot forward, disappearing around a curve.

Jessica stopped the car next to Damon. He ran to the driver's side. "Move over," he said sharply.

Jessica scrambled back into her seat. Damon jumped inside and the car leaped forward once again. But, when they rounded the curve around which the truck had disappeared, there was no sign of it. It had somehow vanished in the middle of Peshawar.

Damon drove down the street. "Look for alleys on your side."

But the houses hugged each other, leaving no space big enough for a truck to drive through. Fifty yards further, at another intersection, Damon parked the car and got out to question several men waiting for the light to turn.

"Nothing," he said when he returned. "No sign of Asadullah or his truck."

"And no sign of Peter, either." Jessica's voice was but a whisper, her eyes wide with apprehension.

Damon gathered her close, pressing her head into his shoulder. "Peter may have decided to wait for us on the outskirts of Peshawar.'' It was all the comfort he could give her.

Jessica closed her eyes, praying that he was right. For a moment she leaned on his strength. Then she pushed herself away, settling back into her seat. "Let's drive on and find out." Her voice was low, and tight with fear. But her head was held high and her shoulders were drawn back.

"You're quite a woman, Jessica," Damon said huskily. He had never admired her more than at this moment. Some women would have shouted abuses at him for being too slow to catch the truck. Others would have dissolved in tears and clung to him. But Jessica didn't break under the pressure of adversity.

Jessica turned to look at him. "And you're quite a man. Trying to catch a moving truck and fight armed Pushtuns with bare hands."

"I'm sorry," he whispered before his lips fastened on her mouth in a kiss filled with desire and desperation.

The desperation startled her. Jessica wound her arms around his neck and gave in to his need.

"I'm not," she breathed when they broke apart. "I'm not sorry you didn't catch them. I can handle another lost shipment." Her voice cracked a little and her hands tightened in his hair. Taking a shaky breath, she continued, "I'm glad you're all right."

But as Damon drove through the streets, Jessica worried about Asadullah. The driver was not a man to meekly watch thieves steal his truck. If it hadn't been for Peter and the other two trucks, she would have insisted on going to the police. But, from experience, she knew that nothing moved fast in this country, not even the police. She could spend hours at the station, repeating their story over and over again, while Peter might be waiting for her, a sitting duck for another attack.

I should've accepted the major's offer. With each heartbeat, those words pounded in her head, heaping guilt upon fear. Her burning eyes searched the madcap traffic for a sight of the convoy, tensing every time she spotted a blue truck. The first one she saw carried no cargo—its platform crowded with Pakistanis hitching a ride. The next truck was filled with melons. At every pothole several of them tumbled off between the missing slats, one of them almost hitting her car.

As the streets widened into boulevards, the shops disappeared and whitewashed villas surrounded by high walls and even higher palm trees took their places.

They raced past ricefields and fruit orchards. They flew past a small caravan of camels and by an old pickup truck that had lost a wheel. Damon drove on, past where the irrigated land stopped and lush green turned to dusty brown.

Peshawar became a sprawling, hazy shadow in the rearview mirror. Before them rose the mountains. Ragged rocks and shadowed crevices.

They had reached the Khyber Pass road without a sign of the convoy.

Chapter 9

Damon turned the car off the road, stopping in the shade of a tall, dusty oak tree. "Now we wait."

"Wait for what?" Jessica shook her head impatiently, words of protest hovering on her lips.

"If you were Peter, what would you be doing now?" Damon turned in his seat, folding his arms across his wide chest.

Jessica considered his question with a frown. Peter might not know about the theft of the truck, and could believe that they had only become separated in the old part of town.

"I'd drive on to the camp. Or wait at a point where we'd have to pass." A smile of understanding lit her tired face. "The last crossroad is about a mile behind us. I should've thought of that myself."

Shaking his head, Damon said quietly, "You can't think of everything. This trip is getting to you." Her eyes were dark with worry, her body tense. "You're exhausted." He lifted her as easily as he would a child, settling her on his lap. "Close your eyes for a few moments. I'll keep watch."

She buried her face in his neck. For a while she drew from his strength, tension flowing from mind and body under the rhythmic strokes of his hand.

A long while later she stirred, refreshed, as from a deep sleep. She looked at him, a rueful smile curving her lips. "Believe it or not, this was supposed to have been a minivacation. I'd planned on shopping for rugs after we'd delivered the supplies." With the tip of her finger she traced the curve of his beard. "But I thank the fates for sending you to the right place at the right time." Her thoughts flew back to their early morning breakfast and Damon's concern for her safety. It was almost frightening the way he had predicted trouble. "Are you sure you don't have a second sight?" she teased.

Damon caught her wandering hand and kissed her palm. "Nothing so spectacular." His face wore a strangely sad smile, shadows clouding his eyes. "Just a little imagination."

"And a whole lot of information," Jessica added dryly. Damon seemed to draw on sources even Jessica didn't have access to. Who had been his source this time?

Damon didn't acknowledge her indirect question. Instead he drew her into his arms, kissing her.

Warm sensations radiated through her and she wound her arms around his neck, opening her mouth with a small sound of pleasure. His arms tightened and his tongue slid past her teeth, feeling texture and movement, the warm eagerness of her response. His hands moved powerfully down her back, cinching her waist, cupping the curve of her hips, lifting her until she sat more comfortably over him.

The intimate touch released a surge of longing in Jessica. "Damon, we can't." There was a strange roaring in her ears.

Abruptly she raised her head, looking down the road. In a fluid motion she sat up. "That's Peter's car." Pointing at the white Ford with one arm, she hugged Damon with the other. "And the two trucks."

Her face radiated joy and she kissed him. Sliding over her seat, she opened the door and ran to the side of the road, waving.

"Jessica, stay back." Damon jumped from the car and ran to her side, shielding her with his body. "Get back," he ordered. His eyes tightened against the silver glare reflecting off the tarmac.

Without protest Jessica obeyed, taking shelter behind Damon. "I know that's Peter," she said firmly.

"It's his car," Damon agreed. "But someone else may be driving it."

"Then wouldn't we be safer in the Mercedes?" It seemed dangerous standing out here, an easy target beside the road.

"No. If they begin shooting, run and hide behind the trees," Damon said.

"All right," Jessica promised quietly, watching as the white car came closer.

Moments later she felt Damon relax. "You can come out now." He stepped sideways to give her a good view of the convoy.

Peter had spotted them and was honking and waving. With a burst of speed he closed the distance, then came to a dusty stop next to them.

"Thank God you're here." His face seemed to have aged over the last hour. Climbing out of the car, he hugged Jessica fiercely and shook Damon's hand. In his relief he seemed to have forgotten his animosity toward the older man.

"What happened?" he asked as he searched for the third truck. "Where's Asadullah?"

"We don't know." Swiftly, Jessica filled Peter in on the events since they had become separated.

"In the middle of Peshawar. I bet the road we normally take wasn't being repaired. Someone set us up. So what are we going to do now? Look for him? Or drive the last few miles to the camp?"

"We'll deliver the supplies first," Jessica decided. She didn't want to risk the other drivers and their trucks searching for Asadullah. It was not an easy decision to make. She worried about the loyal Pushtun's fate. With troubled eyes she looked at Damon, hoping he would offer a better solution.

"Seems to be the best thing," Damon agreed. "Unless we divide our forces. I can supervise the unloading of the trucks. But I don't know Peshawar well enough to search for Asadullah."

"Great." Jessica's eyes sparkled with relief. She doubted that Peter would be able to find the supplies. But as long as Asadullah was safe, she could write the theft off to experience. "Do you mind?" she asked her friend.

"Aren't you going to miss your flight?" Peter asked. He was reluctant to hand over his job to Damon.

Damon shrugged his shoulders. "Let me worry about it."

After a brief hesitation, Peter agreed. Looking at Jessica, he said, "I'll meet you at the Dean's Hotel." Then he handed over the briefcase containing the invoices. "I still have your lunch." He held out the larger of the two coolers.

"I completely forgot about food." She rarely ate between camps. Aya packed the cooler mostly for Peter's benefit. She turned to Damon with an apologetic smile. "Why didn't you remind me to get it out of Peter's car earlier? I didn't mean to starve you."

"I wasn't hungry." He took the cooler from Peter and carried it to the silver Mercedes.

Jessica followed his tall form with troubled eyes. Something had upset Damon. She could sense the tension carefully controlled within him. Was he worried about Henderson catching up with him? Or had he missed his appointment with Ahmed Khan because she had involved him in her troubles? She stifled a sigh of impatience. The wall of silence Damon surrounded himself with was frightening, the uncertain secrets threatening. If Damon had given her the slightest encouragement, she would have broken her promise not to probe into his affairs.

But he didn't. As they drew up at the next camp's administration building he hesitated briefly, before leaving the car.

"Don't do anything I wouldn't approve of," he said quietly.

Jessica grimaced at the provocative statement. Then she met his eyes. They gleamed wickedly. She caught her breath as a wave of desire swept over her. She wanted to kiss him, but Dr. Brooks was already coming down the steps. "I'll be as careful as you are," she promised him huskily, then slid from the car to greet the British physician.

"You're late. I was worried about you." Steve Brooks was an athletic-looking man in his mid-thirties. Blond hair curled damply on his forehead, blue eyes narrowed against the glare of the sun. When he spotted Damon leaving the car, he asked, "Where's Peter?"

"He's gone back to Peshawar." After introducing the two men, she reported what had happened.

The doctor shrugged his shoulders. "Those bloody thieves. I could've used those extra supplies. Don't worry about Asadullah. He'll be careful until they've unloaded the crates. If you see a truck fuming down the road, it'll be him, trying to pursue the men."

"Just what I need to hear," Jessica said sarcastically, staring at Damon. "Men don't know when to quit."

Grinning, Damon laid an arm across her shoulders. "Your claws are showing," he warned. Then he turned to Steve Brooks. "Where do you want me to unload the trucks?"

Dr. Brooks gave him directions, adding, "If you need any help, let me know."

With a nod, Damon turned toward the waiting trucks, hitching a ride on the first one.

"We got a new X-ray machine from Germany," Dr. Brooks said as he preceded Jessica into the building, a big grin splitting his face. "Come, let me show you what other improvements we've made since your last visit."

An hour later Jessica said her final goodbye, handing her friend two bottles of Scotch she had hidden in the cooler. "If you need any more, Peter will get it for you."

"This should last me for a day or two," Steve Brooks joked. "Good luck. And thanks." He shook Damon's hand, his voice deep with regret. "I don't know where we'll find someone else as dedicated as Jessica."

With a final wave, Jessica climbed into the car. She sighed sadly as they drove through the camp for the last time. Another chapter of her life had ended. The future was as hazy as the sky above her, uncertain and vast. For a moment she wanted to turn back the clock and cling to the familiar life. Dark clouds formed on the horizon. Had her decision to take the U.N. position been wise? Would she adjust to the crowds and noise of New York City? Would she be able to help the refugees as effectively? Or would distance and a desk job dull her concern for the plight of the people in the camps surrounding her here?

Damon covered her hand, pressing it reassuringly. "You'll be back." His dark eyes had softened with understanding. "Even if you stayed here in Pakistan, you wouldn't be allowed to make another trip. Not after today. It's too dangerous."

"After today, the convoy will be safer." Jessica smiled weakly. "Security will be so tight, not even a fly will get near the trucks."

"To hell with the convoy. I'm talking about your personal safety." His mouth was set in grim lines.

Dust rose all around them as they reached the dirt track leading to the Khyber Pass road. Jessica rolled up her window before answering calmly, "To hell with the convoy? Do you know what a convoy means to me? It means months of work. Writing hundreds of letters, raising thousands of dollars, sweating in customs, arguing until I could scream with frustration. How can I forget about the convoy? And how could I forget the people depending on the supplies?"

With a shake of his head and a rueful twist of his mouth, Damon picked up her hand and placed a lingering kiss in its palm. "Lost equipment and supplies can be replaced. You can't," he said huskily. "I'm glad you're returning stateside soon."

"In two weeks," Jessica said, wishing that Damon could return with her instead of vanishing into the mountains.

"And no more trips?" Damon asked tersely.

"Only to the embassy and the shops. I'm on vacation starting next week."

One powerful arm closed around her slim shoulders and drew her close. "I've left instructions at my office to give you the key to my apartment if you need a place to stay in New York."

Jessica hesitated briefly before thanking him. If their relationship had been based on friendship, she would have accepted the offer gratefully. But moving into Damon's place would indicate a commitment she wasn't sure she could make. Already the future promised a bag of uncertainties. Until she knew what she wanted and what to expect from their relationship, she was reluctant to take that step. "Ali's expecting me to stay with her until I've found a place."

Damon shot her a look as unreadable as the darkness of night. "If you need a refuge—some privacy—it's yours. No strings," he said evenly.

A slow smile curved her lips. "Thanks," she whispered, pressing closer against him. Suddenly she felt the strong muscles quiver with tension. Damon leaned forward, wiping the windshield and squinting through the cloud of dust. With easy grace, Jessica scooted away from him back into her seat, her eyes also searching the flat brown landscape spreading before them.

Two trucks were racing along the Khyber Pass road not too far away from them. Black fingers of smoke rose above the cabs, flags of fury against the hazy sky. They chased toward the foot of the mountains, until they vanished between the rocks.

"One of them looks like Asadullah's truck." Damon's face was hard as rock.

"It could be," Jessica confirmed tersely. She, too, had caught a glimpse of blue. "Do you think the other truck carries the missing supplies?"

Grimly, Damon nodded. "I'm almost certain. Hold on," he ordered as the car shot forward.

Suddenly a white flash streaked across their vision, pursuing the trucks into the mountains.

"That's Peter," Jessica groaned.

"That damn idiot," Damon swore viciously, hurtling the car over the dips and rolls of the dirt road until the Mercedes groaned in protest.

Jessica swayed with the motion, one hand clenched around the door handle. Glancing at her watch, she said, "They'll never get past the checkpoint at Fort Jamrud. The Khyber Pass road closes in an hour." Driving across the long pass at night was dangerous, so ingoing traffic was stopped early in the afternoon. There were too many bandits lurking among the rocks, waylaying, robbing and killing travelers blinded by darkness.

"The first truck is headed for Landi Kotal. Most likely he's familiar to the guards," Damon pointed out. "The guards may turn Asadullah back, but they won't stop Hallam. Not if he gives them a baksheesh and flashes his passport."

Jessica didn't answer. Her eyes were glued to the track. When they finally joined the Khyber Pass road, there was no sign of Peter.

Minutes later they reached Fort Jamrud. Against the backdrop of the mountains rising behind it, the massive structure looked like a toy castle. Next to the guardhouse stood Asadullah's truck. Of Peter and the first truck there was no sign.

Damon stopped, rolling down the dust-coated window. Angry, heated voices floated from the guardhouse. Damon honked his horn.

Moments later Asadullah shot from the building, his body shaking with fury, the end of his turban flapping behind him. "Those thieving dogs. May Allah spit on them. *Hanum* sahib they stole my crates," he cried, looking at Jessica. "If it hadn't been for this idiot, I would've caught up with them." He stabbed an accusing finger at the guard following closely behind.

"Did you get hurt?" Jessica asked anxiously.

Asadullah shook his head. "They stole my crates. But, by Allah, I will get them back. You tell him to let me pass. They will listen to you, *hanum*."

Jessica said soothingly, "It wasn't your fault that you lost the crates. We saw what happened. But you'll never catch them now. Sahib Damon and I will follow Sahib Peter. The Mercedes is a faster car. I want you to return to Islamabad."

Asadullah shook his head, a fiercely determined look on his face. "I go with sahib. *Hanum* drive my truck to Peshawar."

"The hanum is too weak to drive such a big truck," Damon said firmly.

Despite her anxiety, Jessica had to bite back a smile at Damon's deviousness. Asadullah snorted with frustration. His honor had been smirched and he wanted his revenge, but his pride of possession was as strong as his thirst for vengeance. He had no intention of abandoning his truck. After a moment he gave in to the inevitable. *"Hub,"* he growled, turning away. Throwing another insult at the guard, he walked to his truck.

Damon watched him climb into the cab. Turning to Jessica he said quietly, "I want you to go back to Peshawar with Asadullah."

The quiet intensity of his voice told Jessica more about the possible dangers ahead than graphic descriptions could have done. Her stomach tightened but she shook her head firmly. "Peter is my responsibility. You're not dumping me like some parcel into Asadullah's lap," she said with a stubborn look on her face. This was one time she would not stay behind and wait, fearing for Damon and her friend. If Damon left her she would follow him in Asadullah's truck.

For a moment Damon looked grim. Their eyes met in a silent battle of wills, until a glimmer of a smile curved his firm mouth. "I'd rather have you here beside me," he said softly, reading her intention in the firm set of her chin. One finger touched her mouth in a tender caress. "If I left, you'd follow me anyway."

"Yes," she said simply, kissing his finger with a tender smile.

Damon's eyes darkened with longing. His hand curved around her chin with tenderness. Then he turned toward the guard standing next to the car, talking to him until the man agreed to lift the crossing barrier for them. He paid the toll, adding a generous baksheesh to the small amount. Then he watched the guard's slow strut toward the red and white striped beam. Beyond, the mountains rose in stark relief. "It's not too late to change your mind."

Jessica's eyes followed the road until shadows closed in on it. Fear tightened her throat when she said, "Let's go."

With a grim look Damon started the engine. The car shot forward, beneath the raised beam. A roar came from behind as Asadullah tried to gain enough speed to follow on their bumper. But the guard must have anticipated the Pushtun's move. He swiftly lowered the barrier before the truck could slip through.

The road rose steeply, drawing them into sun-baked cliffs and shadowy crevices. There was only rocks and silence and the purr of the engine for company. Fear curled in Jessica's chest.

"Don't worry." Damon's deep voice flowed over her. "The way Hallam was driving, he's going to overheat his car within minutes. We'll catch up with him soon."

Jessica smiled tightly. Peter was more competent than Damon thought. She'd always known his behavior was a cover for other activities. But even to Damon she couldn't reveal Peter's true identity. The decision rested with Peter, not with her.

"What about your plans?" she asked softly, watching him round several hairpin curves with skilled ease.

Damon shrugged his broad shoulders. "They're flexible." After a moment's pause, he added quietly, "I was going to meet Ahmed in Landi Kotal. I may be there sooner than he anticipated."

Jessica's eyes widened at the news. To soothe her fears Damon had broken his silence. Reaching out, she covered his strong, tanned hand with gratitude. Suddenly the mountains didn't seem so terrifying in their stark splendor or so filled with hidden dangers. Somewhere at the end of this road a friend was waiting.

"You could've told me before," she said, her voice a mixture of exasperation and relief.

Damon raised her hand to his lips. "Don't you trust me to keep you safe?"

"I wasn't worried about *my* safety," she said softly, bending toward him. For a moment she nestled against him in complete confidence. No one would touch her with Damon at her side. But strong and powerful as he was, there was a limit even to his abilities. "Landi Kotal isn't exactly friendly territory," she commented. The town was infested with drug dealers and gun runners, men who shot first and asked questions later.

"If you don't ask questions and stay away from certain quarters, the town is perfectly safe." Damon kissed the top of her head before concentrating once again on the road. They sped around the curve of a rock face, the road snaking before them like a silver ribbon past deep abysses, hugging sheer cliffs. Damon's lips tightened. "Hallam is a better driver than I gave him credit for," he said, scanning the area with narrowed eyes. "We're slowing down because of the air conditioning. I have to turn it off. Open your window, but only part of the way."

Jessica nodded, doing as he asked. Hot air flooded the car, making it almost impossible to breathe. Relieved of the excess drain, the car shot forward. With the sinking sun, the shadows grew longer and darker. The mountains rose all around them, stark and forbidding, without vegetation, not even a small bush or blade of grass. It looked like a lunar landscape and appeared uninhabited.

But that was an illusion.

For the last few miles, Damon's sight had grown sharper, his mouth tighter. Jessica, too, had the uncanny feeling of being watched. Searching the cliffs, she at first saw only flashes of light, like sun reflecting off mirrors. She tried to focus on the source with binoculars, a task made impossible by the car's fast movements. When Damon slowed down to ease the car over a wide crack in the asphalt, she saw a figure standing on a ledge, his dark clothes and orange vest blending into the reddish-brown sun-baked cliffs. But for the light reflecting off his ammunition belt, Jessica would have missed him.

"We're being watched," she said calmly. The Pushtun was some distance away, separated from the road by a gorge.

"They've been watching for quite some time," Damon agreed. "No one invades their territory without them knowing." He watched her raise the binoculars again. "I think you're more intrigued than scared."

"Only for the moment." Jessica grinned, looking at him. "I'll scream if they leap on top of the car."

"Keep looking at me like that and I'll stop the car," Damon said as he negotiated a seemingly endless number of hairpin curves.

Minutes later, they sped past a crawling truck loaded with fruit. Two men sat on top of its hood, one of them pouring water into the engine while the other steadied him. They waved, smiling and shouting, their shirttails and turban ends flapping like friendly flags. Jessica waved back until the car rounded the next curve.

Suddenly Damon braked sharply, pulling the steering wheel to the left. The car bounced and began to skid as a choking dust enveloped them in a thick, beige cloud. Blinded, Damon steered into the skid, the car sliding across the road.

Jessica was thrown forward, then bounced back against the seat as the belt tightened across her shoulder. She rolled up her window to keep out the dust, then clung to the door to keep from bumping into Damon, holding her breath, praying.

After what seemed an eternity, Damon brought the car under control and it jerked to a halt. For several seconds there was only silence, then the harsh sounds of long held breaths finally released. Damon turned his head, looking at her searchingly. "Are you hurt?"

She shook her head. "Only shaken. What about you?"

"Fine. But I'd feel a damn sight better if the dust would settle." He leaned forward and wiped the windshield, peering into the swirling brown fog.

"What happened?" Jessica asked, sneezing as dust particles tickled her nose.

"We almost hit a rockslide blocking the road."

Slowly the cloud surrounding them cleared and the scene before them came into focus.

Jessica gasped. They were facing a valley, beautifully painted with the brush of the afternoon sun. Orange, henna and black, with a splash of green amid the earthtones.

And a thousand-foot drop.

"That was close," Jessica whispered, awed and shocked. No more than two feet of solid ground separated them from the valley below. Shaking, she turned to Damon. "I'm glad you were driving. I would've sent us flying."

Damon shook his head. "I doubt it. I've seen your control in an emergency. I expected you to scream."

"I felt like it," Jessica admitted. "But I didn't want to startle you."

His dark eyes caressed her face, admiration gleaming in their depth. "I've been in a lot of tight places with a lot of men," he said quietly. "I couldn't ask for a better companion than you."

Jessica smiled with pleasure. "You're one hell of a driver."

Damon slid his hand over the steering wheel. "The car is easy to handle." He cupped her chin, placing a tender kiss on her lips. Jessica's mouth softened in response. For a moment their lips clung, pulsing with life and longing, desire simmering, but swiftly dammed. This was not the time to celebrate life.

Damon drew back. Reaching under the seat, he drew out the gun he had hidden there that morning. Jessica watched him check it, then slide it in the back of his belt. "I have to warn the truck driver," he said, opening the door. "Don't leave the car until I come back."

Fear leaped into her eyes. Nodding, Jessica turned her head, straining to see past the back of the seat. Releasing her seat belt, she gazed through the rear window at the pile of rock blocking the road and shuddered. "Those boulders came down recently. There's no way a truck could get past them."

"Right," Damon agreed grimly. "I'll be back soon. If you see anything move, honk the horn. And lock your door." He slid from the car, locking his door. For a moment he stood, searching the rocks above them. When nothing stirred, he ran down the road.

Jessica watched him until he disappeared around the curve. Then she turned back to the mountain, looking from rock to rock, from shadow to shadow, recalling stories of unnatural rockfalls, of Pushtuns robbing travelers thus stopped.

She slumped with relief when Damon reappeared moments later, running with an easy grace. "The lorry apparently has run out of water. It's stopped about a mile down the road, fuming like a dragon."

"I have some flares in the trunk," Jessica said briskly. She did not want Damon to walk down the road to warn the driver. Yet, on the other hand, they couldn't drive off without leaving a warning.

"Where?" Damon reached for the key.

"Next to the spare tire. On the right." Jessica got out of the car and followed him, watching him take one of the flares and go to the curve, planting it in the middle of the road.

While Damon lit the flare, Jessica examined the cliffs. The rockslide might have been started by natural causes, like the mountain sighing or shifting. Or it could have been started by bandits to slow down any pursuers of the escaping truck.

When Damon returned, he walked around the rubble to the other side of the waist-high barrier. "I don't see any tire tracks in the dust. Hallam must have passed before this lot came down." He walked a few steps further up the road, then turned abruptly.

"Let's get going." With long swift strides, he returned to the Mercedes. Helping Jessica into the car, he closed the door and checked the lock. "Leave your window closed."

Jessica bit back the protest that they would suffocate in this heat. She shut the window tightly. When Damon had joined her and secured his side, she asked, "What did you see?"

"Nothing." Damon started the car, and carefully inched it past the rubble of broken rocks. Once they had passed the tight spot, Jessica noticed that he kept away from the mountain and drove along the cliffside of the road, reducing the risk of being hit by anything but bullets.

Suddenly the road widened, following a dry riverbed. The mountains receded, opening into a wide valley, barren, without trees. Sun etched the crests with slivers of fire, setting the rocks glowing.

"How much further is it to Landi Kotal?" Jessica asked. With evening approaching, the smuggler town seemed like a haven.

Damon drove over the bridge spanning the riverbed. "Another ten, fifteen miles. We'll be there before nightfall," he promised, sending the car up again into the mountains. Rounding another curve, he suddenly tensed. Out of the corner of his eye he saw something flash, perhaps a signal warning of their arrival. He slowed down, peering through the dusty windshield.

Suddenly, like pebbles rolling downhill, men jumped onto the road.

"Get down," Damon ordered, braking sharply.

With stiff hands, Jessica pressed the release button of the seat belt, sighing with exasperation when it wouldn't give immediately. Seconds seemed like minutes before she was free. But as she doubled forward to slide into the space in front of the seat, she caught a flash of white behind the human barrier.

"I see Peter's car." A hoarse cry broke from her throat.

"Get down." Damon's voice cut like a knife through her horror. He brought the car to a full stop, inches away from the Pushtuns.

Jessica watched him reach for his gun and unlock the safety latch.

And then, to her utter amazement, he secured it again. "It's all right," he said, smiling broadly and opening the door. "Those are Ahmed's men."

Jessica scrambled up into her seat, leaning back, dizzy with relief. As Damon left the car, a tall man stepped forward, slinging his rifle over his shoulder.

"You took your sweet time getting here." Ahmed held out his arms, a white grin slashing his full black beard.

"Didn't you get my message?" Damon asked, embracing his friend.

Startled, Jessica blinked. Despite Peter's description, the uncanny resemblance of the two men amazed her. Both were tall, both had the same powerful, lean build. They moved with the fluid grace of an athlete. Despite their different dress, they might have been brothers.

Jessica tore her eyes away from the two men, searching for Peter's craggy face among the Pushtuns. When she couldn't find him, she opened her door and raced toward the white car.

The Ford was empty, its windshield shattered, as if it had been pounded with rocks. "Peter," she yelled, her voice hoarse with fear. She jumped up on a boulder on the side of the road, clinging to the top of the car to balance herself.

"Down here." Something moved beneath the car. Like a prairie dog coming out of his hole, Peter stuck his head out. He shook himself, stiffly getting to his feet in a cloud of dust. "Damn it, what are you doing here?" he asked angrily.

"Coming to your rescue, what else? We saw your charge up the Khyber Pass," Jessica explained heatedly.

Peter's face softened. "You look like the angel on top of our Christmas tree. But a little dusty. And about to fall down."

Too happy to hold on to her anger, Jessica chuckled in response and fell into Peter's arms. "I don't know whether to kiss or strangle you."

"Definitely a kiss." Peter caught her, kissing her before putting her down.

"What happened to you?" She raised her finger to wipe a smudge off his face. "What were you doing under the car?"

"Checking for an oil leak. I drove into a rock fall. Barely made it through. My windshield has had it. I must have also damaged the oil pan when I drove over the rocks already on the ground."

"It must've been the same one we almost ran into," Jessica said. Swiftly she described the incident. "How did you meet Ahmed Khan? Did he stop you, too?"

Peter shook his head. "I had stopped to brush out glass splinters when he and his men crept up. Scared the hell out of me. I'm afraid I lost that lorry. It was about a half mile ahead when the rocks started falling."

"And just what would you have done if you'd caught up with it?" Jessica asked, her voice rising with exasperation.

"I had no intention of catching them. I wanted to find out where they were taking our stuff," Peter explained. "If we can find out who's behind the thefts, we may be able to stop them."

Damon watched the reunion, his face as hard as his eyes. He detected nothing even slightly sexual about their embrace and their exuberance after the brush with danger. All he saw was a strong bond of shared laughter and shared work, a firm friendship forged by years of common experiences, problems solved together. In this, he was the outsider. He didn't belong to that world.

Not yet.

Chapter 10

There's something fishy going on," Peter said to Jessica, shifting uncomfortably on the ropes of the charpoy. "Trucks don't just vanish into thin air. And Ahmed Khan and his Pushtuns popped up like magic out of nowhere. The whole thing stinks of conspiracy with your friend Noble right in the middle."

Jessica turned toward the smoking light of the oil lamp, staring at the flickering shadows dancing on the whitewashed mud walls. "Damon had nothing to do with the theft of the supplies," she said firmly. "He risked his life chasing after the truck." Even now the scene chilled her with fear.

"And geese lay golden eggs," Peter snorted, pushing away the remains of the meal as if the sight of it made him sick. "He arrives unexpectedly the night before we leave. Then there's that mysterious business he has to take care of—at five in the morning." His narrowed eyes searched Jessica's face. "Did you ask him where he was going?"

Jessica shook her head. "I guess he went back to his hotel to pick up his bags," she said firmly. "The time of his arrival was merely coincidence. Besides, he was still in the States when the last truck was stolen."

"But Ahmed Khan was here," Peter pointed out quietly. "Don't try to convince me that their meeting is another coincidence, because I won't believe it."

Jessica shrugged her shoulders. Under different circumstances she might have confided in Peter. But her friend would feel compelled to divulge his knowledge to his superiors. They, in turn, would add it to the files of Damon Noble and Ahmed Khan. Top secret files to which Colonel Henderson might have access. She wouldn't risk Damon's safety just to allay Peter's suspicions. "I admit I don't know all the answers," she said softly, "but I trust Damon with my life."

With a low voiced muttering of disgust about the blindness of love, Peter rose to his feet. "It wouldn't surprise me one bit if there were guards posted outside this door."

"I'll bet you a dollar you're free to leave." Jessica grinned, stacking the plates.

Peter shrugged his shoulders. "Perhaps this room. But what about the courtyard?" Without waiting for an answer, he opened the door to the outer courtyard, lit dimly by low banked fires. No one guarded the door. At the far end of the courtyard, Ahmed's Pushtuns squatted in a circle, each with his rifle at his side.

Sitting cross-legged on charpoys, Damon and Ahmed were talking to their host, Rashid Masjedhin. No one guarded the tall gates. No one paid attention to Peter as he stepped outside.

"Guess I owe you a dollar." Peter's tight face relaxed into a smile. "I'm going to turn in. See you in the morning."

Alone, Jessica sank into the chair. Her body felt like deadweight, but her mind was flashing images, recalling the scene at the camp, the theft of the truck.

Peter was dead wrong. He had not witnessed the fight. He had not seen Damon charging after the truck. Peter's suspicions were based on conjecture alone.

She had sat next to Damon. She had witnessed everything from beginning to end. At no time had she noticed anything but his concern and his desire to help. Everything was easily explained.

Except Damon's uncanny warning this morning.

Wearily, she got to her feet. The charpoy at the other end of the room had been made up with a soft cotton pad to cover its netting. The pillows looked fluffy and tempting, yet Jessica hesitated to lie down. She knew that the moment she slipped under the quilted blanket she'd be fast asleep, and she didn't want to waste this last night with Damon.

She reached for her shirt, gritty with dust. She'd had no opportunity to take a bath. A young boy had brought a bucket of water shortly after their late arrival and an invitation that she was welcome to use the washroom in the *hurja*, the women's courtyard, whenever she pleased. Hunger, and the knowledge that the lamb stew served would be inedible once the fat had congealed, had driven her to the supper table instead.

She slowly reached for her hair, taking the pins out. Raking her fingers through the dusty strands, she recalled the events after her meeting with Ahmed Khan.

At a snail's pace, they had towed the Ford up the steep winding road to Landi Kotal. The repair shop had already closed for the day and they waited almost an hour before one of Ahmed's Pushtuns returned with the mechanic. The discussion about the necessary repairs had been endless. When it was finished, Damon had driven at walking speed behind the small caravan of Ahmed's men. By the time they had reached Rashid Masjedhin's home, it had been close to midnight.

With a brief knock, Damon entered the room, carrying her overnight bag. "I thought you might need this," he said, placing the bag next to the door. His dark eyes searched her face, noticing the lines of exhaustion and the pallor beneath her tan. "Why aren't you resting?"

He wanted to cradle her in his arms until she relaxed. He understood what she was going through. He had lived with the warring sensations of a body's total exhaustion and the brain's feverish search for understanding and solutions for years.

"I was debating whether to take a bath, or drop on the bed filthy as I am." She grimaced. "You've made up my mind for me. Definitely a bath."

Damon had washed and changed into Afghan clothes, a wide collarless shirt, its long tail covering the broad folds of baggy pants. He had a disturbing bitterness in his eyes. "What is troubling you?" she asked softly.

"I'm worried about you." He silently crossed the space between them, his sandaled feet soundless on the hard-baked floor.

"Don't be," Jessica said firmly. "There's nothing wrong that a bath and a good night's sleep won't cure."

"Has Hallam been pestering you with his suspicions?" he asked roughly, searching her face.

"No."

The flat tone of her denial told him the truth. "I should've forbidden him to enter this room," Damon said harshly.

Jessica stuck out her chin. "Forbidden?" she asked coldly, staring at him as if seeing him for the first time. The flickering light heightened the contrasts of his harsh, proud features. The Afghan clothes stripped him of the veneer of their western culture. His full, clipped beard deepened the projection of power and danger.

This man was not the sophisticated and gentle Damon Noble she had met at Aunt Gloria's party. For the first time she understood why Peter was reluctant to trust him, why he was suspicious. She sighed in exasperation. "I'm the only one to *forbid* Peter this room. If I didn't know you, I wouldn't trust you, either. You'd scare me to death."

His eyes softened with amusement. "You're made of stronger stuff. Remember our first meeting? I felt the bruises on my shins for days." He reached for her hand, his thumb drawing circles into her palm. He kissed each finger. "I'll bet these can throw quite a punch."

Heat spread up her arm like wildfire. Her face began to glow under the almost palpable caress of his eyes. Swaying toward him, she said huskily, "You deserved everything you got, attacking me from behind like that."

"If I'd followed my baser instincts I would've carried you off caveman-style." He drew her closer, his arms tightening around her softness and warmth.

Jessica leaned her head against his broad chest, inhaling a seductive mixture of tangy soap and fresh mountain air. "I'd make a very disagreeable prisoner," she warned, drawing away from him. With each movement fine dust chafed the tender skin of her breasts and stomach. "I need to wash."

"This place has no running water," Damon warned. "All you can expect is a bowl of cold water and a hole in the ground."

Jessica grimaced. "And no electric light."

He smiled slowly. "It's not the Plaza Hotel, but it's the best we could find at such short notice."

Jessica shrugged her shoulders. "I'll manage. Considering the alternatives, this house is a haven of warmth and safety." She lifted the overnight bag to the empty charpoy and took out a change of clothing. "I won't be long," she promised.

Damon strode to the door opposite the one leading to the outer courtyard. The young boy who had served their meal rose from his squatting position. Damon talked to him softly, asking if the women of the household were asleep. Nodding his head, the boy explained swiftly that he was waiting to show the *hanum* to the washroom.

The *hurja* was bathed in darkness. Except for the closest male relatives, no man was allowed to enter this part of a Pushtun home where the women moved freely without their veils. Once a girl reached adulthood, only immediate family members were allowed to see her face. Friends, even the closest of them, saw the women only as veiled shadows.

Jessica peered curiously at the largest of the dark and silent buildings, the main house where Rashid Masjedhin lived with his wife. The other, smaller buildings most likely housed the families of his four sons.

The boy had picked up a lantern and now guided her silently along a high wall until he came to a narrow door. "This is the washroom," he said.

Jessica noticed the way he avoided looking into her face. To look upon another man's woman was an insult punishable by death. She reached for the lamp he held out to her, thanking him gently.

As Damon had warned her, the toilet was but a hole in the floor. The remainder of the room was equally primitive. Tubs of various sizes stood against one wall. Earthenware bowls had been stacked on a table standing near a wall from which sprouted a small hand pump. The pump gushed glacier-cold water when Jessica swung its handle. Swiftly she filled a bowl.

Wincing when the water hit her skin, she refilled the bowl twice to remove the dust. With her skin feeling tough and dry and her teeth chattering in the cool mountain night, she swiftly slipped into her clean clothes, grunting with relief at their residual warmth. Her hair still felt like a sandbox, gritty and coarse, but the air was too frigid and the towels too thin to wash it tonight. With strong strokes she tried to brush out the grit and dust. Soon the strands crackled with life. When she'd cleaned up the washroom, she opened the door.

Her young escort had waited for her patiently. Taking the lamp from her hand, he escorted her back through the quiet courtyard to her room and bid her good-night.

Damon had removed the stacked plates and leftovers. A steaming teapot, sugar and two cups sat on the table. He took one searching look at Jessica's pinched face and poured the strong hot brew into the metal mugs.

"I thought you might need warming up." He added a lump of brown sugar, stirred it and handed her the tea. "Their water supply comes from glaciers. It's pure but cold."

Jessica carefully cupped her drink, savoring the heat flowing into her frozen body. The tips of her fingers began to tingle. She sipped the sweet, cardamom-flavored liquid, feeling the warmth spread with each swallow.

"How do you know that the water is pure?" she teased Damon. "I've seen mountain streams with outhouses placed over them close to the glacier."

Damon raised one dark brow questioningly. "Here? I don't think so. Besides, this water has run over seven rocks. Mohammed said that makes it clean. Are you doubting the word of the prophet?"

Jessica nodded, saying lightly, "I guess I'm an infidel. I boil water for ten minutes and eat hot dogs and ham." Unconcerned, she finished her tea. Few germs could survive both freezing and boiling temperatures.

"Darling infidel," Damon said softly. He came up behind her, enveloping her in his arms. His hands ran up and down her body, spreading a different kind of heat.

With a sigh of pure bliss Jessica leaned against him, closing her eyes. Her skin tingled wherever he touched. With slow, sinuous movements she curved into his hands, seeking his touch until a moan broke from her lips.

"Warm enough?" His warm breath blew into her ear.

She nodded, shivers of desire puckering her skin. "Don't stop," she whispered, twisting around. She opened her eyes and stared straight into his. They were blazing with fire, flames leaping, reaching for her.

"I won't," he promised huskily, his hands sliding sensuously up and down her spine. "I've shared you all day with a thousand people and a world of threats. Tonight is ours."

"No wake-up calls at three in the morning?" Jessica kissed the corners of his mouth, teasing him with the tip of her tongue. She raised her arms, drawing his head down, closer, until her body arched into him.

"Not tonight," Damon agreed huskily, capturing her lips.

Smiling, Jessica closed her eyes, letting her senses take over. The softness of his hair was smooth beneath her palms. His mouth tasted of the cardamom-flavored tea. Her hands slid beneath his shirt.

Tension coiled beneath the tips of her fingers. Even under her soothing strokes the steel ropes did not soften. "Why are you so tense?" she murmured. "Did Ahmed Khan bring bad news?"

Damon made a sound of denial deep in his throat and shifted, pressing his body against hers. He was determined that nothing would come between them tonight. No bad news. Not even a breath of air.

But what about his conscience?

He could almost hear the jeering laughter of fate. Take her tonight and she'll hate you forever.

Shutting out the voices, he raked his fingers through her hair, enjoying the flow of silk on his hands. He whispered her name before claiming her lips. Gently, powerfully, he kissed her, drugging her senses until nothing existed but the heat of desire.

Jessica wanted to stay there forever, with his mouth searing hers, his arms holding her. She wanted to forget about vague dangers and whispered threats. But with each kiss, with each caress, his tension flowed into her, until she began to tremble.

"You go to my head." He pushed her face into his shoulder, his fingers ruffling her hair. "You seep into my blood until nothing matters but my desire to love you."

Jessica froze at the rough, harsh sound of his voice. "Tonight, that's all that matters," she said fiercely.

The hold of his arms around her tightened. Moments later he expelled his breath. "Is it?" he asked softly into her hair, struggling with his conscience. Damn Ahmed. And damn the fates that played such cruel games with him.

"Yes," Jessica said firmly. "I wish you could talk to me." Her eyes were filled with unasked questions, fear lurking in their depths.

Damon stared at her, his eyes hard. He saw warmth and softness, her desire to share his troubles tonight. He was tempted to ease his burden.

His face became a mask. Not tonight. Not now. Tomorrow would be soon enough. For a moment he played with the thought that even tomorrow she need not find out. Who would tell her the truth? Not Ahmed, not his men. Hallam? He almost laughed at the thought. Only one outsider guessed at the truth. Henderson. But at this moment Henderson was no threat. Ahmed had made sure of that.

Abruptly he turned away. "Wrong time. Wrong place."

Jessica stared at his strong back, her eyes shimmering with tears. Had there ever been anything but wrong times and wrong places for them?

If Peter's car was repaired, she would leave tomorrow. Another parting, followed by more waiting for the right time and right place. Waiting for letters that never came.

"Is there a right time for us, Damon?" She flung the question at him. "A right place? What if September never comes?"

He smiled thinly at her. His eyes were dark and very intent. His voice was as clipped as hers. "September always comes. Time doesn't stand still."

"But sometimes, it comes too late."

"That's in the hands of fate."

"You decide your own fate," Jessica threw back at him. "You decided to follow me that day in May. You involved me in your life. Don't shut me out now." Would she ever be anything else to the men she loved but someone to play with then leave? Would she ever experience the partnership her parents had? Sharing the good times as well as the bad. Sharing life, not just a bed.

"When my husband died, I thought, this is it. No more loving. No more planning ahead. Just living from day to day, waiting until the pain would lessen. Finally it did. I was doing fine. I was content. Why did you come into my life and make me feel again?"

"Because I couldn't help it. Your warmth and laughter drew me like the evening follows the day." He smiled crookedly. "I've camped at many fires but none warmed me. None reached the cold deep within me. Your warmth and softness wraps around me on cold mountain nights, the embers still glowing in the darkness." He reached out and framed her face. "You're right, my love. I should've turned away. But I couldn't. I needed your warmth."

"And now you don't need it?" Jessica asked gently, responding to his need with all her womanly softness.

He bent his head and touched her lips. "I'll always need you. Too much to endanger the flame."

With a sigh of exasperation Jessica protested, "I don't need a keeper."

Damon wrapped his arms around her and drew her close, saying between kisses, "You need someone...to protect you...from your own...unselfishness."

Frowning, Jessica drew away. "No one takes advantage of me. I can be quite ruthless when I feel I'm being used."

Damon only smiled crookedly, brushing his beard across her lips. The short, soft bristles sensitized her mouth. Then his tongue softly traced her lips with tantalizing strokes. He touched the hollow beneath her cheekbones then gently blew into the shell of her ear.

Jessica's arms tightened around his neck at the stab of pleasure running through her. With a moan she arched against him, feeling the heat of his body under the thin clothes. Her hands slid into the opening of his shirt and moved over strong fluid muscles, her fingernails raking the curls on his chest.

Jessica closed her eyes against the overwhelming sensation. Suddenly she felt herself being lifted and carried the short distance to the charpoy. Gently he placed her there. Jessica could feel the strength of him sliding against her and she clung to his broad shoulders.

Damon sat down on the wooden frame, drawing her between his legs. He tilted his head and kissed her breasts. Through the material of her blouse Jessica could feel the sudden moist heat of his mouth.

"I've dreamed of making love to you, of touching you and caressing you until you cry, 'enough,'" Damon said hoarsely against her sensitized skin. His fingers opened the buttons of her shirt, peeling the material slowly away from her shoulders until it fell behind her. Her bra followed. His hands reached out to cup the smooth whiteness of her breasts, tracing the darker aureoles with his thumbs until they had hardened and stood up, begging for his touch.

His lips touched her, the sucking motion making desire flow hot through her. Jessica slid to her knees, leaning backward over his thigh and arm, holding on to his broad shoulders, trembling with desire.

"Enough," she cried, hurting with longings. "I can't bear the teasing anymore."

He laughed softly, his breath flowing over her like tiny butterfly touches. "Too soon, my love," his deep voice soothed her. But his hands went on touching her, driving her wild.

She gasped, fighting the desire flooding her, her fingers digging into strong shoulders to keep sensation from taking over. Somehow she had to hold on to her sanity. She opened her heavy lids.

His face was hard with restraint, the flickering light touching high cheekbones, straight drawn brows. The hollows were shadowed, dark as his beard. His eyes were black, twin flames of fierce desire burning in their depth.

Her hands slid under his shirt. Her fingers moved up and down his back, delighting in his response. Slowly she straightened, sitting on his knee to raise the shirt over his back. Lifting it to eye level, she blinded him for a moment. Jessica bent and gently bit his neck.

"Vixen," he growled, his hands tightening around her waist. "Just wait. In a few minutes I'll make a meal out of you."

She tightened the material over his eyes. "In that case I'll keep you blinded."

"Blind or not, I'll find you, wherever you are." His deep voice was raw with emotions. Jessica shivered under the threat.

He raised his arms and shrugged off the shirt. Moments later he lifted Jessica and gently laid her on the bed. Then he straightened, loosening the tie of his wide baggy trousers.

Jessica watched the material slide to the floor, catching her breath when he stood before her in his naked splendor. She watched the oil lamp's flickering shadows dance over sculpted muscles. Tall and powerful, he was her warrior king.

As he reached for Jessica, the light flickered one more time. Then the room was plunged into darkness. Jessica felt the rough touch of his hands slide over her skin. He cov-

ered her with smooth movements, finding her mouth with
unerring accuracy. Her lips parted, drawing him into her.

Damon wrapped his arms around her soft warmth, never
breaking the kiss while his hand unsnapped her waistband
and slid down the zipper of her jeans.

For the last time he battled with his conscience and his
need. But Jessica was his weakness. He'd known that from
the moment they'd met. He had fought against that weakness. For her sake, not for his.

He groaned at the thought of leaving her now. Involuntarily his hold tightened around her waist. With hands, hard
yet gentle, he stroked the jeans from her hips. What difference would it make if he left her now? Would she feel less
pain? Would she remember his noble gesture and understand why he had left her tonight?

No.

Nothing he did now would lessen the sense of betrayal she
would feel if she found out the truth. Leaving her now
would only fill her with bewilderment and rejection. Unless
he explained himself.

And that was the one thing he could not do. Silently he
jeered himself. He'd give his right hand to spare her pain.
But nothing could stop the wheel fate had spun into motion eleven years ago. Would he ever be free of the past?

The only thing left to him was hope.

And the rest of this night.

"I adore you." His lips moved down her neck to her
breast, tantalizing her with his tongue, stroking the sensitive skin, her hard nipples begging for his lips. He caressed
them with an intensity that sent stabs of hot pleasure
shooting through her.

"Damon." Her voice was husky as she arched her body,
her flesh quivering with desire. Her arms reached for him,
sliding over his strong back, raking her nails gently over his
skin.

She stared into the darkness, wishing she could see him.
But there was nothing. No moon. No stars. Not even the
outline of his face. Only the black void of night.

Then she felt him slide from her grasp, stroking the sensitive skin of her stomach with the sable brush of his beard. With a moan Jessica arched into the sensation, once again reaching for him. But he moved further down, out of her reach.

"Stop." She cried out hoarsely, feeling herself drowning as he touched the warm center of her. "Enough."

"Soon." His voice soothed her once again. But his tongue continued its torture. He sensed the resistance in her, as if she were afraid to give herself completely. "Let go, love," he groaned hoarsely. "Come to me."

Jessica tossed her head from side to side in wild abandon. Her hands reached for him and drew his head closer to her, her lips moaning his name. Shifting, Damon entered her smoothly, surging deeper than before as if he wanted to possess her, touch every part of her.

Gasping, she moved with him, pleasure expanding with every movement of his body until she cried out and came apart in his arms. Damon filled her, covered her. Only he existed. She cried out his name.

Damon smiled in the darkness. A tight smile, hard with the intensity of his feelings. Suddenly he shuddered. With a hoarse sound, he let go of control, merging with her liquid fire.

For a long time after, the ragged sound of their breathing filled the air. Damon held Jessica tightly, feeling the tremors subside slowly. He cradled her head in his shoulder, stroking her hair until the shudders had passed.

"I wish we had a light," Jessica spoke softly. She was turned into him, her arm across his chest, and one leg thrown over his. With satisfaction she noticed that the disturbing tension she'd felt earlier was gone. Damon lay as relaxed in her arms as she in his.

"Are you afraid of the dark?" His arm tightened around her, his free hand stroking the wild mane from her forehead.

Jessica shook her head. With Damon holding her the darkness held no threats. "No. I just like to look at you."

"Why? I haven't changed. I'm the same man you spent all day with." He kissed her lightly. "Go to sleep. You've had a hard day."

Same man, but different faces. Drowsily she wondered why she had been afraid to let go, to give herself to him, body and soul. Jessica smiled sleepily. She had always known that she had nothing to fear from him. His concern wrapped around her like a warm blanket on a cold winter night. "I love you," she whispered before sleep claimed her.

Damon lowered the lids over burning eyes, feeling no triumph. The whispered words he had waited to hear echoed, mocking him. He lay awake, listening to Jessica's breathing, holding on to his dream. He did not want to miss a moment of her warmth. He kissed her gently.

Throughout the night, he tried to think of a way that would change the course of events. But the wheels had been set into motion too long ago for him to slow them down.

Chapter 11

Just before dawn Damon heard a soft knock on the door. For a moment he tried to ignore the intrusion. He wasn't yet ready to leave the warmth of Jessica's body. He wanted to be beside her when she opened her eyes.

But the knocking continued, softly, insistently. With a sigh he stirred. He moved carefully, sliding smoothly from the bed and shivering when the cool morning air hit his warm skin.

He reached for his wrinkled clothes. He shook them until he was certain that neither scorpion nor snake had hidden in their folds. Then he dressed swiftly and opened the door.

Ahmed Khan leaned against the wall, his arm raised to knock once again. At Damon's appearance, he dropped his hand, waiting until his friend had almost closed the door behind him.

"Good morning, my friend." His blue eyes searched Damon's face. Seeing the softness in the harsh features, he smiled, his scar curving wickedly into his bushy beard. "I'm sorry I had to tear you from the soft arms of your woman, but I wanted a few private words with you before everyone stirred."

He turned and let his eyes run over the courtyard, crowded with charpoys and men wrapped in blankets sleeping on the ground.

"Good morning." Instantly alert, Damon followed Ahmed's glance. "Your speech gets more flowery every time we meet," he said mockingly.

Ahmed studied his friend with searching eyes. It wasn't like Damon to be disgruntled in the morning. "You didn't sleep."

"No."

"I wish there was something I could do." Ahmed shrugged his shoulders. "Have you come up with anything?"

Damon shook his head.

The stars were already fading in the sky, yet none of the sleeping men stirred. Lined up in rows, the head of each Pushtun pointed the same way. Southwest, toward Mecca. When the pink of Aurora touched the mountaintops, the men would rise. They didn't need alarm clocks. They always woke with the rising sun to bow in prayer toward Mecca. Their faith was the center of their lives and the core of the tribal law.

"Where's Hallam?" One charpoy was empty. Damon knew it wasn't Ahmed's because the khan preferred to sleep surrounded by his men on the ground.

"He's outside the walls. Hallam, too, seems to suffer from insomnia," Ahmed Khan said dryly. "Or perhaps his sleep was disturbed by the green-eyed monster."

A horse whinnied softly. Other animals behind the wall stirred restlessly. Muffled curses broke the silence. The big gate creaked open. Peter tumbled into the courtyard, as if he'd been propelled into it. The gate groaned shut behind him. For a moment he stood, as if deciding what to do. Then he silently crossed the few steps to his bed and lay down, wrapping the sheet tightly around him.

"We're leaving soon," Ahmed said, smiling slightly. "Everything is ready to go."

"I'm not going with you," Damon answered. Yesterday evening the two had agreed to send an armed guard with Jessica and Hallam down the Khyber Pass. But during the night Damon's plans had changed.

Gravely, Ahmed looked at him. "I don't think that's wise. Not that I blame you for wanting to stay. In your position, I, too, would prefer to spend the day with my woman. But it isn't safe to linger. The events of last night drew attention to us. Now everyone in this town knows we are staying at Rashid's home." He paused for a moment, willing Damon to change his mind.

"Will Rashid suffer if I stay another day?" Damon asked.

"No. Rashid is safe. I wouldn't have asked for his hospitality if I had thought otherwise."

"Then I'll stay," Damon said firmly.

Once more Ahmed tried to convince his friend to leave. "Henderson is not far behind us. Last night he rented a car in Peshawar. He will be in Landi Kotal before the noon prayer."

"All the more reason to stay." Damon's voice was even, despite the bad news. He had hoped to delay the man for at least one more day. "I'm sure he was behind the attempt to kidnap Jessica yesterday. I won't give him another chance to lay his hands on her."

Ahmed's face was impassive. He, too, suspected Henderson behind that move. "I understand. Better than most. Farah's death stains his hands. I wish I could stay and take revenge now for my wife's suffering but the caravan must move out this morning. I don't want unpleasant surprises on the way. I can only pray that the day of *pushtunwali* will come soon."

Again, Damon looked at the sky. The stars were fading and a shimmer of pink heralded their imminent departure. "I will follow you tomorrow." He thought of Jessica lying asleep in the charpoy behind him. He couldn't leave her, vulnerable and unprotected. He would see her safely to Peshawar before he returned to the mountains.

With the impassivity of his race, Ahmed accepted the decision. "I will leave Gorband and Ismail behind to guide you through the mountains to us. May Allah be with you, Damon."

Damon looked at his friend, his lips curving into a smile. "May Allah guide you safely."

"Perhaps Allah will enlighten me how infidels, even those as strong and wise as you, my friend, can become weak-kneed and softheaded over a woman." He bowed with a flourish. "Take care."

Damon chuckled. "Someday you'll meet a woman who will turn your head."

"I hope I am forever safe from that fate. I am told that protection lies in numbers," Ahmed answered lightly. "Perhaps I should take four wives. A wise man divides his attention equally between his women. Thus is he saved from pitfalls. I am striving to be very wise."

"You'll be wise and poor," Damon pointed out dryly. "How many goats does a wife cost these days? And how many camels and horses?"

Ahmed laughed softly. "You have a point. No wife is cheaper than four." Then his face became serious. "My love for Farah was warm and gentle. With her death something died within me. I have nothing to offer a woman but the harshness of these mountains and my thirst for revenge." He embraced Damon. "The men are stirring. Go back to your bed. I will see you in a few days."

Damon watched him as he moved between the charpoys, a tall, lonely man in black robes. The gate creaked open and shut, and then he was gone. As Damon turned away, a movement caught his eyes. Peter Hallam had raised his head.

Frowning, Damon watched Hallam get to his feet. Should he stop him? He shrugged his shoulders. There was no need. Ahmed would hear the protesting sound of rusty hinges should the man follow him.

The room was warm and dark as he closed the door behind him. One lone window, placed near the ceiling and small to ensure privacy, shed rapidly brightening daylight. Silently he walked to the bed.

Frowning, Jessica watched Damon's approach. She had been awake since he had left her side. Through the half-shut door she had listened to the conversation between the two friends. She bit her lip, trying to control the emotions churning within. Was Henderson responsible for yesterday's kidnapping attempt? He'd been at the camp. Despite her dislike of the man, she found it difficult to believe that the colonel would risk his career to even his score with Damon. His career would be ruined once he released her. If he released her. With a shiver she remembered Ahmed Khan's accusation. How had Henderson been responsible for Farah's death?

Was Henderson also behind the theft of the crates?

Damon was in the middle of all the violence. Not to observe but to trap the man.

Blood, hate, revenge.

Damon's world. It was a world totally alien to her. All her life she had worked for peace. She knew that she could never share his life-style.

Damon had removed his shirt and trousers and walked to the bed.

"What are you doing?"

"Coming back to bed," he said quietly, lifting the cover. Before Jessica could protest, he lay down. His arms reached for her, pulling her on top of him.

"You're cold," Jessica said. His skin felt like ice.

"Warm me," Damon whispered into her ear, his hands moving with long, caressing strokes down her back. His hands were very sure, very gentle. "Do you know what time it is?"

Jessica shook her head. Her heart ached with pain, yet her body moved with a will of its own, responding to his touch.

"It's five o'clock in the morning. Not even the roosters are up." He framed her face with heart-stopping gentleness. "I promised you a whole night together."

One whole night. She wanted a whole life. "We have two hours left," she whispered. "Let's make the best of them."

She bent her head, her tongue tracing his mouth. She would tell him of her decision later. She could live in his world for one more day and give him the warmth he craved.

His lips opened to draw her within. His hands tightened around her face with possessive gentleness. She kissed him with a sweetness he had never known. As if it was the first kiss. Or the last one.

A hunger shot through him, tearing at his determination to treat her gently until he could feel only the deep, sharp pain of need. In one powerful movement he shifted, capturing her body with his weight.

Looking into Jessica's eyes, he saw they were troubled. He realized then that she must have heard all of the conversation with Ahmed. He sensed the fear, confusion and pain.

"Promise me you'll wait for me," he said, his voice gritty with emotion. "There are things I can't explain right now. But when this is all over I want the chance to show you that I'm not quite the savage you think me."

"I don't think you're a savage," Jessica protested. "But I can't live in your world. War and peace don't mix." And that would never change, no matter how long she waited for him. She looked at him, tears filling her eyes and pain stilling her breath.

"Don't cry," Damon said hoarsely, catching the falling tears with his tongue. "After this summer things will change."

With a twist of her head Jessica pressed her lips to his. She had known Damon such a short time, yet he had breached all her defenses. He made her laugh and he made her cry. He had frightened her and protected her. He was gentle, yet hard; dangerous, yet kind. Her lover, yet a stranger.

He had turned her well-ordered life upside down. He had shaken her out of the cocoon she'd wrapped around her like a second skin. Because of him she was truly alive again. She owed him something for that gift.

"I'll wait," she promised. Her arms tightened around his neck.

With a groan, Damon gathered her into his arms, repeating his promise without words.

Jessica shivered as his hard body settled over her. Gone was the gentleness. As if wanting to place his brand all over her, his mouth blazed over her skin, his beard fanning the fire. Her fingernails moved up and down the strong cords of his back, raking his shoulders until she felt him shudder in response. Wonder changed to fierce exultation as she realized her power to stir this hard, tough man. Her caresses grew more daring, more stimulating, until he groaned against her flesh. His mouth moved lower. Her nipples were soon standing hard and erect.

"Demon," she gasped as the burning sensation spread through her body. She arched under him, increasing the pressure of his need.

"Red-haired witch," he growled deep in his throat. His lips leisurely explored her stomach, his tongue spreading fire, fanning the heat over every inch of her skin until she felt like a furnace on the point of exploding. Between moans she begged him to give her release, but Damon prolonged the heavenly torture with his mouth, his hands and his body. Jessica felt her body tighten like a bowstring, but soon he damped the fire. Her body was responding with a will of its own to his expert touch.

She heard his exultant laugh, then felt him filling her, moving deeply within her. Her legs tightened around him, wanting to increase and prolong the heat. Her lips feverishly tasted his skin as her breathing quickened.

"Easy, my love," Damon warned hoarsely, noticing her shallow gasps for air. "Slow the flames with a few deep breaths."

She tossed her head from side to side. "But I don't want to lose the heat."

"You won't," he promised, setting a slow rhythm, refusing to give in to her urgings to quicken the pace. But her passionate response sorely tried his control. The heat inside her reached a level almost unbearable before the fire exploded into a million sparks. "Hold me," she cried out hoarsely.

With a final thrust, Damon stiffened. His powerful arms reached for her, holding her, cherishing her. Then, rolling over until she was lying on top of him, he held her until the tension flowed from her body, leaving her drained and quiescent.

Watching the deepening rise and fall of her chest, he hugged her close. For long minutes he held her, stroking her thick mane, running his hands over her smooth firm body, so small against his great size.

"Did I ever say you were out of condition?" His deep voice held a hint of laughter. "I take it back now, my love."

"I think I pointed out to you that your legs are twice as long as mine. But you didn't believe me." She laughed softly, rubbing her cheek against the curls on his chest. She was too exhausted to even raise her head.

"I believe you now. If you were any fitter, I might not survive the next time we make love. Or did you use a witch's magic?"

"If I did, you drained me of all my power. I don't think I can move." She tried to shift her legs. They felt too heavy to be moved. What was happening to her? She felt drugged. She had never abandoned herself to passion as she had with him. Damon had thrown her off balance until she didn't recognize herself anymore.

"Sometimes I think I must be dreaming all this." Her fingers gently moved the dark curls on his chest. "But if it is a dream I don't ever want to wake up."

Damon laughed softly. "It's no dream. You hit me like a blow torch." He lifted his head, gently kissing her mouth.

Jessica responded, desire quickening once again. "Damon," she whispered, inviting him closer to her fire.

"We can't," Damon protested hoarsely, trying to hold onto reason. "You're not strong enough."

"I feel strong enough to move mountains," Jessica assured him.

"I don't know about mountains." Damon smiled tenderly. "But you certainly move me." He loved her then, slowly, sweetly, asking little of her, but giving all of himself.

They dozed, wrapped in each other's arms, until the rooster crowed. Soon low-voiced prayers drifted into the room. Then children's voices mingled with the Pushtuns' deeper ones. Goodbyes were shouted. The thunder of hooves rent the air as Ahmed Khan's caravan moved out.

"How will you follow Ahmed?" Jessica asked when silence once again filled the room. "Did he leave you a camel?"

Grinning, Damon shook his head. "Never again. Ahmed brought me one of his stallions." He groaned. "I haven't ridden in months. Just as well that Ahmed went ahead. I don't think I could've kept up the bruising pace he sets."

"With a caravan?" Jessica raised her eyes questioningly. "What does he carry?"

Damon cursed silently. Jessica was by far too perceptive. "Supplies."

Jessica didn't need to ask what kind of supplies the khan carried. She had a fair idea. Guns and ammunition. Explosives that could light the sky like fireworks on the Fourth of July. And death.

"What would you like to do today?" Damon could feel the tension flow through her. "We have a few hours before Hallam's car will be ready."

Jessica knew he was changing the subject, drawing her thoughts away from unpleasantness. "I still need to buy some rugs. Could we go to the bazaars here and see what they have to offer? Or will that be too dangerous?"

Damon shrugged his shoulders. "Dangerous? Not if we only look for carpets." He looked at her steadily. "No searching for the crates," he warned. "The town is littered with drug dealers and gun runners. Men here answer questions only one way. With their guns."

"I'm not going to stop every man we meet and interrogate him," Jessica said calmly. There were other ways of finding out if the supplies were being sold in the bazaars although she didn't know what she would do if she stumbled onto them. Could she notify the authorities? Was there a government station in Landi Kotal? It was more than likely, so close to the Afghan border.

"What about Henderson?" Jessica asked quietly, knowing that the colonel posed the biggest threat.

Damon looked briefly surprised that she knew that information. But he only shrugged his shoulders and said, "Like Ahmed said, he won't be here until noon."

Jessica tossed her head. "How do you know? He may already be in Landi Kotal. If Henderson is ruthless enough to have killed Farah and have me kidnapped, one guard at Fort Jamrud is not going to stop him."

Damon's face hardened. "The moment Henderson sets foot in this town, I'll know," he said firmly.

Muttering an oath, Jessica got swiftly to her feet. "I'm getting tired of your puzzles." She picked up her clothes and slipped into them before facing him. "I'm tired of half-truths and half-lies. I want hard, cold facts, all of them. Like, why does Ahmed believe that Henderson killed his wife? And why should the colonel risk his career trying to abduct me?"

Damon stared at her in grim silence.

"Damn you, answer!" Jessica cried, frustration and anger shaking her voice. "If you didn't want me to know, why didn't you close the door?"

Damon rolled onto his side, propping his head on his elbow, his eyes narrowed dangerously. But still he said nothing.

"Okay, then. What role do I play in this game?" Jessica challenged his silence. "I believe I at least have a right to know how, and why, I got involved in this mess."

"Your role is that of an innocent bystander. And I plan to keep it that way," Damon said harshly.

Furious, Jessica spun around and picked up her bag. "I'm going to wash," she said between clenched teeth. "This isn't the end of our conversation," she warned with her hand on the door latch.

Coolly, Damon cocked one brow. "I didn't think so," he said calmly, covering himself.

Warm sunshine greeted her as she entered the *hurja*. Closing the door, she took a deep breath, trying to control her lingering anger. Curiously, she looked around. She'd

never been in a typical Pushtun home before. Customs in
Islamabad were more relaxed than up here in the mountains where strict purdah still prevailed.

Jessica noticed that everything was scrupulously clean.
The hard ground had been washed down and swept. The
charpoys, used during the night, now stood against one
whitewashed wall. The sheets, pads and blankets were airing on a clothesline. Several children were playing catch,
hiding behind the covers and linens, tossing them high as
they charged between and beneath them. Their yells and
laughter made her smile.

"*Hubasti, hanum* sahib." Jessica turned her head toward the sound. A slim young woman stood before her.
Large brown eyes studied her with a mixture of shyness and
curiosity, one hand drawing a long white scarf over the
straight blue-black hair. A flowery, long-sleeved tunic covered her modestly. Bare feet peered from beneath the hem
of wide, startlingly white pants.

Gravely, Jessica returned the greeting. This beautiful girl
must be the wife of one of Rashid's sons.

Within moments three more women had joined them, all
young, like the first one. The children stopped playing and
ran toward them, swelling the crowd. At the door to the
main house, yet another woman appeared. With graying
hair and a lined face, unhurried and stately, she crossed the
courtyard.

The younger women and children respectfully parted,
then closed around the mistress of the house. "Welcome to
my home," Zaira Masjedhin said, bowing her head regally.
"I am sorry that I did not greet you last night," she said in
heavily accented English.

"It is I who must ask your forgiveness for invading your
home at such late hour," Jessica replied in Pushtu, bowing
her head with equal formality. "Thank you for opening
your home to strangers."

"You speak our language well," Zaira said, her face relaxing with a mixture of approval and delight. "I am glad.
It has been a long time since I spoke English. I have lost

much of my ability. Where did you learn to speak Pushtu so well?''

"As a child I lived in Kabul," Jessica explained. By Pushtun standards she already would have been considered an adult at fourteen, almost old enough to be married. She felt certain that Zaira's daughters-in-law were younger than she herself. Despite the wrinkles and gray hair, Zaira was probably only in her mid-forties.

"My husband's brother lives in Kabul," Zaira said. "It is not a good place to live right now."

Jessica agreed with her. Then she asked if she might use the washroom.

"Of course, *hanum* sahib." Zaira walked her to the door of the room, the family following them.

"My name is Jessica."

She smiled. "And I am called Zaira. Would you honor us with your presence for the first meal of the day?"

Jessica accepted the invitation with a smile. She would have preferred to share her breakfast with Damon, but she guessed that Damon and Peter would be entertained by their host in the outer courtyard.

When she joined the women in the sunshine a little later, a long table had been set close to the main house. The meal was simple. Bread, butter and honey. Cheese, grapes and tea. The bread had been freshly baked. It was still warm and crisp. The flat, twenty-inch pieces were ruffled and slightly curved. Earlier, Jessica had seen the fresh dough spread onto cylindrical clay forms that were then placed into the oven. The ruffled surface kept the dough from falling off.

The grapes were sweet and huge. Some of the single berries were as large as her thumb. The climate in the mountain valleys was perfect, ensuring plentiful, superior crops. Wines made from these crops might have surpassed anything else produced in the world. But since Muslims didn't drink spirits, whatever fruit wasn't eaten or dried to raisins rotted away.

Little by little the younger women lost some of their shyness. They smiled and giggled, offering Jessica more food, asking her questions about the United States.

During their meal the children played at the far end of the courtyard. When the adults finished eating, Zaira called them to the table, and they came running, reaching for the bread and fruit with dirty little hands hastily wiped off on their clothes. One of the girls snuggled up to Zaira and whispered something into her ear. The woman turned to Jessica, her dark eyes laughing. "Afram, my granddaughter, asks if she may touch your hair. She also wants to know how often you use the henna. She says that the beard of her uncle—my brother—never looks so good. He uses the henna to ward off evil."

Smiling at the little girl, Jessica explained, "I don't use henna. Allah gave me this color. And, yes, you may touch my hair."

Within moments not only Zaira's little granddaughter, but the other children surrounded her as well, their fingers curiously gentle as they touched her hair. Jessica ruefully suffered their explorations, and the awe and wonder in their high-pitched voices brought a grin to her face. Nevertheless she was relieved when Zaira finally called a halt.

"You are very kind, Jessica *hanum*." Zaira smiled with gratitude. "Thank you for being so patient with the little ones. Do you have children of your own?"

Jessica shook her head. "My husband died soon after we were married."

"The friend of Ahmed Khan is not your husband?" Zaira asked with a mixture of puzzlement and sudden reserve.

"Damon sahib is a friend of my family," Jessica explained, feeling slightly uncomfortable. How could she explain to a woman living in purdah that morality in the western world was very relaxed compared to the stringent rules that governed her life? "My family's friend watched over me last night."

After a moment of indecision, Zaira accepted the explanation, her face brightening once again. "My husband said that you were very tired when you arrived. Are you feeling better today?"

Jessica slowly exhaled her breath. She didn't want to see the friendly face tighten with disapproval. "The trip from

Islamabad was long and dusty. But after a night spent on your comfortable charpoy, I feel fine. You have a beautiful home.''

"Allah has been kind to me. I am very fortunate," Zaira agreed. "And it is a pleasure to welcome you to my house. I hope you will stay with us as long as it pleases you."

"Thank you. I would love to stay," Jessica said gently. "But as soon as the car is repaired we have to leave. The man promised to fix it by noon."

"Insh'Allah." Zaira smiled doubtfully. "Today is our holy day and few men are willing to work. I would be delighted if you honored my home with your presence for another night. Would you like to see my house?"

Jessica was aware of the kindness Zaira showed her. "The honor is mine. I would love to see the rest of your home."

She accompanied Zaira through immaculately kept rooms, a living room, a bedroom and a storage cubbyhole. Brightly colored woven rugs, *kelims*, covered the floors. In the bedroom the whitewashed walls were bare. The few possessions were stored in two large chests at the foot of a wide charpoy.

The living room, Zaira explained, served as the center of family life during the cold winter months. When snow covered the ground they would eat grouped around the large *sandali*.

Jessica looked around the large pleasant room. Colored cushions were placed against one wall. Two intricately etched brass trays on plain wooden stands served as tables. Another chest stood against a wall.

A big pottery vase drew Jessica's attention, its black design over a deep turquoise-blue background very familiar to her. Her mother owned several bowls made in Istalif, the summer resort of the wealthy, an hour's drive outside of Kabul. She was careful though, not to voice her pleasure out loud. Zaira would have given her the vase she obviously valued highly. The law of hospitality demanded such sacrifices and rejecting the present would have been an insult. Jessica kept her admiration to herself.

"If you can spare the time, I would like to show you around the other buildings," Zaira offered. Nodding, Jessica followed her outside. The place was built like a fortress. Along one high wall surrounding the property were the rooms her four sons and their families occupied. Several storage rooms stretched along another wall. Farthest away from the living quarters was a chicken coop housing at least ten hens and a rooster. The large kitchen was next to the washroom.

"The stables for the animals are in the outer courtyard," Zaira explained proudly. "My husband is the biggest landowner in the village."

"You have a beautiful home," Jessica commented. Even with no electricity or running water, everything was stark and clean. The women worked hard with century-old tools. Yet, as they wandered from place to place, laughter followed them everywhere.

Despite the restrictions of purdah, despite the lack of modern conveniences, they were happy. They seemed to have so little freedom compared to American women and so few luxuries. But in the turmoil of world change they lived in confidence, free of responsibilities outside the home, secure in their faith that their way was the correct way to live. Their lives had a measure of permanence and security, Jessica reflected, that her own life had always lacked.

Before returning to her room, Jessica asked Zaira information about the bazaars.

"You will have to ask my husband," the Pushtun woman answered, shaking her head. "We women are not allowed to go shopping in Landi Kotal."

"Not even with the protection of the *chadris*?"

Zaira smiled. "A good wife does not talk to strangers even when covered by the *chadris*."

"Then how do you buy shoes?"

"My husband takes the size of my foot on a sheet of paper. Then he buys the slippers. He is generous and buys good shoes, but," she sighed, "sometimes I wish for some pretty ones, like the ones my daughter wears. My daughter works in Peshawar as an *amshida*—a nurse."

Jessica was startled at the revelation. Since no one had mentioned a daughter, she had assumed that Zaira had only sons. She had forgotten that once a daughter reached maturity, her name was mentioned only among family members and here in the *hurja*.

"Is your daughter married?" Jessica asked.

Zaira nodded, a proud look on her face. "She studied in Paris. She went as a companion for her cousin, Farah. There she met Muir Osman, Farah's brother. He is now a surgeon at the Afghan Hospital in Peshawar."

"Then you come from the same tribe as Farah?"

"Yes." There was sadness in the Pushtun woman's eyes. "Poor Farah. She was a lovely woman, so sweet and gentle. It is two years since her death, but Ahmed Khan still mourns for her." Then she shrugged her shoulders. "It was Allah's will. While Farah was alive, the khan would not leave her to lead the Holy Warriors in their fight for freedom."

"But Ahmed Khan is a physician," Jessica protested weakly. "Why did anyone expect him to fight?"

"The prince is a good healer," Zaira agreed. "He saved my oldest grandson's life last year. But his birth chose him to be our khan, our leader. Our tribes look to him for guidance." She paused and then continued with a sigh. "Every doctor here has to be a warrior, too. The infidels hunt especially for them. Without their knowledge and medicines, many more of our men and children would die. And the more men who die in sickness, the fewer who can fight the holy war. For the last two years the khan and his men have been living like dogs in caves. I beg the prophet with each prayer that the time will come soon when all our men can walk the land with their heads held high."

"In our faith, we light candles when we pray," Jessica said softly.

Zaira's eyes sharpened with interest. "It is a good custom, *hanum* sahib. Light to brighten the darkness of despair."

"When I return home, I will burn a candle every night and pray," Jessica promised her solemnly.

"You are a good woman, *hanum* sahib. May Allah bless you for your kindness and give you a good husband and many sons."

Chapter 12

When Jessica finally returned to the guest room, Damon was waiting for her. He had washed and changed into a fresh set of clothes and sat writing at the table in black Afghan robes and black boots. Their high tops gleamed in the sunlight shining into the room through the open door.

"Did you enjoy yourself?" he asked.

"Zaira gave me the grand tour. This place is very impressive. What are you writing?" she asked tentatively, hoping he'd forgotten her anger earlier that morning.

Shrugging his wide shoulders, Damon got to his feet. "A short note to my parents. Would you mind mailing it for me when you get back to Islamabad?"

"Of course not," Jessica assured him.

"Just give me another few minutes," Damon said gratefully. "I'm almost finished." He sat back down and picked up his pen.

Jessica noticed that he had straightened out the room. The pad and cover had been rolled up and the sheets neatly folded. Her suitcase stood next to the door. It all looked rather desolate.

Had it been only an hour since she had lain in Damon's arms? So little time remained before they once again would have to part. Soon these moments spent together would be just memories, memories hoarded against lonely nights so she could reach into a full bag of stored remembrances to ward off the cold.

Was her life going to be a collection of one-night stands?

She wanted permanence. Not necessarily a house in the suburbs where she would stay and never move, she had inherited too much of her father's wanderlust for that, but she had also inherited some of her mother's longings.

Jessica dreamed of a home, a house somewhere in the world with Damon at her side. But she doubted that just visiting new places would ever be exciting enough for him. And boardroom battles were a tame substitute for the exciting life he now led. Could office politics ever wholly satisfy him?

She looked down at the dark head bent over his notebook, her throat tight with pain. She loved him enough to hide her agony for their few remaining hours here. But was her love strong enough to spend the rest of her life waiting for him to knock on her door for a few days of warmth? Only the future could tell.

"Where's Peter?" she asked when Damon stopped writing.

"He's taken the Mercedes to supervise the repairs to his car," Damon explained lightly, tearing the sheet out. Handing it to her, he said, "I wrote the address on top of the letter."

Jessica folded the sheet. "Is Peter all right?" Somehow Peter's behavior had seemed odd. It wasn't like him to go off and leave her without a word.

"He's fine." Damon got to his feet, and walked toward the door. "Since he took your car into Landi Kotal, we'll have to go on horseback." He looked at her questioningly. "How well do you ride?"

"I won't fall off," Jessica said lightly. During the cooler winter months, she had frequently ridden with Barbara and Peter. "Did Peter leave a message?"

Damon shook his head. "If you want to talk to him, we can ride by the repair shop."

"Thanks. But that won't be necessary." She didn't believe that Peter would be anywhere near the repair shop. At this moment he was most likely searching for the stolen supplies. Be careful, my friend, she prayed silently. Despite her trust in Peter's abilities, she worried about his safety. One wrong move and he might easily disappear without a trace. "I have to put up my hair," she said, hiding her fears.

With two long strides Damon crossed the distance between them. Tilting her head back, he stared down into her face. "Don't worry about Hallam. He can take care of himself."

"That's not what you said yesterday."

"I've changed my mind," Damon said coolly. "Or rather, Hallam changed it for me."

Jessica's face tightened. "What do you mean?"

"You know his job with you is a cover," Damon stated coolly. "I should've seen through his disguise from the beginning. He's not the first agent masquerading as low level embassy personnel." His eyes narrowed. "Why didn't you tell me?"

Jessica said firmly, "I don't know what you're talking about. Peter is my assistant."

Damon smiled at her crookedly. "Your reticence is very commendable, if slightly misplaced. Hallam carries a service revolver. Since when are such guns issued to diplomats?"

Jessica shrugged her shoulders. "Perhaps he borrowed it from a friend," she pointed out lightly.

"A service revolver?" Damon asked dryly. Then he bent his head and kissed her lightly. "Put your hair up and meet me outside."

Jessica watched him stride to the door and leap lightly down the two steps into the courtyard. She folded the letter and placed it with her passport. Then she put up her hair, covering it with a scarf.

A few minutes later she crossed the outer courtyard to the gate where Damon was waiting for her. Four horses stood saddled, munching on the sparse grass growing along the high wall. Two Pushtuns sat on the ground, talking, their ammunition belts glinting in the sun. Rifles lay close to their hands.

At Jessica and Damon's appearance they rose to their feet, their rifles in their hands. They greeted Damon, but ignored Jessica. To acknowledge her without an introduction would have been an insult to Damon.

"This is Gorband," Damon said, introducing the taller and older of the two men. "He speaks some English, which is one of the reasons Ahmed left him with me. Ismail is his nephew."

Jessica smiled at the men and greeted them in Pushtu.

Gorband grinned through his bushy, black beard. "The *hanum* speaks our language much better than you, Damon, sahib."

"True," Damon admitted lightly. "I'm still a little rusty. But I ride better. So watch out for the *hanum* and don't go too fast."

Jessica tilted her head and looked at him teasingly. "I may surprise you. I've ridden since I was a child."

"Want to race?" Damon's eyes danced wickedly, walking toward a sturdy-looking mare.

Jessica's glance shifted from the comfortable girth of the small horse to the tall, sleek stallion, grazing a few feet away. "Only if we switch horses."

Chuckling, Damon shook his head. "You wouldn't be able to control Sheitan. He is bred for *naiza bazi*."

"Really?" Jessica asked. "I've watched *buzkashi* in Kabul, but I've never seen *naiza bazi*. What happens in it?"

"The goal of the game is to beat the enemy by removing as many tent pegs in a camp as possible with a three-pronged lance," Damon explained. "It's even more dangerous than *buzkashi*"

Jessica shuddered. "At the *buzkashi* game, one man died." Turning, she stroked the mare's neck. "I think I prefer her to your stallion."

Slowly the crooked smile appeared once again. "I'm relieved. The mare's too small for me. I would have looked ridiculous with my feet trailing in the dust." With his hands around her waist, he lifted her into the saddle. "She's more your size."

With a smile curving her lips, Jessica watched Damon walk up to the stallion and gather his reins. He stroked the satiny dappled neck, his voice a gentle song. As he swung lightly into the saddle the stallion tossed his head, prancing and kicking up dust. Jessica watched him, admiring the elegant curve of his neck, admiring, too, Damon's easy seat and his gentle but firm hold. Then she saw the rifle and ammunition belt attached to the saddle, and her smile froze.

"I've never ridden with an armed escort before," she muttered.

Damon rode to her side, his mouth a straight, firm line. "You have a choice."

"Some choice. I've no intention of spending the morning behind walls."

"Then ignore the rifles," Damon advised softly. "They're a part of Pushtun life."

Silently, Jessica stared at him. Apparently rifles were a part not only of Pushtun life, but of Damon's, too. Would she ever be able to accept that fact?

"I'll try," she promised huskily.

A slow smile spread over Damon's face. "Let's go." He turned to Gorband and Ismail.

With a shrill cry, Gorband urged on his mount, digging in his heels. His nephew was right behind him. Jessica and Damon followed slowly.

Zaira's house stood on a rise at the end of the valley of Landi Kotal. The fortresslike home was surrounded by green fields of sugarcane and wheat. In the distance Jessica could make out the town, shimmering in the morning sun.

The trail leading to the village wound its way along the foot of the mountains. For a while she rode silently, her eyes sliding over giant boulders, deep crevices and sheer rockfaces reaching for the sky. Jessica tilted her head to the cloud-covered peaks. "It's beautiful," she whispered. "So harsh and majestic."

Damon smiled, his dark eyes caressing her face. He, too, had whispered when Ahmed had first introduced him to the mountains. He, too, had felt awe. "I thought you might enjoy the ride. Seeing the mountains from a car is like viewing the Grand Canyon from a helicopter. All you get is a glass bubble effect, no more exciting than looking at a picture."

"But it's certainly safer," Jessica pointed out dryly. "Not everyone can climb down the walls of the canyon or hire armed escorts."

"Would you climb down the cliffs of the canyon with me?"

"I would have ridden with you without escorts," Jessica answered his question simply.

Damon reached out and touched her cheek. "Alone, I might not be protection enough for you. You're very important to me, Jessica."

A sweet smile curved her lips. "You do have a way with words."

A little while later they passed two young children herding a flock of fat-tailed sheep. They waved and called, knowing no shyness of strangers. Damon and Jessica waved back.

"Does Ahmed Khan have any children?" she asked, turning to Damon.

"No." Damon's easy smile vanished abruptly. "Farah wanted children desperately. But even she agreed that times were too dangerous to raise a family. Ahmed's prominent position has always made him a prime target for assassination, although, before Farah's death, he played no major role in the resistance movement. He supported it only with advice, some funds and medical help."

"How did Farah die?" Jessica asked quietly.

"She killed herself."

"Dear God. No." Jessica's eyes widened with horror. "But, I don't understand. Why did Ahmed accuse Henderson?"

"Farah was raised in purdah. When she went to Paris to study nursing, she became used to the freedom of western women. After her marriage to Ahmed, she went with him, over his objections, everywhere, helping him. More than once Ahmed threatened to send her to the States. I can still hear her protest that she was perfectly safe, that men don't make war on women." His face hardened until it was a mask carved from rock. "Pushtuns don't. But others do. One night, when Ahmed had been called away, she went to help a wounded foreigner. That same man handed her over to the Russians, who put her in prison. Ahmed got her out a few months later, getting wounded in the attack on the prison. Farah nursed him until he was out of danger, then she took an overdose of sleeping pills. She had been made pregnant and couldn't live with the shame."

Jessica's face was frozen with shock. Her white lips barely moved when she whispered, "Poor Farah." No woman survived violation unscarred, but most learned to live with their private nightmares. Had Farah lived in the States, she, too, might have survived the ordeal.

"What would have happened to her if she hadn't committed suicide?" Jessica asked.

"Before the rescue, Ahmed had already made arrangements to send her to a sanitorium in Switzerland. She couldn't have stayed here in the mountains."

"Exile," Jessica said, her voice rough with frustrated anger. "Your friend, I assume, would have remained behind."

Damon stared at her broodingly. "Yes."

"Shamed, exiled and abandoned," Jessica hissed. "No wonder she killed herself."

Damon smiled tenderly. "If I had known you then, I would have suggested to Ahmed to send her to you." Then the smile vanished. "Despite his western education, Ahmed is Pushtun. He judges and is judged by tribal law. Farah was his property, therefore her shame was his. In Pushtun eyes he had lost his honor. He was judged a weakling because he had been unable to keep his wife in her proper place and protect her. In peace time, he, too, might have been forced to leave."

"But he is the khan," Jessica protested.

"Under *pushtunwali*, all men are equal," Damon pointed out softly. "No honorable man would follow a weakling, because then he would also lose face."

Which, Jessica thought, explained the khan's disappearance. He had been dead to his tribe until he had cleared his honor, fighting in the holy war, wreaking vengeance on his enemies.

For a time they rode quietly side by side, Jessica staring blindly ahead. A wave of sympathy washed over her for both Farah and Ahmed Khan, two people trapped by conscience and tradition.

As hate for the man who had delivered the Pushtun woman to the Russians curled in her stomach, she asked herself questions. What had happened to the man? Why had Damon broken the silence he had insisted on until now? And what was his purpose? She was sure his revelation had not been accidental. Damon rarely left anything to chance.

With painstaking thoroughness, she searched through the puzzle pieces, fitting them together one by one. Jessica stiffened as the last piece fell into place. Ahmed Khan held Henderson responsible for his wife's death. The colonel must have been the injured foreigner Farah had gone to help.

She turned her head and stared at Damon's sharp profile while her shocked mind tried to absorb yet another horror. Why would an American officer kidnap Ahmed's wife and hand her over to the Soviets?

It didn't make sense. Unless—she shook her head, unwilling to accept the logical conclusion—Colonel Henderson was a double agent.

"How long have you known?" she whispered.

"Known what?"

"That Henderson works for the Soviets."

"I've suspected it for eleven years," Damon said soberly. "Henderson is very clever. He's avoided trap after trap. So far we've always been one step behind. Farah might have been able to help us, but she died before she could testify against him."

"Who is us?" Jessica asked. But her question was drowned out by the stamping of hooves as Gorband came riding toward them.

"Sahib, we are close to town." He pointed at the nearby village.

Damon looked at Jessica's pale face. "Do you still want to visit the bazaars?" he asked.

Jessica's first impulse was to return to the house. She wanted answers to the many questions somersaulting in her head. But one look into Damon's hard face told her that the time for confidences was over. He had wanted to warn her, had wanted her to be aware of Henderson's divided loyalties. In that, he was successful.

"What else is there to do?" Jessica challenged grimly. "Who else knows about this?"

With a warning look, Damon swung out of the saddle. He reached for the ammunition belt and fastened it across his chest. From one of the saddlebags he took a long black shawl and a small skullcap.

Jessica watched him put the cap on top of his head. Its color was black, with a scroll of green and orange design. Gold threads had been woven into the orange, catching the light of the sun. With twists of head and arms, Damon skillfully wound the black shawl several times around the cap. He secured the end with a knot, a small piece fluttering at the back of his neck.

From his horse, Gorband eyed the turban critically. "Very good, sahib," he finally approved. "Not even the khan would find fault with you. If you don't talk too much, everyone will take you for one of us."

"That bad?" Damon cocked one brow, grinning. He turned to Jessica, "What do you think?"

Jessica stared at the transformation, her breath catching at the sight of him. The black turban rode low on his brows, throwing his harsh features into prominence. His eyes seemed darker than ever. The straight mouth seemed firmer above his jutting, bearded chin.

The third face. The thought flashed across her mind. Ruthless, harsh and frightening. Darkness was closing in.

With a shake of her head she tried to rid herself of the frightening thoughts. "I'll bet even your mother wouldn't recognize you now."

He changed subtly, always sensitive to her thoughts. His lean body stiffened, head poised. Dark eyes burned past her weak smile, reading her confusion and fear. "I'm still the same man," he said softly.

His deep voice brushed over her, a gentle breeze dispersing the threatening cloud. "You look like a Pushtun prince," she teased, swaying forward.

"He is the khan's brother," Gorband agreed.

Jessica drew back. She had completely forgotten the Pushtun's presence. "What does that mean?" she asked, turning to the Pushtun.

"Ahmed Khan loves him like a brother. He is one of us."

The words were so simple, but their meaning was disturbing. "One of us" meant the same friends and the same enemies. Sharing of shelter, possessions and ideals—and blood vengeance.

A chill crept over her.

Damon said briskly, "When we enter town, we'll leave the horses with Rashid's cousin. From his house it's only a small distance to the bazaars. No matter how thick the crowds, try to keep us in sight."

Jessica nodded, looking down at him. The sun reflected off the brass cartridges in his ammunition belt onto his harsh face. "Is the disguise necessary? I didn't know that a visit to the bazaars was so dangerous."

"It's just a precaution." He swung back into the saddle with easy grace, the gold in his cap glinting dangerously as he moved.

It was a precaution that served them well, Jessica admitted later. In the dark maze of crowded streets, men, women and children stopped and stared at her, but no one made a threatening move toward them. The mass of people parted respectfully wherever they went.

The bazaars were divided into sections. Staples like rice and grain, sugar and flour, raisins, nuts and tea were sold on one street. In the fruit and vegetable lane, Damon bought her a bouquet of flowers—zinnias, daisies, roses and carnations—shaped artistically into a large cone.

Her eyes bright with pleasure, Jessica thanked him. "They're beautiful."

She turned to Gorband, cradling the flowers against her. "Do Pushtuns court their woman with flowers?"

Gorband nodded. "When a Pushtun is interested in a girl, he sends flowers to the house. But only after the bride price has been agreed upon will he be allowed to talk to her."

"How does a man choose his bride if he cannot see or talk to her? I know that some marriages are arranged by relatives or for political reasons. But what about the others?"

Gorband's eyes twinkled. "A Pushtun, rich enough to marry, watches the young girls at play before they wear the *chadris*. Then, when the girl is grown, he talks to the father."

Jessica grinned at the deviousness of such action. "Is the girl allowed to say no?"

Gorband chuckled. "Yes, *hanum*. My daughter has refused three good men. The one she wants to marry is not rich enough yet. But the khan has promised to help."

"Your daughter is blessed to have such a considerate father," Jessica approved.

Gorband shook his head, smiling slightly. "An unwilling wife causes much misery. The three men who wanted to marry her are my friends. They do not deserve to suffer such a fate."

Jessica laughed softly, knowing that she was being teased. Like fathers the world over, Gorband obviously loved his child. "You are a wise man."

"Also a very troubled one," Gorband said. "My daughter's willfulness has given me many bad dreams."

"I think she has also given you much joy," Jessica said.

The Pushtun nodded, then looked past her to Damon. "Some day, Damon, sahib, you must bring the *hanum* to my home." Then he added firmly, "But not before my daughter is married. In her willfulness, she may admire your western ways and become discontent with our Pushtun ways."

Damon looked at Jessica, caressing her face. "Some day, when it is safe, the *hanum* will come with me."

As they rounded another corner, Jessica found herself in the street she had been looking for. The shops here sold cosmetics, drugs and perfumes. Small plastic bags of henna and kohl nestled among silver and gold glitter along with various herbs, vials of perfume, pink curlers and plastic combs. There was even a solitary, dented can of hairspray in one of the stalls.

Abruptly, Jessica stopped. "I need some hairspray."

Damon raised one brow in question. He knew she didn't use anything but shampoo. "Go ahead," he said, stopping some feet away from the stall.

Jessica stepped forward and picked up the can from the slanting board on which the wares had been arranged.

"How much?" she asked the merchant, holding up the can. The man was richly dressed. A vest embroidered with gold thread covered his Afghan clothes. From one of the pockets dangled a heavy gold watch chain. A *culla*, a cap of finest Persian lamb, sat rakishly on top of his head. Behind him, unmarked cardboard boxes rose from the floor to ceiling. Contraband, Jessica thought.

"Five dollars, *hanum*, sahib," he said swiftly, a gleam in his dark eyes.

Jessica was used to people stating their price in hard currencies like U.S. dollars and West German marks. "Three dollars," she countered easily.

"Four dollars. It is the only can in the bazaar."

"Three fifty," Jessica said firmly. When the merchant agreed swiftly, Jessica knew she had paid too much for the can. "Do you have any Band-Aids," she asked, searching in her purse for her billfold as if the Band-Aids were an afterthought.

While the merchant got to his feet and slowly went into the back of the room, Jessica examined the stacked boxes more thoroughly. She found some inscriptions. One read Fragile, another had a Russian label. She could feel Damon's eyes boring into her back, but refused to turn around to meet his disapproval. She wasn't asking suspicious questions. When the merchant returned, handing her a small box of British adhesive bandages, she was disappointed. It was contraband, the small white box was labeled for hospital use, but it was from a British shipment, not theirs.

At the next store she asked for aspirin. They were of German origin. The disinfectant she bought next was of French make. At the last stall she asked for Silvadene, a burn ointment. But the merchant shook his head in bewilderment. He had never heard of the cream.

With a sigh of exasperation, Jessica turned to Damon, who had followed her. "Nothing. Not one sign of the supplies."

Damon took the purchases from her, his face hard. "Let's go," he said, his voice tightly controlled. When they were some distance away from the shops, he said, "There hasn't been time for them to reach the bazaars. If they ever get here."

"But where else—?" Abruptly she stopped, searching his hard face. "Afghanistan," she answered her own question. "Why didn't I think of it before." A slow smile curved her lips. "Somehow I don't mind it so much now. If I knew that the supplies wouldn't be sold at exorbitant prices and instead were used to help people in need, I would let them steal more crates."

Damon slowly shook his head. "I think you actually mean that."

"Of course I do. Don't you see. It's the perfect solution. As long as congress is undecided about sending food and medical help to the Afghans, our hands are tied. But if crates simply disappeared—" She grinned.

"Thank God, you're returning to the States," Damon said roughly, shaking his head. "How would you distinguish between thieves and *mujahidins*? Or would you drive up the Khyber Pass and deliver the crates to the border yourself to make sure they got into the right hands?"

His sarcasm flowed right over her. "There are other ways," she pointed out gently.

"Not any you're going to get involved in," Damon said firmly, taking her arm and leading her away from the shops.

In a side street, he held up the supplies. "Do you really want these?"

"Maybe I should keep the aspirin," she said tartly.

Immediately his hard eyes softened. "Headache?"

"No. My arm hurts." She looked pointedly at the tight hold of his hand biting into the soft flesh of her upper arm. "I don't plan to run away."

With a rueful grin, Damon eased his grip. "Reflex. Sometimes, my love, you scare me with your impulsive actions."

Jessica wrinkled her nose. "It was just a thought. And you can let go of my arm. I promise I won't disappear."

"No more searching," Damon warned softly, slowly releasing her.

"All right," Jessica agreed.

Before they reached the carpet merchants, they passed stalls selling sweets. Jessica stopped and bought a bagful of sticky honey confections for the children. From a nearby bazaar, she bought scarves for Zaira and her daughters-in-law.

"I hope you remember that we came on horseback," Damon said, looking at the mounting purchases.

"You can give the Band-Aids away," Jessica said lightly. "They've served their purpose."

Damon promptly dropped the bag at a beggar's feet. "Carpets," he said pointedly.

Jessica's smile vanished. She had been enjoying this brief interlude of carefree shopping. Moving from stall to stall she could pretend that this was nothing but an ordinary shopping spree. Two lovers enjoying themselves, tasting Turkish honey and arguing about the color of silk scarves. By looking only at Damon's dark face, she could ignore the ammunition belt slung across his chest and the rifle in his hand. She could even disregard the silent watchful presence of the armed Pushtun guards.

She knew that once she had visited the rug dealers she and Damon would ride back to the house. End of pretense. In the privacy of their room, she would have to face the ugly reality of the colonel's betrayal.

With a sigh, she agreed. "Let's look at rugs."

The street of the carpet merchants was not far away. With a cry of delight, Jessica watched an old Pushtun unroll rug after rug. King Mauris. Saruyks. Prayer rugs. A profusion of jewel colors: royal purples, celestial blues, holy greens.

A large Saruyk carpet, with hexagonal designs the color of copper against a background of deep blue, caught her eye. From the silky luster of the wool, Jessica could tell that it was quite old. The many rows forming the border around the center design were intricately knotted.

"I've seldom seen anything more beautiful." Jessica looked at Damon, her eyes glowing with pleasure and excitement. "I wonder how much he wants for it."

"I don't see any blemishes. The color is clear, not mottled. No frayed edges. And still the original fringes. He probably wants an arm and a leg," Damon quipped.

"You're probably right." Jessica smiled ruefully. "But if he accepts a check I'm going to buy it." She reached for a corner, turning it over with an experienced flick of her hand to test the tightness of the knots. The edge held its position for a moment, then rolled smoothly back. The knots were very tight indeed.

"Turn it over," Jessica told the merchant.

"The *hanum* knows how to shop," the Pushtun chuckled softly. "This jewel is flawless. No holes. See for yourself." He turned the carpet.

On her hands and knees, Jessica examined every inch of it. Her fingers slid over the back with caressing hands. The knots were so small and tight that there was little difference between the right and wrong side except for the luster age had wrought.

"How much do you want for it?" she asked.

"Three thousand dollars," the Pushtun said promptly. "I am giving it to you because the *hanum* knows how to appreciate a piece like this."

"Two thousand," Jessica countered immediately, wondering how much the merchant had paid the poor Afghan refugee who had sold it to him. He'd probably offered no more than five hundred dollars, which was only a fraction of its worth.

"But *hanum*," the merchant wailed, "have you looked at the twenty-two stripes?"

Each stripe in the border increased a carpet's worth as the intricate design was more difficult to knot than the larger center.

"They are very good," Jessica agreed. "But the price is too high, even for a beautiful piece like this."

"Perhaps the *hanum* needs time to admire its beauty a little longer. I will bring some tea." Before Jessica could protest, he rose and went to the back of the store.

"It's worth every penny," Damon said when they were alone, his tanned hand stroking the velvety softness with sensuous delight.

"It is," Jessica agreed. "But if I accept his price now, will he sell it to me? He is planning at least an hour's worth of entertainment and may feel cheated if I agree too soon." It wouldn't be the first time a merchant refused a sale because his customer didn't have the time or the inclination to play the polite game. Especially when he knew that he could easily sell his wares to someone else.

She pointed at a King Mauri of very fine quality, exactly what her father was looking for. "That one's for Dad. And Aunt Gloria would love the small prayer rug."

Damon leaned against the wall, his arms folded across his chest, a small smile of amusement curving his lips. "And how are you going to get them back to the house?" he asked her softly.

"Sling a roll behind each saddle," Jessica said, smiling. "Or we could pass the repair shop and put them into the trunk of the Mercedes."

After the old merchant returned with tea in an old brass samovar nothing was said about carpets for quite some time. He directed most of his questions at Jessica. Where did she come from? How did she like to live in Pakistan? What was she doing here in Landi Kotal?

Jessica answered easily. Most of the questions she had been asked a thousand times before. "I am visiting the par-

ents of good friends here in Landi Kotal. And because I've
heard that you have the best carpets of anyone here.''

Once the conversation returned to business, they haggled
amiably. In the end Jessica bought all three rugs at a rea-
sonable price. When the matter of payment was discussed,
the merchant readily agreed to take her traveler's checks and
a personal one for the rest of the sum. Apparently, Jessica
had proven during their conversation that she was honest.

The mullah was calling for noon prayers as they left the
shop. Both Gorband and Ismail were kneeling with their
heads toward Mecca, bowing repeatedly. For a moment
Jessica wondered if Damon would join the Pushtuns to keep
up his disguise. He didn't. But Damon wasn't the only one
ignoring the mullah's call. A scribe, squatting in a nearby
doorway, kept on writing a letter for a customer. Across the
street two women still haggled with a vendor through the
thickness of the *chadris*.

Jessica guessed that most of them would pray later at a
more convenient time. Pushtuns were devout Muslims and
rarely missed the five prayers each day.

When Gorband rose to his feet, Damon asked him to get
some boys to carry the rugs for them. Within moments the
Pushtun returned with two ragged-looking youngsters.
Bowls, hanging by a strap from their hands, pronounced
them beggars. They were empty as yet, because the merchants did not give baksheesh until after they had made a
profit. Later in the afternoon the beggars would swarm
from store to store. Now they tried to earn a few coins by
carrying purchases for those who could afford to pay them.

At Rashid's cousin's house, they strapped the rugs behind the saddles. Within minutes, the town lay behind them.

Gorband and Ismail once again rode ahead. Jessica and
Damon followed more slowly through the haze of the noon
heat shrouding the valley. They didn't speak, both reluctant to break the companionable silence.

Only as the house came into view did Jessica realize that
Damon had not taken off his turban or his ammunition belt.

Chapter 13

After the hot, blinding sun, the room was blessedly cool and dark. Jessica put the flowers on the table and sank into the chair, stretching her legs. She had not realized just how tired she was until she had slid from the mare's back into Damon's arms.

Riding and walking in the high altitude had drained her of her strength. Or perhaps, she thought with a grin, it was the unusual and vigorous exercises she and Damon had indulged in that had tired her.

The smile vanished as quickly as it had appeared. Frowning, she stared through the open door into the outer courtyard where Damon was talking to Rashid and two of his sons.

Upon their arrival, the three men had drawn Damon into a shady spot, leaving Gorband and Ismail to carry her purchases into the room and tend the horses. Whatever they were discussing must be serious. Jessica could not hear their voices, but their vigorous gestures and the tense expressions on their faces spoke as loud as words. Something had happened. But what?

Jessica could think of several possibilities, all of them urgent and none of them pleasant.

Something could have happened to Peter. She knew he had not returned because her car was still missing. Or perhaps Colonel Henderson had been seen in Landi Kotal. The possibility worried her more than Peter's continued absence.

Wearily she got to her feet. She might as well wash and change into her last set of clean clothes instead of stacking worries as high as the surrounding mountains. She reached for her suitcase, lugged it across the room and lifted it to the charpoy.

Opening the zipper, she noticed that her hands were quite steady. Only yesterday she would have been shaking with fear at the dark cloud of danger gathering above them all. Now the threats did little more than tighten her stomach in knots.

People, she thought grimly, adapted quickly—and she was no exception. If she stayed any longer around guns and violence, she might pick up a rifle herself one day soon. She shuddered.

She took her clothes, the gifts she had bought and her purse, and marched from the room, slamming the door.

In the courtyard the women were preparing lunch. The aroma of freshly baked bread filled the air, mingling with the smoke of grilling kabob.

"I see the *hanum* has returned from the bazaars," Zaira called from the kitchen door, wiping perspiration from her face. "Was your trip successful?"

"Very successful." Jessica smiled. "The bazaars have many things for sale. I couldn't resist buying these scarves for you and your daughters-in-law."

Zaira's dark eyes lit with pleasure at the sight of the long pieces of silk. She wiped her hand on a rag wrapped around her waist, then touched the soft material with delight. "Thank you, *hanum*, for your kindness."

"The pleasure is mine," Jessica assured her. Handing her the bag with the honey candy, she said, "I hope the children will enjoy these."

Zaira opened the bag and smiled. "They will not eat them until after the meal," she said firmly. "Will you join us here? Or would you prefer to eat with your friend?"

Since Jessica believed that Damon would eat with the men, she said, "I will join you, if I may."

"We're honored." Zaira bowed. "And thank you for your gifts."

In honor of their guests, the women had prepared a delicious meal, Jessica's favorite. They served kabuli—rice cooked with raisins, carrots and piñon nuts—and kabob—skewered lamb meat marinated in garlic-flavored yogurt. Zaira smiled with approval as Jessica skillfully used pieces of freshly baked bread to scoop up the rice and slide the meat off the skewers.

"I have a spoon, if the *hanum* prefers."

Smiling, Jessica shook her head. She liked eating Afghan food Afghan style. When she rose from the table, stuffed like a goose, she went straight to her room, spread out the padding and stretched out on the charpoy.

She slept deeply, so deeply that she did not stir when Damon entered the room and shed his turban and ammunition belt. Laying them on the table, he closed the door before joining her.

He didn't touch her, didn't draw her close. In a few minutes he would have to rouse her. It was almost time to leave for Peshawar if they wanted to reach the town before dark. He had planned to leave an hour ago, but Hallam's absence had made their departure impossible.

Right after their meal, he had sent Gorband and Ismail to the repair shop to find out what was going on. They had returned a few minutes ago with the news that Hallam's car was ready. But Hallam was missing, as was the Mercedes. The news had not surprised him, only confirmed his suspicions.

A grim smile twisted his lips. Hallam had outsmarted him. The man's foolish behavior had been as much a disguise as his role as Jessica's assistant. Very effective and very convincing.

He had a fair idea of Hallam's location. He was some-where between here and Ahmed's village. Damon was sure that the Mercedes was parked somewhere, hidden behind rocks. He knew it was within easy reach of the house, be-cause Hallam had doubled back and taken one of Rashid's horses. If he had followed the trail of the caravan, he wouldn't have gotten very far. Damon knew that Ahmed had men guarding the trail.

Suddenly the faint purr of an engine disturbed the si-lence. That could be Hallam now, returning from his little jaunt. Shifting, Damon turned on his side until his back was toward the door. He looked down at Jessica. He was tempted to kiss her awake and watch slow pleasure replace her drowsiness. Reaching out, he gently trailed one finger over her mouth. She stirred, her lips moving uncon-sciously, parting slightly. With a slight groan he gave in to temptation and bent his head.

The door to the outside courtyard opened stealthily.

Cautiously, Peter slipped into the dimly lit room, paus-ing briefly to adjust his eyes to the dim light after the glare of the sun. Then he closed the door behind him and bolted it, wishing that he still had his gun. But the revolver had been lost in a mad scramble to get away from Ahmed's men.

His hand tightened around the handle of the flashlight he had found in Jessica's car. It was not as useful as a pistol, but better than empty hands.

The charpoy creaked. Peter tensed, his gut instinct tell-ing him that Noble was awake. He didn't underestimate the man. Anyone who had lived among terrorists for years and had survived unscathed was well trained and dangerous. Too dangerous to give him the advantage dark adaptation provided. His thumb pushed the button of the flashlight, flooding the room with its powerful beam.

Damon moved with the swift reflexes of a man used to unexpected attacks. He spun around and swung his legs to the floor, his body coiled. Then he sat utterly still, assess-ing the situation, a man used to facing danger with cold reason not heated blindness, and waited for Hallam's next move.

"Get out, Hallam." His voice was a low, menacing growl.

"How did you know it was me?" Peter asked, amazed. Noble couldn't have seen past the blinding torch, not clearly enough to identify him.

"No one else would have the effrontery or the stupidity to invade the privacy of another man's room," Damon said. "Here in the mountains it can mean death."

Jessica sat up, rubbing the sleep from her eyes. "What's going on?" She pushed herself to her knees and peered over Damon's shoulder. Shielding her eyes, she snapped, "Damn it Peter, lower the light."

The beam wavered slightly, then settled on Damon's stomach. "I'll turn it off in a moment," Peter said roughly. "But first I have to know that Noble doesn't carry a gun."

"You're crazy," Jessica said flatly. "Damon has no weapons. Not in this room." Her voice sounded very certain. Knowing how much she hated the sight of guns, Damon would never bring one to their bed.

"I want you to make sure. Frisk him," Peter ordered.

"Do it yourself." Jessica slid past Damon, getting to her feet. Then she calmly walked over to Peter and took the flashlight from his hand.

Placing both hands on her hips, with the light pointing at the ceiling, she asked curtly, "Would you mind telling me what's happening? And where have you been? Why do you charge into this room like a bull into a china shop?"

Peter twisted his lips. "I was quieter than that."

"Not much," Jessica snapped. Her eyes narrowed as she looked at him. Peter was filthy. His hair was matted with dust and sweat. His shirt was stained dark with perspiration and ripped in several places. The knees of his jeans were scuffed to threads as if he had crawled miles over rocks. His face was streaked with dust and a big bruise darkened his chin. He looked tired and ready to collapse. But his lips were firm and his hard eyes glittered. "My God, what happened to you?"

"Ahmed Khan's men, that's what."

"They did this to you?" Disbelief and anger filled her voice. She turned to Damon, still sitting on the charpoy. "Is that possible?" she challenged.

"Very possible." His voice was light, as if he found the situation amusing.

Jessica did not. "Please explain."

Damon slowly rose to his feet and came to her side, wearing his crooked smile. "I think I'll pass that honor over to Hallam." He bowed his head in ironic deference toward the younger man. "He's earned it." Then he stood with his feet planted apart and his arms crossed over his broad chest, outwardly relaxed. But his guts had tightened like coils as he prepared himself for the blow that would turn his dreams into illusions and Jessica's love into hate. Until Hallam's disappearance he had hoped to have the chance to explain everything to her himself.

He had been waiting for the right time and the right place. Especially the place. He had put off telling her what had happened to the crates until they returned to Peshawar. If then she had decided to storm out after his explanations, blinded by anger and pain, she would not run straight into the colonel's arms.

No. That was not quite true. If concern for Jessica's safety had been uppermost in his mind, he would have left her with Asadullah at Fort Jamrud. But he had wanted to prolong their time together. The truth was that he had deliberately put off the moment, hoping that he would not have to tell her anything at all. He had gambled and lost. *Insh'Allah.* It was the will of God.

"I found the supplies," Peter said, bitter triumph glittering in his eyes.

For a moment Jessica's eyes brightened at the news. "Where are they? Any way we can get them back?"

"You'll have to ask Noble that," Peter spat.

Turning to Damon, she noted the hard distant look in his eyes and was puzzled by his lack of enthusiasm. And what had Damon to do with the recovery of the crates? Unless— no, not Damon. "I don't believe it." She rejected the idea in a flat voice, her eyes begging him to deny Peter's absurd charge.

For a moment she saw Damon's hard eyes soften and his lips move. Then his mouth again firmed into a straight, forbidding line.

"Are you so much in love with him that you can't see the truth when it hits you right between the eyes?" Peter demanded hoarsely, the words rushing out with the speed of a waterfall. "Think, Jessica. Remember what I told you last night. When he left your house, he had more than enough time to set the whole thing up. He knew enough to rob the whole damn convoy."

"He's also the man who risked his life running after the truck while the thieves took pot shots at him." Jessica rejected Peter's accusation, her eyes still pleading with Damon to defend himself. To deny the charge. Say something. Anything. Only one word to keep their love shining brightly, untarnished.

But Damon said nothing in his defense. He met her eyes calmly, as if Peter's accusations were nothing but a storm in a teacup that would pass in an instant.

"Didn't you find it too pat that the khan and his men were waiting for us on the road? That meeting was no coincidence." Peter drove on relentlessly.

"It wasn't," Jessica agreed, taking a deep breath. If Peter had based his suspicions on mere coincidences, she could refute those charges easily enough. "I knew that Damon had come here to visit his friend."

For a moment, Peter looked startled. "You knew? Why didn't you tell me?"

"Never mind. Is that all the proof you have? Suspicions? Nothing more?"

"Of course not," Peter shouted angrily. "I'm trying to tell you why I snuck out last night and tried to get a look at the caravan camped a few hundred yards outside the walls. It was too well guarded to get close to and that made me even more suspicious. Why would anyone guard food so heavily? So this morning when the caravan moved out, I followed it. I had to track it for hours before I got a look at some of the stuff. They moved fast, so fast that if they had carried food, they would have crushed every bit of it. Finally, unnoticed, one of the boxes fell off and the contents spilled on the trail. Cans of Silvadene. The same stuff that I found when I opened one of the crates in customs."

Fog swirled around her, a thick numbing mist. Jessica shook her head to clear it. "Ahmed could have bought those supplies in the bazaars," she said hoarsely.

"Then why did the Pushtuns chase me when they discovered the loss and turned back for it?" Peter asked grimly. "Why did they beat me? If the khan hadn't intervened, who knows what might have happened to me. He sent me back under escort."

Jessica barely listened to Peter's last words. She stared at Damon as if she had never really seen him before.

She closed her eyes and tried to recall the details of the last days spent with Damon. Damon coming in late at night. His warning to her that the trip might be more dangerous than previous ones. His concern when he learned that their escort ended before they reached the last camp and the offer to drive with her. And Damon sprinting after Asadullah's truck.

Contradictions existed everywhere she turned. Who could she trust? Damon, the man she loved, who lived in a world ruled by violence and deceit? Or Peter, who had worked at her side for years?

What did she really know about Damon, apart from the fact that he could make a woman feel like a queen? Only she didn't feel like a queen right now. She felt used—and filthy.

She looked at Damon with bitterness and shame. "Tell me that the supplies Peter found are not part of our shipment."

"The supplies belong to us," Damon said firmly, his eyes hard and unflinching, and seemingly without regret when Jessica blanched.

"Sure they do," Peter mocked him coldly. "If those three big crates were yours, why didn't you just say so? Why stage a robbery for something that belonged to you in the first place? All you had to do was show us your invoices, bills of lading or receipts and we would've handed the stuff over to you. But you don't have anything, Noble. Not one damn bit of proof.''

Damon stood unmoving, a statue carved out of rock. Only his eyes moved from Hallam's heated, dirty face to Jessica's frozen mask. "No proof," he agreed mockingly, as if he thought this scene nothing but a spoof. "Only a fool would leave papers lying around, which if found, could blow this whole operation sky high."

Suddenly a sharp knock shook the door. "Open up," a harsh voice demanded.

Neither Jessica nor Peter moved. But Damon turned his head sharply, grim amusement curling his lips. As he walked toward the door, Peter warned him, "Don't open it."

Ignoring the warning, Damon reached for the latch. With a muttered curse, Peter stormed toward him.

"Don't, Peter," Jessica cried out in alarm. Damon was a head taller, more powerful and infinitely more experienced than her friend. In a fight between the two, Peter would be hurt. She had seen Damon in action, downing three men within seconds.

Jessica's cry slowed Peter down but did not stop him. He charged Damon at the same moment Damon flung the door wide, catching Peter in his shoulder, spinning him around. The sudden sunlight flooding the dim room reflected off the flashlight in Jessica's hand. Before Jessica could stop him, Peter had torn it from her grasp, swinging it toward Damon's head.

"Stop it, Hallam." The new voice of authority thundered through the room, freezing Peter with his arm raised.

Jessica's eyes widened at the sight of the man filling the door, dressed in dark turban, dark clothes and dusty black boots. The ammunition belt slung across his chest glinted dangerously and the rifle in his hand was cocked.

"*Hubasti*, Jessica, *hanum*," he said politely, his blue eyes raking her frozen face. "Please excuse the intrusion of your quarters."

"*Hubasti,* Ahmed Khan," Jessica said grimly, wondering if he also asked a man's forgiveness before he hurt him. Then her eyes moved from man to man. Peter stood open-mouthed, looking like a goldfish gasping for air, his arm still frozen high. Damon stood frowning at his friend, and the khan's blue eyes took in the situation with mocking amusement.

"Is this a drama or a comedy?" he asked, raising one bushy brow.

Under different circumstances Jessica's sense of humor might have brimmed over. They did look like players frozen on a stage. Only this wasn't a farce. No comic misunderstanding was about to be dissolved.

"I'm not laughing," Jessica said, eyeing him coldly. "And neither will my government when I make my report."

Ahmed Khan hesitated briefly, his eyes silently questioning his friend. In answer, Damon shook his head. Shrugging his shoulders, the khan turned back to her. "If we win the jihad—the holy war—your government will forgive and forget, Jessica, *hanum.* And if we don't, it won't matter." His gaze moved to Peter. "Hallam, lower your arm before you get a cramp."

Then he once again turned back to Damon. "If I had known that you were still here, I would have detained Hallam for a few hours. I thought that you had already left for Peshawar."

"That's all right," Damon said wearily. "Jessica would've refused to leave without him. Why did you come back?"

Briefly the blue eyes raked Jessica and Peter. "I will tell you later."

Even in her shocked state, Jessica sensed the danger lurking behind the brief words. For a moment fear flickered in her eyes, but she firmly extinguished the tiny flame. Damon's welfare did not concern her any longer. Why should she care for a man who had lied to her, used her and cheated her? Why should she feel anything but disgust at her own gullibility?

"I want to talk to you," said Damon, staring at Jessica.

His firm deep voice pierced the shield of numbness that had sustained her through the ordeal. Prickles of emotion washed over her. "But I don't want to listen to you. Unless you've decided to return the crates to us," she grated, her eyes bright green with anger.

"I can't do that," Damon said quietly. "But I can explain—"

"Explain what?" Jessica turned on him, her eyes flashing green fire. "That you didn't know about the crates, until it was too late?"

"Yes," Damon said steadily.

Jessica laughed jeeringly. "You're a fool if you think I'd believe you now." If he had told her the truth when she had first mentioned the three extra crates, she might have believed him. But now it was too late.

"Let's go outside, Hallam," Ahmed prodded the younger man.

Peter grimly refused to go. "I'm not leaving Jessica alone with Noble." His hand clenched around the long handle of the flashlight as if he considered using it.

"Don't do anything foolish," the khan warned softly. "Move." He stepped aside to reveal Gorband and Ismail with their rifles raised.

"Go on, Peter," Jessica said firmly, looking at the grim expression of the two men she had joked with only a little while ago. No laughter relieved the harsh planes and angles of their faces now. They were ready to use force if the khan ordered them to.

"Don't worry about me," she added. She was not afraid of Damon. She knew with a certainty that Damon would never harm her physically. Besides, she wanted a few minutes alone with him. She had a few choice words to say to him, too.

After a moment's hesitation, Peter walked out into the sunshine. Ahmed Khan followed, closing the door behind him.

Jessica stared into the dark face looming above her as if she had never seen it before. Was this cold stranger the same

man who had made warm, beautiful love to her? Not this
man, with eyes as cold and hard as rock. Not this man, with
a mouth drawn into a thin straight line and whose hands
were reaching for her, hurting her now, biting into her with
a strength he had not shown her since their first encounter.

No, this was not the Damon she knew. This was the ruthless man she had sensed beneath the gentleness. The man she
feared.

"You're hurting me," she said. His hands eased instantly and she spun away from him. "You wanted to talk?"
she jeered, her eyes flashing with rage in her ice cold face.
"I can't imagine what else you have to say. But talk away."
She turned away. If she had to look much longer into his
hard face, she would lose control of the pain and rage boiling inside her.

Damon tried one more time to reach her. "The three
crates belong to us." His eyes followed her across the room.
"They were shipped to the embassy, not to you. I was going
to get them out of customs yesterday morning."

"At five?" Jessica challenged coldly. "Wouldn't it have
been a little difficult without papers?"

"No more difficult than it was for you," Damon said
quietly.

Jessica was unwilling to believe him any longer. Their relationship had been built on trust. And with that founda-
tion gone, it fell apart like a house of cards. "But it was even
easier to steal them from me. And I played right into your
hands. That was quite a performance you gave, trying
to catch Asadullah's truck," she said coldly. "You used
me."

"No." Damon harshly rejected her accusation. "Henderson used you, you little fool. He was sitting on a ware-
house full of electronic equipment. He had no way to ship
it out of the country, and he knew we were getting close. On
his trip to Pakistan a few months ago, he found the perfect
solution. Your supplies. Crates of food, clothing, medical
equipment, crates that no one ever checked. When you told
me about your shipments, everything fell into place."

"So you latched on to me, trying to find out if I was involved," Jessica said harshly. Lies. Deceit. Every smile. Every kiss. Oh, yes, she had been a fool.

"I had you checked out the night you left. I had to be sure," Damon said levelly. "Jessica, I never lied to you."

Her lips twisted with disbelief and bitterness. Perhaps on a personal level Damon had not lied to her. Not once had he said that he loved her, and he had never made any promises. It was not his fault that she had asked more of their relationship than he was willing to give.

He desired her, but Jessica doubted that he would have become involved with her if she had not become entangled in this mess. She finally accepted what she had always feared. On Damon's list of priorities she ranked second.

"What was in those crates?" she asked tersely, needing to know the whole truth.

"Which ones?" Damon asked, his voice rough with frustration. He could feel her slipping away from him. "We don't know about the last shipment. My guess is that it contained nothing important because, in a way, it was a trial run. The information came too late to check your shipment, or to prevent the theft. We would've let it go through in any case. Our main objective is to catch Henderson—before he defects to the other side."

"Your crates."

"We replaced Henderson's stuff with bandages, syringes and antibiotics."

"And guns, explosives and hand grenades," Jessica added, filling in the items he had not mentioned.

"Is that what you believe?" Damon asked quietly.

Grimly, Jessica noticed the evasion. She stared at him unblinkingly, rage and pain tearing her apart. She knew that the *mujahidins* needed both medical supplies and weapons if they were to go on fighting. But, by using her supply transports, Damon had jeopardized her own work. If the Pakistani government suspected that her shipments were being used for anything but the stated purposes, they would demand control over the supplies. That would mean only half of every shipment would actually reach the camps.

She glared at him. "It took me three years to establish a smooth supply system," she said, her voice vibrating with fury. "And you may have ruined everything."

But despite all the evidence mounted against him, she hesitated to answer his question. What if she was wrong? What if everything he had told her was true? Her head was spinning with the tangled web of denials, evasions and evidence.

And Damon was asking for her blind trust and unconditional acceptance, despite everything that had happened. It was irrational, illogical, downright impossible.

And yet she couldn't say the words that, yes, she believed bullets were mixed with bandages.

"No wonder the colonel is constantly snapping at your heels," she snapped instead.

Seemingly unmoved, Damon quietly repeated his question. "Is that what you believe?"

Jessica hesitated briefly. Pain was tearing her apart. She didn't know how much longer she could look at him and not break down. "Yes," she finally said firmly, cutting the last threads tying them together. "Any man ruthless enough to make a woman fall in love with him to further his own ends, would use my transport to smuggle weapons."

For one moment Damon stood unmoving, staring at her in disbelief. Then he swore, his calm restraint evaporating in a string of vicious curses. But he didn't deny her words.

"It's so glaringly obvious," she said with aching calm. "A woman with more experience would've seen through you from the beginning. That's why you picked me, didn't you? I was so damn stupid, a crass innocent who fell for a trick as old as time." She turned around and walked to the door. If she stayed any longer in this room, she would break down in front of him.

Damon followed Jessica with long lithe steps, stalking her. With her hand on the handle, she sensed his presence and spun around, pulling the door open at the same time. "May Allah be with you," she said quietly.

"No," Damon said curtly, kicking the door shut again with such force that the frame shuddered in protest. "I'm not leaving. Not yet anyway. Not until I've convinced you just how wrong you are.''

''You're wasting your time. Nothing you say will change my mind.''

Damon looked at her with narrowed eyes. Jessica was too hurt and angry to listen to reason. Unfortunately he could not give her time to cool down and consider the facts calmly. He knew of only one way to reach her. ''This will,'' Damon said with calm certainty, his hand closing around her arm. Drawing her against him, his free hand caressed her cheek.

''No,'' Jessica said harshly, pushing against the hard wall of his chest.

She might as well have swallowed the words, because Damon was not listening. He bent his head and found her lips, easily overpowering her resistance.

Until now Jessica had tried to be calm and rational but all restraint left her at the first touch of his lips. She kicked and clawed, as determined to free herself of Damon as she had been to escape her kidnappers.

But Damon was prepared for her actions. With a single shove he pushed her off balance, then he lifted her and tumbled her backward on the charpoy. He followed her down, controlling her struggles easily with his greater weight and power. He waited until her rage and strength had been depleted, until she had stopped twisting, turning and trying to buck him off.

Finally she gave up the futile struggle. She took a few shallow breaths, prolonging each exhalation phase to calm herself. Damon lay on her chest like the rock she had so often likened him to. But when she did not renew her struggle, he shifted his weight to his elbows, sliding down until his hips rested on top of hers. He bent his head, his breath flowing over her heated face, stirring memories of their night spent on this bed.

For one startled moment she met the knowing darkness of his eyes. Then she turned her head away in dismay. She still ached for him. ''I want you,'' Damon murmured, his lips touched her ear, spreading tingling heat down her neck.

Jessica stiffened, appalled at the wild longing coursing through her.

"And I could make you admit that you want me as much as I want you." Damon nibbled at the tight rope of her neck, his beard like a sable brush, soft and exciting.

Jessica felt the growing hardness of his hips spreading liquid fire to her loins. She bit her lip against the cry of protest and despair. Her body was betraying her.

"I could take you now and you would moan in response," Damon said, his voice hard and certain. With his bearded chin he brushed aside the flaps of her shirt that had become unbuttoned during the struggle. He kissed the swelling flesh of her breast with tantalizing sweetness. The satin material did not hide her instant reaction to his caress. "You see what I mean. Admit I'm right."

Jessica bit her lip.

Firmly he slid one hard hand under her cheek and forced her to face him. "Admit it," he said roughly.

Jessica's eyes were bright green with rage and humiliation as she fought against the knowledge that he was right. "No," she lied.

With swift, sure movements Damon peeled back the material, his thumb stroking the hard pink nipple. "I could prove it now," he said, determination to wrest the admission from her stamped on his face.

"Yes," she hissed between clenched teeth, fighting the passion he stirred in her. "But I'll hate you."

"For a while," he agreed, watching the green eyes flash fire and her tongue moisten her lips. "But I don't know of a more effective way to rid you of the notion that I've been using you." His mouth slid hot and moist over her breast as he watched her eyes flare wildly. With a gleam of satisfaction, he raised his head. "We'll continue this conversation tonight in Peshawar." With powerful, sensuous movements, he slid over her body before getting to his feet. "Now I'm going to the bazaars with Hallam to get the car."

For several minutes after he had left, Jessica lay on the bed, the heat of his body and the touch of his mouth still lingering. Tears, laughter and screams alternately warred for release. Her body trembled with the force of the emotional struggle. When she heard the clatter of hooves, she calmed herself. Getting to her feet, she buttoned her shirt all the way to the top with steady hands.

She was not going to wait for Damon to drive home his point. When he returned from Landi Kotal, she would not be here. She was less afraid of driving down the Khyber Pass than of finding out what her reaction would be if she spent tonight in his arms. In broad daylight she stood a good chance of reaching Peshawar without incidents. But hating Damon meant hating herself, and that would ultimately destroy her.

Swiftly she left the guest room and crossed the courtyard. The Mercedes was once again parked where Damon had left it last night. Looking around, she saw no one. Ahmed Khan and his men must have accompanied Damon and Peter into Landi Kotal.

The keys to the car were gone, but Jessica had a second set taped beneath the front bumper. She took them from their hiding place and opened the trunk. She made several trips, filling it with her suitcase and the carpets. After one last look around the room, she picked up her purse, hesitating briefly. She hated to leave without saying goodbye to Zaira. Swiftly, Jessica estimated how much time it would take for the men to return. An hour at the most. If she didn't want to meet them on the narrow road to Landi Kotal, she had to leave right now. Resolutely she closed the door to the room, crossed the empty courtyard and shut the tall gates.

When she started the car, she noticed that the needle of the fuel gauge pointed to empty. She thought of the ten liter canister in the trunk, then decided against taking the time now to fill the tank. With luck, she would make it past Landi Kotal.

But, only a mile down the road, the Mercedes spluttered to a stop. Swearing at her previous foolishness, Jessica got out of the car and hauled the heavy canister out. She poured the gasoline, keeping one eye on the road ahead. When the canister was empty, she locked the gas cap into place, breathing a sigh of relief.

Suddenly men slid from behind the boulders to her right and rose from between the high stalks of the sugarcane to her left, surrounding her.

Shocked, Jessica stepped back until she bumped into the side of the car. "Who are you?" she whispered hoarsely, her eyes moving from man to man.

They were dressed as Pushtuns, their turbans tied in Pushtun fashion. Even the ammunition belts were slung across their chests, cocked rifles pointing at her. But they were smaller in height and finer boned, their slitted eyes and broad, flat cheekbones reminding her of the five men who had tried to kidnap her the day before. They were Turkomans.

She took a deep breath, searching for the face of Colonel Henderson. Stay calm, she told herself. There's nothing to worry about. Damon will be here soon. Damon, Peter and Ahmed Khan.

"Ah, Mrs. Stanton." The colonel strolled toward her, his cold eyes narrowed against the sun. He wore Afghan robes like his men. "What an unexpected pleasure to find you alone, without Noble."

Hysterical laughter bubbled inside her. The colonel was behaving as if they were once again at the party. Only this time she was alone. Her fingers clenched around her keys, their serrated edges biting into her skin. "Damon is not far behind," she said slowly. "What do you want?"

"The three crates you took out of customs with your shipment," the colonel said calmly. "They belong to me."

Jessica's eyes widened, wild laughter filling her. She wondered who would claim those damn crates next. "I don't have them anymore. They were delivered to the camp yesterday afternoon."

"To which camp?" the colonel asked sharply.

"The one close to Fort Jamrud," Jessica said, hoping that he had not heard about the theft of Asadullah's truck.

Colonel Henderson shook his head. Stepping closer, he took one of her arms in a bruising grasp. "We checked every one of the camps you visited yesterday." Still smiling coldly, he raised his free hand and slapped her across the face. "Now, Mrs. Stanton, who has the crates?"

Her ears rang from the blow. Fear curled inside her, choking her. Jessica stared at him silently. All she could think of was that the longer she delayed him the better her chances were that Damon would come. She winced as the grip of his hand tightened cruelly.

"Mrs. Stanton, where are the crates? The sooner you tell me where they're hidden, the sooner you'll go free."

His words did not fool her. Jessica knew that the colonel would never release her. He would not hand her over into Soviet hands, as he had done with Farah. She was not a Pushtun woman, the wife of a rebel leader. She was an American diplomat with high ranking connections that could only prove embarrassing to the Soviets. "I have no idea where the crates are," she said with perfect honesty. "They were stolen yesterday in the middle of Peshawar."

"Now we're getting somewhere," he said silkily. "I know that Noble stole the crates. Where did he hide them?"

Jessica closed her eyes against the sudden tears. Every one of the colonel's words was proving Damon's innocence. "And you stole my truck a few weeks ago," she accused him.

"You didn't leave me any choice. It would've been so much easier if you had cooperated with me. You and I could have had a lot of fun together."

Jessica's lips curled. "You don't know me very well, colonel. Even for love I wouldn't betray my country. But I was never in any danger of falling for you. Frankly, Henderson, you only disgust me."

The colonel's face tightened, but his voice was just as silky as before. "By tomorrow you'll sing a different tune," he promised.

"If you kidnap me," Jessica said as calmly as she could, "you invite more trouble than I'm worth."

"Ah, but that's where you're wrong." The arctic eyes warmed with anticipation. "Eleven years ago, Noble stole my woman. Now I am taking his. I've waited a long time for my revenge. I only regret that I won't be there to see his face when he finds out that you're with me."

Panic welled up in her, making her weak. She wanted to plead with Henderson to let her go. But one look into those cruel eyes steadied her. "Damon is not in love with me," she said quietly.

For one long moment, he searched her face thoroughly, reading the truth in her face. For one long moment Jessica thought that she had won, that he would release her. "Very clever, Mrs. Stanton," he sneered. "But I don't believe you." His hand jerked her forward. Opening the door, he pushed her into the car. Then he gave some rapid orders in Russian. Two men jumped in the back seat from the driver's side, their rifles aimed at her head. "If you make one wrong move, they have orders to shoot," Henderson said. "Dead, you're less trouble to me than alive. Remember that." He slammed the door and walked around the front.

Suddenly a shot rang out. A Turkoman in the road cried out and fell. The colonel spun around, his hand reaching for the gun in his belt.

"Henderson. Let her go." Damon's voice came from somewhere behind the rocks.

At the sound of Damon's voice, Jessica felt new life flow into her. Her eyes moved from the colonel's position to the nearest boulder, three feet away from her seat. In the rearview mirror she could see that the Turkomans' attention was focused on the outside. Her hand inched to the door handle, gripping it tightly. The long rifles were unwieldy inside the car. She might have a few seconds before they could shoot at her.

Outside, one Turkoman raised his rifle and fired a shot in the direction of the voice.

Rifle shots came from the sugarcane field, hitting two of the colonel's men. The others ran for cover, leaving only the two in the back seat of the car and Henderson crouching low.

"One more shot, Noble, and I'll order my men to kill Mrs. Stanton."

"You're surrounded by my men," Ahmed's voice came from somewhere behind the rocks. "If you kill the woman, you're going to die, slowly, like the dog you are."

Henderson raised his head over the hood and fired in response. In that instant Jessica threw open the door and slid from the car. With three swift steps, she reached the boulder, crouching low as a shot sizzled past her head.

"Jessica, get down," Damon called harshly, firing more shots.

Bullets flew like hail, passing over her head. Jessica covered her ears, crouching and praying.

"Damn it, he's getting away," Ahmed swore from somewhere behind Jessica. "Gorband. Ismail. Follow him."

A dark shadow slid into the space next to her. Jessica spun around, ready to kick, hit and claw. "Thank God it is you," she sobbed in relief when she recognized Damon's face.

"Running from the car was a brave thing to do," Damon said quietly while shots rang out once again. He raised his head to look over the boulder, then lowered it with a grunt of satisfaction. "The two Turkomans just left the car."

Jessica stared at his dusty face, words of apology trembling on her lips.

But Damon wasn't looking at her. He was moving to the side of the boulder. "Hallam is trying to get into the car. The moment he's inside, run to it. And keep your head down." Over his shoulder he looked at her.

Jessica nodded, her eyes meeting his. Damon swore at the sight of the bright red print of Henderson's hand staining her cheek. "He's going to pay," he promised with quiet rage, touching the bruise tenderly. Then he called, "Hallam," and raised his rifle, firing a volley of shots above the boulder.

"Okay," Peter called, starting the car.

Bullets whizzed around the boulder. Damon threw her to the ground and covered her. "In a moment it will be over. Once you're in the car, stay down until Hallam tells you to come out."

Jessica nodded. She wanted to tell him so many things. To ask his forgiveness. To apologize for doubting him. Above all, she wanted to tell him that she loved him and would wait for him. But there was no time. She felt Damon move and fire again. "Run, Jessica."

Blindly, she obeyed. Ducking, she ran toward the car. She heard a shot rip the open door and threw herself onto the seat, slipping down in the footspace to make room for Damon.

"Stay down," Peter ordered, leaning over her to grasp the handle.

"No, Peter. Wait for Damon," Jessica cried, trying to stop him from closing the door.

"He's not coming." Peter slammed the door. The Mercedes shot forward as gunfire exploded all around them once again, bullets hitting the car like hailstones. Peter swore and floored the gas pedal, hurtling them down the road. Jessica hung onto the seat, pressing her head into the cushion. Tears were running down her face. "Too late," she whispered. Too late to take back her words. Too late to turn back the clock. Damon had sent her to safety without the one word she needed to hear. She knew that September would never come for them.

Chapter 14

"Why didn't you tell me that Noble is one of us?" Peter challenged some time later. They were coasting down the steep road to conserve fuel, weaving their way past lorries and cars, tires screeching. In bright daylight the traffic was heavy.

"Because I wasn't sure," Jessica said quietly. Subconsciously she had always known that Damon was involved with the Agency, but she had ignored all the signs. It had been so much easier to pretend that he was an observer and not a participant. "How did you find out?"

"Ahmed Khan told me when he returned my pistol." He braked gently as they reached the place of the rockslide. The road had been cleared, only piles of debris indicating the spot where Peter's car had almost been buried.

"What will happen to your car?" Jessica asked. "How are you going to get it back?"

"One of Rashid's sons will drive it down in a day or so," Peter said, glancing at her frozen face. Her unnatural calm worried him. He would have preferred tears and arguments, even sharp demands to drive back to Landi Kotal.

"We never made it into town. Apparently Henderson did not come up the Khyber Pass. He must have climbed one of the mountain treks the smugglers use. Ahmed's men spotted him and the Turkomans and went to warn the khan. Then Ahmed and some of his men tracked Henderson to the town. When we left the house to get my car, one of Ahmed's Pushtuns came to warn us that Henderson was on his way back. Rashid, who knows these mountains like the back of his hand, led us around the Turkomans." He shook his head. "I still can't quite take in Henderson's defection. I didn't really believe it, until he stopped you on that road."

"He didn't stop me," Jessica explained. "I ran out of gas. I didn't see anyone until I emptied the spare gas into the tank. Then I was suddenly surrounded by Henderson and his Turkomans. If only I had stayed at the house." Her voice was filled with bitter self-recrimination.

Peter shrugged his shoulders. "Don't blame yourself too much. In the end, things worked out better this way. I understand why you wanted to leave before Noble returned. If I hadn't—"

"It doesn't matter," Jessica said wearily. She could not blame Peter for the events. She blamed herself for not trusting Damon. Peter had an excuse for his behavior. She had none.

When Fort Jamrud came into view, Peter gave a sigh of relief. "I'm glad we made it without a hitch. I hope you realize that I'll have to file a report. It will mean a lot of questions for you. Most likely security will insist that you leave Pakistan almost immediately."

For the first time Jessica showed some animation. Her eyes glowed and her chin thrust out stubbornly. Shaking her head, she said hoarsely, "I'm not leaving." As long as she was anywhere within reach, Damon might contact her.

Peter stared at her, but did not argue. He knew that nothing he said would change her mind. Others could do that much more effectively, men with more authority and enough clout to send her home to safety.

* * *

The questioning Peter had warned her about lasted almost two hours. When it was over, the three men facing her knew everything—every word the colonel had ever spoken to her, Ahmed's story, and how much time she had spent in Damon's company. The only secret she was allowed to keep was the number of times Damon had made love to her.

"I want you out of the country," the man she had known until now as Curt Pearson, Internal Revenue, finally said. "Can you be ready in three days?"

"No." Jessica shook her head firmly. "I still have to pack and sell my car. I need at least a week." She did not tell him that she planned to stay even longer. Delaying tactics were always more successful than outright defiance. In five days she could plead that her car had not been repaired in time to sell it. Later she could pretend to have dysentery, which would make the long flight impossible. When she ran out of believable excuses, she still could try outright disobedience. But for a while at least, she planned to stay where Damon could contact her easily.

"A week," Curt Pearson said dryly, his gray eyes piercing the bland facade of her face. "I strongly suggest that you're ready then. I don't want to use more drastic measures to see you safely out of here."

Jessica decided to take his advice. She sorted and packed. She sold her furniture and accepted a tentative offer for her car. In the oppressing heat she worked ceaselessly from morning to sundown. At night she went to farewell parties given in her honor. She pushed herself to the edge of exhaustion, hoping each night to drop into dreamless slumber. But each night the nightmares came, haunting her, waking her with volleys of shots still ringing in her ears.

Two days before her scheduled departure, the movers came and sealed her belongings into large containers. With only two suitcases of clothes, Jessica moved into Barbara's guest room. That night the nightmares were worse. Jessica saw a cave filled with ghostly shadows wading through blood. She screamed so loud Barbara rushed to her side.

"If this is love, I'll make darn sure to fall for a guy with a nine to five job," Barbara said quietly after she had calmed her friend.

Remembering her own similar thoughts, Jessica smiled weakly. "Famous last words. Someday you may have to eat them. What about Peter? He is in love with you."

Barbara abruptly got to her feet, a closed look on her face. "There is nothing between us," she denied firmly. She looked at her watch. "Let's try to get some sleep. Do you want me to stay with you? I can sleep in the other bed." She nodded toward the second twin bed beneath the window.

"Thanks, but that's not necessary. I'm going to read for a while." Jessica knew she could not go back to sleep. She intended to spend the few hours until dawn in a chair.

"Well, if you're sure," Barbara yawned. "I'll leave the doors open."

Jessica hugged her friend. "Don't worry. I'm all right."

"Yeah," Barbara said doubtfully. "Wake me at six. I wish someone would bring back Peter's car. I hate getting up early every morning to pick him up."

Jessica, too, waited anxiously for the return of the Ford. She hoped that Damon would send a note for her with Rashid's son. Since her return she had clung tenaciously to that hope. She knew that Damon wanted her. What she didn't know was how much.

When Peter returned from work the following afternoon, the car stood in its usual parking spot. Barbara brought the news, dropping a paper bag into Jessica's lap. "This is your stuff. Peter found it in his car."

For a moment, all blood left her face. Jessica clutched the bag, afraid to open it. Then she rose to her feet and walked to her room, seeking privacy. She closed the door and emptied the bag on the bed. With shaking hands she sorted through maps, a pair of sunglasses, old receipts and road passes. At the bottom of the stack, she found a sealed envelope, a little grubby and wrinkled, as if it had passed through several hands. With her heart in her throat she reached for it and tore it open.

A white sheet of paper fell out. For a moment Jessica stared at it, her hands trembling as she unfolded it. Nestled within its folds lay the small curl of her hair.

For long minutes she sat frozen in shock, staring at the wisps of coppery hair. Then she closed her eyes against the onrush of tears. She could see Damon on that magical day in May, his thick black hair ruffled by the wind, his shirt unbuttoned halfway down his chest. She recalled the tender caress of his strong long fingers as he shaped the curl, and his promise that September was just around the corner. It was at that moment that she had realized how much he cared for her. What she had not known was that she would always be second best to him.

"Damn you," she sobbed, reaching for the curl. She got to her feet and dropped it into the wastebasket. Deep down she had always known the truth. Damon desired her, but he loved the excitement of his job more.

Stiffly, she picked up the sheet and envelope, examining it closely. Blank envelope. Blank sheet of paper. Not one damn word. But the message was clear. "Go home," it said. "Don't wait for me."

With a strangled sob, Jessica jerked her suitcases from the closet and began packing her few belongings.

The next morning she finalized the sale of the Mercedes. She also visited her servants to say goodbye to them. With tears running down her wrinkled face, Aya pressed a shawl into Jessica's hands. It was beautifully embroidered with her name. Gulmahmad handed her a coffee can filled with Pakistani soil and a package of mixed seeds from the garden. Jessica didn't have the heart to tell him that it was illegal to bring foreign soil into the States.

Jessica had given them their gifts a few days ago. A golden chain for Aya, a watch for Gulmahmad and money and clothes for them both. She had also made sure that they had good jobs waiting for them.

At the airport, friends and colleagues waited to see her off. Among them was Curt Pearson. He looked tired. His pale eyes were rimmed with red, as if he hadn't slept in days.

With a ghost of a grin, he said, "I'm glad you changed your mind about staying on."

Jessica managed a smile. Then she turned to exchange hugs and promises to write, her hands filling with letters she agreed to mail the moment she arrived in New York.

Peter was more subdued than she had ever seen him, his face gray beneath his tan. "I spent all night mopping floors," he explained with a tired smile. "The pipe in my bathroom broke."

"You should've called for help," Jessica said. "I would've come over."

"Thanks, but I managed. Take care of yourself," he said quietly. "I'll see you on my next leave."

The final boarding call prevented her from answering. She hugged him, then turned to Barbara. "Thanks for everything." Fearing she would break down and cry any moment, she tore herself away and rushed through the gate.

On the platform leading to the plane, Jessica paused and turned for one final look at the mountains. Dark clouds, heavy with rain, shrouded the range even to its foot. Fear ran down her spine. Something was holding her, calling her back. The first drops of rain hit her upturned face. With a muttered oath, Jessica dashed for the plane, the drops streaking down the frozen mask of her face. Behind her, the skies opened in a torrent of rain. The monsoon had finally arrived.

"Where are you?" Gloria's voice was tinged with exasperation. "You promised to be here today. Tomorrow is your mother's birthday."

"I didn't forget. My van broke down somewhere near Lexington. I'm calling from a garage right outside of town. I won't make it until after dark, though." Jessica looked through the dirty glass of the phone booth at the van still parked where the tow truck had left it an hour ago.

"That's fine," Gloria said. "We are going out. You're sleeping in your old room. And don't wait up for us. We'll be late."

It was almost midnight when Jessica parked the dusty van in the circular driveway of the big old mansion. Getting out, she stretched her tired limbs. She had driven nonstop since leaving Lexington. Lord it felt good to be home.

Upon her return to the States, she had spent one week in Washington with her parents. After the first three days, Jessica had felt like screaming. No, she had no interest in buying new clothes. No, she did not want to go apartment hunting. She wanted to be alone and to stop pretending that she was glad to be back.

Aunt Gloria had seen past the lines that jet lag and sleepless nights had stamped on her face. "What happened?" she had asked gently. "The last time I saw Damon I could have sworn that he was in love with you. When he mentioned that he was going to visit you, I had such great hopes. I expected to see you getting off the plane, glowing with happiness. Instead you look frozen to your soul."

Jessica had shaken her head. The emotions Aunt Gloria sensed had been desire and need. If Damon had loved her, he would have forgiven her. "Irreconcilable differences," Jessica had replied.

After one searching look, Gloria had accepted the explanation. "Go away for a few weeks," she suggested gently.

Jessica had agreed. She needed solitude in which to cry; if the tears ever came.

The next day she rented a van. Days and nights she had driven, exploring her country, eating when she felt hungry, sleeping when she was too tired for nightmares to haunt her. For six weeks she wandered from coast to coast. Like most of her friends in foreign service she had seen the Taj Mahal, the Eiffel Tower, Athens and Rome; but she hardly knew her own country.

She had avoided cities. Instead she went camping near mountain streams and at the edge of the desert. With each mile the ice coating her heart melted a little.

The night after her visit to the Grand Canyon, she cried herself to sleep. The sheer cliffs and stark beauty of the landscape reminded her of the Khyber Pass. Millimeter by slow millimeter the cap on bottled memories opened, memories of the joys and agonies of loving Damon.

She still arose each morning with traces of tears to face another lonely day. But as September had drawn closer, hope had begun to kindle, its tiny flame growing steadily. Perhaps some day...

Jessica turned back to the van, filled her arms with clothes, and walked the few steps to the front door. The house key Aunt Gloria had given her upon her return from Islamabad was sliding into the lock when the door was flung open from the inside.

Startled, Jessica stepped back. "You shouldn't have cut your evening—" The words froze on her lips as she recognized the man outlined by the glittering chandelier.

"Damon!" Jessica stood frozen, staring with disbelief at the tall, powerful man who had filled her dreams since their first meeting here. As her eyes adjusted to the brilliant light, the dark outline became more detailed. He had shaved off his beard, had done so some time ago because his chin showed the same color as the rest of his face. His features were also harsher, drawn and thin.

She could sense the power, cloaked by the loose white shirt, and feel his tightly leashed restlessness and impatience.

"You're late." His voice was cold, as hard as the eyes raking her face.

His tone hardly registered with her. "And you're early. Five days early." She dropped her bag, keys and clothes. With a sob she ran to him, throwing her arms around his neck, laughing and crying at the same time. She whispered his name over and over again, still not quite convinced that he was real. But the arms closing around her were hard and strong.

"I've been waiting for a week," Damon groaned against her lips. Then he kissed her as if he had waited a lifetime for her to return.

"I didn't know," she said when the kiss was over. Briefly she wondered what she would have done if she had known that Damon was in Washington. Avoided him? No, she would have driven day and night. She would have run, walked or crawled if she had known he was waiting for her. During the long lonely days and nights, she had come to realize that it no longer mattered who Damon was. She loved him. And as long as he needed her, she would be there for him. Second best was better than emptiness.

A moth brushed across her face. Jessica raised her head and looked at the moths and mosquitos streaming through the open door. With a sigh of impatience, she pushed away. Quickly picking up her clothes, bag and keys, she brought them into the house. "I'm going to take these upstairs," she said, walking toward the wide curving staircase. With one foot placed on the first step, she looked back. "Don't go away," she said softly, her eyes running hungrily over him.

Leaning against the closed door, Damon stared at her soberly. "I'll be here."

As Jessica ran lightly up the stairs, she wondered what had happened to Colonel Henderson. She felt certain that Uncle Howard would have broken the rules and told her if the man had been killed. Which meant that Damon's stay was only temporary. But how long? She stopped to look down at him. He still leaned against the door, as if he intended to wait for her there.

Or as if he needed the support of the door.

For an instant Jessica clung to the railing, then ran back down the stairs, her sneakers barely touching the steps.

"You're hurt!" Up close, she could see the fine beading of sweat on his forehead, and the careful, rapid movement of his chest.

Her fingers gently outlined the bandage spreading from his shoulder across his chest like protective armor. "You should've stopped me," Jessica whispered. She had hurled into his arms with the force of a small tornado.

He straightened with a shake of his head. "I needed that kiss. I needed to know that you missed me as much as I missed you. Your reaction told me better than words that you still want me." His hand touched her face, catching the tears falling down again. "I don't know what I would have done if you had greeted me with a polite smile."

Jessica turned away abruptly, wiping the tears with the back of her hand. "You sent me away," she said, her voice harsh with remembered agony.

"What?" Damon exclaimed, reaching for her shoulder, spinning her around.

She faced him with the same empty look she had worn when she held the curl in her hand. "What else was I supposed to think? A blank sheet of paper wrapped around my curl. No explanation. Nothing to give me hope. Just that damn wall of silence shutting me out, telling me louder than words that you didn't want me anymore."

Damon bent his head until their lips almost touched. "I've wanted you since the moment I met you." He kissed her with hard need. "I thought I had lost the curl. After I was shot, Ahmed hid me in a cave. I remember calling for you, asking for you to wait for me. Before the fever began, Ahmed promised to see to your safety, because Henderson was still free. I guess he sent the curl. He was the only one who knew its significance. Are you sure there was no message?"

Jessica nodded. "Only a grubby envelope and a blank sheet of paper." She frowned. Only three people had known or suspected that she planned to stay. Peter, Barbara and Curt Pearson, who had warned her about taking drastic measures if she was unwilling to leave. Perhaps he had the car searched and had destroyed Ahmed's note. "What happened after Ahmed hid you in the cave?"

"After that, I don't recall anything except cold and darkness." His voice hardened again. "And then I found out you had left Pakistan as scheduled. As if you couldn't wait to put as much distance as possible between us."

"No," Jessica protested hoarsely, pressing her lips against his, kissing him, telling him without words that she would have come to him had she known where he was.

"When were you shot?" she asked when she could talk again. But she already knew. It was the night she had woken Barbara with her screams.

"Two days before you left," Damon said flatly. "Do you mind if we continue this conversation somewhere more—" he managed a small grin "—comfortable?"

Jessica's eyes darkened with concern. "Living room, kitchen or den?"

Damon tensed at her choice of location. Bulky couches, kitchen tables, barriers to hide behind. Was she trying to keep him at a distance? "How about upstairs?" he suggested tersely.

Jessica bit back the question if he could manage the steps. She knew he hated to admit even the need to rest. Nodding, she followed him up the stairs. When he picked up her clothes on the last step, she swallowed the words of caution trembling on her lips. He swung her heavy traveling bag over his good shoulder. "What's in here? Rocks?" he asked, walking toward her room.

The door stood wide open and the bedside lamp was lit. The quilted bedspread still bore the imprint of his body where he had spent the last hours waiting for her.

He laid her clothes over a Queen Anne chair and put her purse down on the seat. Finally he walked toward the bed and stretched out on it, his good arm propping up his head.

Jessica followed each of his slow, measured movements. She tightly clenched her hands by her side to keep from tearing off his shirt and his bandage to see for herself how badly he was hurt—and to stop herself from strangling him. His gesture of independence and pride had been stupid and unnecessary. She understood his need to test his strength, the pride of the injured warrior preparing for his next fight.

"I've a van full of clothes and presents that need unloading," she said, her voice rough with silent protest. Her eyes moved hungrily over his broad chest, over his wide shoulders and slim hips. She ached with her need to hold him and forget about lonely tomorrows.

"That can wait," Damon said roughly, with a hunger that matched her own, and held out his hand. "I can't."

With a soft cry Jessica went to him, balancing her weight on her knees. She lowered her head and kissed him gently.

Damon's arm tightened around her, pulling her off balance until she lay outstretched beside him. He rolled over, kissing her fiercely. His hand opened the buttons of her shirt, seeking her warm, soft skin. He caressed her with hard possessiveness, stirring glowing embers into bright flames.

"I want to see you," Jessica said, her voice filled with urgency. She reached for his shirt. Damon could have died in the mountains and she would not have known he still cared for her. She opened the buttons, kissing the warm skin above the bandage, her arms tightening around him until he groaned. She moved lower, loosening his clothes, helping him slide out of them. Then she examined him inch by inch, her hands finally stopping at the bandage. "How bad is it?" she asked quietly.

"Almost healed," Damon said, his face tight with restraint. "It won't stop me from making love with you." He reached for her firmly, loosening the scarf in her hair, spearing his fingers through the fiery strands until they fell like glowing silk over her tanned skin. Then he undressed her, slowly, kissing each part of the bare skin, enjoying her convulsive responses. When he would have rolled over her, Jessica pushed him back and slid on top of him, loving him.

Much later, when they lay wrapped in each other's arms, she asked the question uppermost in her mind. "What happened to Henderson?" She had never wished a person dead. But, alive, the colonel was a constant threat to Damon, their country and their happiness.

Damon closed his eyes, remembering the cold nights and pouring rain, men dying and traps set but unsprung. Henderson had been smart. But in the end his personal hatred of Damon had been his undoing.

"He's breathing. And wishing he wasn't," Damon said quietly. "He caught a bullet in the neck. He'll never stand trial for conspiracy." He paused for a moment, then added, "Ahmed found he couldn't finish him or leave him to die. He patched him up and carried him down the mountains to Peshawar." He looked at her searchingly. "My job is done."

"For the moment," Jessica said evenly, averting her face. The world was filled with Colonel Hendersons, terrorists, and wars. "Until your wounds are healed."

"No."

His firm denial brought tears to her eyes. "Don't make empty promises," she said harshly, twisting and rolling off the bed. "I've heard them all—every excuse imaginable." She looked at him with angry despair. "You don't need promises or excuses to get me into your bed."

Swearing, Damon got to his feet. His hand clamped on her arm, shaking her. "Shut up."

She ignored him. "I'll move in with you, if that's what you want. I'll keep your bed warm for you. Until—" her voice broke.

"Until what?" Damon asked savagely.

"Until you don't want me anymore. Until my father or Uncle Howard knocks on the door—or until being second best isn't enough for me anymore."

With a groan Damon gathered her against his chest, his face buried in her hair. "You never asked me what I was doing here. I handed in my resignation five days ago. I've wanted out for quite some time. But until Henderson was caught, I couldn't quit. I knew the man better than anyone else. There was only room for one of us in this world."

"You should've told me." Jessica lifted her face.

"I did. The only way I could. I promised you September." Damon bent his head and kissed her deeply. "But I want more than a month or a year. I want you forever. A lifetime of loving and children." He pressed her against him. "For a while I will have to stay in the States. My father is getting older and I need to take some of the burden off his shoulders. But we will have time for trips, together."

Jessica looked at him smilingly. "I want to keep on working."

"Of course you do." He looked at her lovingly. "And someday, we will return to Afghanistan. When it is safe to send another ambassador and his wife."

"I love you," she breathed against his lips.

"And I love you," Damon said roughly, kissing her.

Silhouette Intimate Moments

COMING
NEXT MONTH

MIND OVER MATTER—Nora Roberts

Aurora Fields believed she was a modern, practical woman who had no time for romance. But when her work as a theatrical agent brought her up against film producer David Brady, he found a way to change her mind.

EDEN'S TEMPTATION—Susanna Christie

Their government assignment brought them together, but treachery forced them to flee into the desert. On the run, Eden and Jake shared many things: exhaustion, hunger, distrust—and love.

COLTON'S FOLLY—Renee Simons

Abby Colton came to the reservation as an outsider, but she won acceptance from everybody—except Cat Tallman, the man she was beginning to love. Cat's mind was sure Abby had no place in his life, but his heart had other ideas....

BAYOU MIDNIGHT—Emilie Richards

Sam Long knew what he didn't want: a relationship that would interfere with his first, last and only love—police work. Then he met Antoinette Deveraux and realized just how wrong a man can be.

AVAILABLE THIS MONTH:

ATTRACTIVE, SPACE SAVING BOOK RACK

Display your most prized novels on this handsome and sturdy book rack. The hand-rubbed walnut finish will blend into your library decor with quiet elegance, providing a practical organizer for your favorite hard-or soft-covered books.

Only $9.95

***Approximately
16" x 8"
when assembled***

Assembles in seconds!

To order, rush your name, address and zip code, along with a check or money order for $10.70* ($9.95 plus 75¢ postage and handling) payable to *Silhouette Books*.

Silhouette Books
Book Rack Offer
901 Fuhrmann Blvd.
P.O. Box 1325
Buffalo, NY 14269-1325

Offer not available in Canada.

BKR-2R

*New York residents add appropriate sales tax.

Take 4 Silhouette
Special Edition novels
FREE
and preview future books in your home for 15 days!

When you take advantage of this offer, you get 4 Silhouette Special Edition® novels FREE and without obligation. Then you'll also have the opportunity to preview 6 brand-new books —delivered right to your door for a FREE 15-day examination period—as soon as they are published.

When you decide to keep them, you pay just $1.95 each ($2.50 each in Canada) *with no shipping, handling, or other charges of any kind!*

Romance *is* alive, well and flourishing in the moving love stories of Silhouette Special Edition novels. They'll awaken your desires, enliven your senses, and leave you tingling all over with excitement . . . and the first 4 novels are yours to keep. You can cancel at any time.

As an added bonus, you'll also receive a FREE subscription to the Silhouette Books Newsletter as long as you remain a member. Each issue is filled with news on upcoming books, interviews with your favorite authors, even their favorite recipes.

To get your 4 FREE books, fill out and mail the coupon today!

Silhouette Special Edition®

Silhouette Books, 120 Brighton Rd., P.O. Box 5084, Clifton, NJ 07015-5084

**Clip and mail to: Silhouette Books,
120 Brighton Road, P.O. Box 5084, Clifton, NJ 07015-5084**

YES. Please send me 4 FREE Silhouette Special Edition novels. Unless you hear from me after I receive them, send me 6 new Silhouette Special Edition novels to preview each month. I understand you will bill me just $1.95 each, a total of $11.70 (in Canada, $2.50 each, a total of $15.00), with no shipping, handling, or other charges of any kind. There is no minimum number of books that I must buy, and I can cancel at any time. The first 4 books are mine to keep.

B1SS87

Name _____
(please print)

Address _____ Apt. #

City _____ State/Prov. _____ Zip/Postal Code

* In Canada, mail to: Silhouette Canadian Book Club, 320 Steelcase Rd., E...
Markham, Ontario, L3R 2M1, Canada
Terms and prices subject to change.   SE-SUB-1A
SILHOUETTE SPECIAL EDITION is a service mark and registered trademark.

FOUR UNIQUE SERIES
FOR EVERY WOMAN YOU ARE . . .

Silhouette Romance

Heartwarming romances that will make you
laugh and cry as they bring you all the wonder
and magic of falling in love.

6 titles per month

Silhouette Special Edition

Expanded romances written with emotion and
heightened romantic tension to ensure
powerful stories. A rare blend of passion and
dramatic realism.

6 titles per month

Silhouette Desire

Believable, sensuous, compelling—and
above all, romantic—these stories deliver
the promise of love, the guarantee
of satisfaction.

6 titles per month

Silhouette Intimate Moments

Love stories that entice; longer, more
sensuous romances filled with adventure,
suspense, glamour and melodrama.

4 titles per month

Silhouette Romances
not available in retail outlets in Canada

SIL-GEN-1A